D0916338

THE LONGEST ROAD

BOOK 2 - EPIC JOURNEY SERIES

DAN WALSH

BAINBRIDGE PRESS

The Longest Road

Epic Journey Series - Book 2

By Dan Walsh

Bainbridge Press

ISBN: 978-1-7341417-4-0

Copyright © 2020 Dan Walsh

All rights reserved

Cover design by Bainbridge Press

Cover photo: Tree Alley, Image ID : 14725932

Copyright: FilmFoto

Licensed through 123rf.com

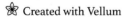 Created with Vellum

1

Late October, 1857
Foster Mansion, Gramercy Park
New York City

THE DREADED DAY had finally arrived.

Laura's eyes panned the room, making mental pictures of the scene. She didn't want to forget a thing. John's childhood bedroom. It had been their living quarters for the past month. A marvelous refuge after the terrific ordeal they'd been through with the shipwreck. It was larger than their master bedroom back in San Francisco which, to that point in her life, had been the biggest bedroom she'd ever seen.

Every bedroom in the Foster Mansion was bigger than every other room in their house. John's parents' bedroom was larger than their entire first floor. But it wasn't the size of the place she'd miss. Or the elaborate furnishings.

It was the people. John's family.

Especially Allison, who'd quickly become the sister Laura never had. Then John's brother Joel, his wife Evelyn and their children; nieces and nephews Laura had only just begun to know. They were the cutest things and had already started calling her Auntie Laura, jumping for joy whenever they saw her. Laura would even miss John's mother.

After today, would she ever see any of them again?

Beyond John's family, there was her "second family." Micah, Eli, and Sally. In some ways, she felt closer to them than anyone. Especially Micah. How could she leave them now?

San Francisco had indeed become her home. The place where she had met John, where they'd fallen in love and gotten married. And John had built her such a nice house. They hadn't even moved in yet. Before their honeymoon trip, she had so looked forward to beginning to furnish and decorate it.

But San Francisco was SO far away. So very far away. She sighed. Perhaps that's what she dreaded most of all. The journey itself.

It wasn't how long it would take. Thanks to the kindness of God, she'd get to spend all that time alone with John. She reminded herself of how very differently these past four weeks would have gone had he perished in the shipwreck, as they had feared. Instead, she and John were starting a new chapter of their lives together. And whatever was contained in those pages, it would be infinitely better than the horrible life that could have been.

But this journey they were about to take, by necessity, must include getting back on a ship and sailing far away from land for days — if not weeks — at a time. She shuddered just thinking about it. The nightmares were not as bad or as intense as the first few weeks, but she was still having them. Stuck alone on a ship adrift at sea. Or like John, floating on a raft but all alone, with sharks circling the waters around her.

John had assured her, this trip would not be anything like the last. She stood next to the dresser, the very spot where John had explained how this time there'd be no disasters or perils at sea.

"I've worked it all out, Laura," he'd said ever so gently. "Believe me, I'm as nervous about getting back on a ship as you. But we're years away from a railroad that connects all the way to California. Even taking those that exist as far as they'd go, we'd still be spending weeks, if not months, in a bumpy uncomfortable wagon riding through hot steamy deserts, crossing rivers with no bridges, through wilderness areas that often come under attack by Indians."

"I know," Laura said.

John continued. "With the plan I've been working on, we'll be riding in first-class accommodations on a train from here to Savannah. That cuts down on two-thirds of the trip on the Atlantic side of the sea and gets us two states south of the place where the Vandervere went down. And from everything I've learned, it's very rare for hurricanes to hit that part of the ocean in late October. Once we get to Panama, we cross over to the Pacific side by train again. You remember the voyage on the Pacific side."

She did. It was mostly calm and peaceful sailing. It all sounded so well and good the way John had explained it. Nevertheless, just thinking about getting on a ship again —

any ship — sent shivers up her spine. The worst part of it was, when the rescue ship had appeared, it was only big enough to save the women and children. Over four hundred men were left stranded on a rapidly-sinking ship. She'd spent all those days living with the certainty that John had perished at sea. She just didn't feel ready to get back out there again. But nothing could be done. They had to get home. And this was the only way.

The bedroom door opened, abruptly ending her thoughts and memories. It was Sally, Micah's daughter, carrying folded sheets and bed linens. Laura turned to face her.

"You didn't have to make the bed, Miss Laura. Mrs. Foster wants me to strip the bed down and redo all the linens."

Try as she might, Laura could never get Sally to just call her by her first name. "I'm sorry. I forgot. Just did it out of habit, I guess." She sighed.

"That's okay." Sally started un-making the bed.

That's when Laura noticed her face, her eyes. Something was wrong. She was trying to cover it up, but something was troubling her. "Are you okay, Sally?"

She kept working. "I'll be fine if I just stay busy."

Laura saw tears welling up in her eyes. "You're not okay. What's the matter? Are you sad because we're leaving today? Because I am."

"Plenty sad because of that." She moved around to the other side of the bed. "Gonna miss you folks something awful. But it ain't that. I don't think I can talk about what it —" The tears flowed. She tried wiping them away but her sadness was too strong.

Laura rushed toward her put her arm around her shoulder. "What is it, Sally? Whatever it is, you can tell me."

Sally turned, put her arms around Laura, and just cried. "Oh, Miss Laura. It's so terrible. I'm afraid Eli gonna go and get himself killed. And there ain't nothing I can do about it."

"Eli's going to be killed?" Laura repeated. "Why? What has he done?"

Sally lifted her head, then stood in front of Laura, wiped her tears on her sleeve. "It's not what he's done. It's what he's fixin' to do. And if he does what he's sayin', none of us will ever see him again. I just know it."

2

Leaving Laura to finish up the packing, John made his way down the main staircase of the Foster home, by itself a work of art. It was funny. As a child, he never appreciated this place. But being back this past month after being gone for two years, he was seeing it in a brand-new light. Probably the way most people view it when they first walked through the finely-crafted front doors.

Very rich people lived here. That would be your first impression.

But John could also say — and this with great clarity — it no longer felt like home. He was most definitely visiting the family manse, as a guest, and nothing more. He cleared the last few steps and headed for the veranda at the back of the house. There he would meet his older brother, Joel, for breakfast. Something Joel had requested yesterday when they parted. It wasn't just a chance for a last goodbye before John and Laura left for San Francisco. Apparently, Joel had "something rather important" to discuss and said he'd come here from his place a few blocks away.

"Meet you there at seven, my good man," Joel had said.

Looking at his watch, John saw that it was five after, which meant Joel would already be in his seat on the veranda, his coffee already poured. This was confirmed after John made it through three familiar doorways and stepped into the nippy morning air. There was Joel at the far end, dressed as though attending a dinner party rather than a casual breakfast. Coffee in one hand, morning newspaper in the other.

As John closed the distance, he noticed a silver serving tray on the mahogany buffet to the left, lid still on, a silver serving spoon beside it on a china plate. A matching silver coffee set was beside that on an ornamental tray complete with a silver creamer and bowl for sugar.

"Oh, there you are," Joel said. "Hoped you didn't forget." He set the newspaper down.

"It's only five-after, Joel."

"Right," he said, sipping his coffee. "I don't know where Sally is. She was supposed to serve us breakfast this morning. She's usually quite prompt."

John glanced at the distance between Joel and the silver food tray. Couldn't be more than twelve feet. "Who poured your coffee?"

"I did. Couldn't wait any longer."

A wonder you survived, John thought. He walked over to the tray, lifted the lid. Wasn't exactly sure what he was seeing, but it smelled delicious.

"Sally should be here in a couple of minutes," Joel said. "Can't imagine what's keeping her."

"Well, how about this?" John said. "I will serve you and me some of this delicious whatever-it-is breakfast stuff here." He picked up the serving spoon. "It'll be great practice for me, since we're heading back to a place where we don't have people who serve you food and pour your coffee."

"I suppose that'll do. But the way things seem to be going for you out there, I expect it won't be long before you and Laura can afford to hire house servants to take care of the mundane things."

John finished putting the breakfast food on Joel's plate. "That almost sounded like a compliment."

"It was, in a way. I have to be honest, John. I haven't said this since you've been back, but I should have. You surprised all of us upon your return. Considering the little you had when you went out there two years ago, it was almost shocking to learn that you and Laura had sailed all this way in first-class accommodations, and that your hardware business was doing so well. Neither Father nor I saw that coming."

John didn't know what to say. This conversation was certainly uncharted territory for him. He finished putting food on his plate, poured his coffee and brought all this to the table. "Here you go, sir," he said serving Joel's plate. "Hope you enjoy your breakfast...casserole?"

"I can't remember what Sally calls it," Joel said. "But I can't get enough of it. There are biscuits in there, scrambled eggs, sausage, some kind of cheese. I've spent very little time in the South, but I have certainly enjoyed the unique southern dishes she brought with her when she escaped."

"That's one thing I definitely haven't missed, being back," John said, "dealing with the injustice of slavery. They don't have it out in San Francisco. It's great to see all the freed Negroes around the city here, but there still seems to be so much tension in the air."

"Things seem to be heating up on that issue," Joel said. "I see it every day in the newspaper. Can't tell where this situation will end up."

"Aren't you and Mother at all nervous about employing Sally and Eli? As you said, she escaped from the South. Eli's a runaway, too, isn't he?"

Joel finished chewing, nodded.

"I was reading an article yesterday," John said, "of some slave catchers from Virginia wanting to press charges against a white couple in Brooklyn, for housing a runaway slave they'd hired and hid the past several months."

"Nothing will come of that," Joel said. "Technically, it is the law. Northerners aren't supposed to help runaway slaves from the South, and we can be arrested or fined if we're caught doing it. I've not been personally involved in any of this, but from hearing conversations between Mother and Allison, sentiments in the North are siding more with the abolitionists. We can't stop the slave catchers from coming up here searching for runaways, but fewer people are cooperating with them, and most of the authorities around here are unwilling to enforce these laws. Against whites, I mean."

"So, Sally and Eli aren't in danger of being captured by these...slave catchers?"

"I suppose they're not entirely out of danger, but it's been over three years for both of them, and no one has come looking. During that time, the organization that Mother's dealing with secured legal-looking papers for them both. So, it seems they're in the clear. At least for now. But like I said, who knows where this whole situation is headed? I heard Mother talking with a neighbor a few weeks ago, who wanted to hire a Negro for her staff but she was saying that most of them—the ones that escape now, I mean—don't stop here in New York any longer. They keep going till they reach Canada."

John sighed. "That's the one part of our trip home I'm not looking forward to. For Laura, it's about being on the ship. For me, it's more about the trip down to Savannah. We'll mostly be on a train, but it's gonna be hard riding through all those slave states, which is most of the trip. Seeing the way they treat people like Micah, Sally, and Eli. I don't know how Laura's going to handle it when we see them mistreated nearby."

"Or how about this?" Joel said, "if the train makes a stop in the center of one of the southern towns — which it most likely will do — and you see slaves being auctioned on the block right outside your window? That could very well happen."

John shook his head. "I know. Not looking forward to that at all."

Joel stood up, carried his plate to the buffet. "I simply must have more of this."

"Look at you, serving yourself," John said.

"You want a little more?"

"No, I have plenty. But what was it you were wanting to talk to me about before I left? You said it was something important."

"It is. And in a roundabout way, we've been edging toward it this whole time."

"I'm not sure I follow."

"It's about your trip back to San Francisco," Joel said. "I've already talked this over with Father. And believe it or not, he's on board with what I'm about to say."

John set his fork down. "Which is?"

"We have a proposal to make that will include...well, it would include you and Laura *not* getting on that train today. And well...*not* going back to San Francisco at all."

3

Harrison Townhome, Gramercy Park
New York City

PRESENTLY, Micah was where he'd usually be most mornings
these days...in the carriage house at the Harrison place.
Doing what he usually did most mornings...getting the
Harrison's horses ready to face the day. Every morning since
he got here a month ago, it be so easy to start the day off
smiling. Just the fact he was a free man was enough. Even
had the papers to prove it.

Could still hardly believe it.

At this age, Micah had never allowed even a hope to
form that he'd ever be free this side of heaven. Figured he'd
end up his number of days serving Captain Meade aboard
the Cutlass. Hard as that was, those three years had been the

easiest to bear since his first memories working out in the cotton fields as a young boy.

But now look at what the Lord had done for him? "Yes sir, Shadrach, these are my best days, for sure. Standing here, brushing your mane, smooth as silk. Can't hardly call it a chore." Shadrach nodded, as if he understood. Fact was, Micah didn't mind any of the work that went along with caring for these horses. Nicest looking creatures he'd ever laid eyes on. Had to be some high breeding at work here. When he first got to the Harrisons, he was led to believe he'd find the horses stubborn and difficult to manage. But after just a few days, the opposite was true.

Shadrach, Meshach, and Abednego were just as calm and good-natured as you'd want horses to be. Course, that weren't their names in the beginning. They didn't even have names. They were just the brown one, the dark brown one, and the black one. That was part of the problem. Creatures this fine and this smart had to have names. Micah knew right off what to call them. Three of his favorite Bible characters from the book of Daniel. Before the first week was out, all three responded to their names like they'd known them all their lives.

"You just needed someone to start treating you right, didn't you boy?" Micah stroked the brush across Shadrach's back. "Give you a little respect. A kind word every now and then never hurt no one, neither." Shadrach was the biggest of the three. The Harrisons had two different carriages, parked up front. Both as fine as anything Micah had seen at the plantation houses down south. The one Shadrach pulled had just the one seat, could hold maybe three people. The other was big enough for the whole family to ride in. Meshach and Abednego shared the load on that one.

Micah glanced up at the clock, wondered what time John and Laura would be leaving the Foster place to start their long journey back home. The thought saddened him. About the only sadness he'd known in recent days. First, that they were going so very far away. And second, didn't know if he'd ever get to see them again. Considering his age, and how long it took folks to get from one side of the country to the other. And he knew how much Miss Laura hated boat rides. Given how bad her last one went, who could blame her?

He sighed. Wished there was some way he could see them both one last time. He owed his entire situation to their love and kindness. No one on earth had ever treated him the way John and Laura had.

Just then, Micah heard a familiar sound at the back of the carriage house. His dog Crabby whining in the little pen he made for her. "You being so patient, girl," he yelled. "I'll be there in just a minute. I promise." Whenever Micah wasn't tending the horses, Crabby got to be with him. But these horses had never been around a dog, and Crabby had never been around horses. For a while longer, he had to keep their getting acquainted times on a short leash. All it would take was one time and one horse getting spooked with Crabby underfoot, and she'd be hurt awful bad, maybe even killed.

But Micah could tell of late, the horses were warming up to ole Crabby. How could they not? She just the sweetest thing.

Three knocks on wood. Micah heard them clearly at the front of the carriage house. Wouldn't be the Harrison's, since it be their place they always just walk right in. "I'll be up there in just a second."

"Micah, that you?" someone yelled back. The voice, southern and familiar.

"It's me," he said.

"I was told I'd find you here, but I didn't believe 'em. Last I heard, you were sailin' on the open seas."

Micah set the horse brush in its place, patted Shadrach on the back, and returned the horse to his stall. He came out, looked down the walkway between the two carriages toward the front, saw the silhouette of a man standing in the doorway.

"Why, it is you, Micah." The man took a few steps forward. "It's me, Josiah Johnson. From Fredericksburg. I come in? Don't feel safe standing out here in the open."

"Josiah? Haven't seen you for so long." Micah hurried toward him. "Sure, you can come in. Safe as can be in here. Just me and the horses, and my dog." Crabby was whining something fierce now, her tail thumping against the pen door. She loved company.

The men met in the middle exchanged hugs and pats on the back.

"Don't think you changed even a little," Josiah said.

"You about the same," Micah said. "Little grayer on top. Few more creases around the eyes."

"Yeah, that's what folks tell me." Josiah looked around. "My, this what they have you doing now? Taking care of horses in a place like 'dis?" He stroked the side of the family carriage. "A very nice situation you got yourself here."

"Don't I know it?" Micah said. "Should see where I stay

now. Got a little place all my own upstairs. Most comfortable bed I ever slept in. You wanna come see it?"

"Wish I could, but I'm kinda in a hurry."

"Oh...so...how life been treating you down in Fredericksburg?"

"Not too good, my friend. Area's come on some hard times. Crops took a real beating just over a month ago when a hurricane came on shore. You hear anything about that?"

"Oddly enough, I did. And in a way, that hurricane — and what the good Lord did 'cause of it — helped me get my freedom."

"You free now?"

"Totally free, papers and all."

"First good thing I ever heard come out of a hurricane. It messed up things for us but good. Bunch-a plantation owners sellin' slaves left and right to make up for they losses, breaking up families like nobody's business. So much heartache and grief going on every day down there ever since."

"Sorry to hear it," Micah said. "How'd you come to be up here in New York?"

"I run away, just like your Eli and Sally did three years ago. Escaped with my wife and son. Got helped by that woman they call Moses, same as Eli did."

"Only Moses I know not a woman," Eli said.

"This one is. On account of all our people she helped get free. Real name Harriet Tubman. Works with the Underground Railroad."

"Now, that name I've heard of. So, what...you all gonna live up here now?"

"Wish I could, but they say we best keep going north, till we reach Canada."

"Why's that? No slaveowners up here. Most folks, I found, either treat you nice or just leave you alone. But nobody's treated me the way things were down south."

"Not the slaveowners we worrying about," Josiah said. "It's the slave catchers. Supposed to be all over the place up here just waiting to snatch any runaway slaves they come across, drag 'em back down to their masters for a pretty penny. You got your papers, so I 'spect you okay. But Micah, Eli and Sally, could be in danger. That's what they tell me anyway."

"I surely hope not. They got papers too, now, say they free. Don't know if they're real or not. But Mr. Joel—the man they work for say no one's gonna take 'em away. He make sure of it."

"Well, that's good to hear," Josiah said. "But we ain't got no one to look out for us up here, so we best keep movin' till we get beyond their reach."

"When you heading out again?"

"First thing tomorrow, is what I hear. But when I heard you were nearby, I had to come see for myself."

"Well, I'm glad you did. Say, since you were in Fredericks-burg not too long ago, hear any news about my youngest girl, Hannah? All I know is what Eli told me, when he escaped with Sally three years ago. Said she wouldn't come with them 'cause of some boy she in love with. He a slave at some other plantation."

Josiah's expression instantly changed. "Fraid I do. And the news ain't good. Fact is, that's part of the reason I came to find you, when I heard you was close by. Hannah went and married that young man she was in love with, about a year after Eli and Sally left. But her master one of the ones who recently lost all that money 'cause of the hurricane. He sold her off to some rich owner from Charleston, tore her right out of the arms of her husband. I was there when it happened. She was screaming and crying like her life was over. And the worst part was, this slaveowner from Charleston not a nice man. Folks were saying — and judging by the other slave girls he bought— I could believe it. All of them pretty young girls. Every single one. Her husband tried to stop 'em, and they beat him unconscious."

Micah's heart sank within him. *Oh, Lord, Jesus.*

Josiah put his hand on his friend's shoulder. "So sorry to be bringin' such terrible news. But I thought you ought to know."

Micah sighed, tried to fight back a surge of tears he felt coming. "Poor Hannah."

"Yep," Josiah said. "An awful thing."

Micah looked up at Josiah. "Could you do me one favor, my friend. If you see my boy Eli before you leave tomorrow, could you hold off on tellin' him this sad news about his sister? I'd rather be—"

Josiah got this look on his face.

"What's the matter?" Micah said.

"Too late. Saw Eli yesterday afternoon. Told him everything I just told you. It was Eli told me where to find you."

4

John Foster looked at his brother for a moment. He was
being totally serious. "You and Father don't want Laura and I
to go back to San Francisco?"

"No, we don't," Joel said. "Me especially."

John didn't know how to take this. Two years ago, when
he'd left home to go out west, he did so solidly branded as
the black sheep of the family. Joel's demeanor then had been
good riddance, who needs you. Now he was in earnest about
keeping John in the fold?

"So, what exactly are you proposing? If we don't go back
to San Francisco — not that I'm agreeing to this, mind you
— but if we stay, what do you think I should be doing
instead?" John took another bite of this delicious food.

"Simple," Joel said. "Sell your house and hardware business out there, stay here and join the family firm. Since the
sinking of the Vandervere and the sudden loss of all that
gold, there's been something of a financial panic in the business world. Oddly enough, that has served to increase the

demand for business insurance. People have had a month to read all the stories of businesses going under because their losses from that sinking were not insured. I can't handle all the calls coming in myself. And clearly, we underestimated your flair for business. There's no doubt in either one of us now that you could handle this job."

John thought it somewhat ironic; had either Joel or his father expressed even an ounce of confidence in him two years ago, John never would've left. As encouraged as he was to learn their sentiments had changed, his own had not. "Joel, I am genuinely touched by your invitation to join you and father in the family firm, but there's nothing simple about this idea. Not for Laura or for me. While I may have gone out there with nothing, we've made quite a life for ourselves now in San Francisco. My business is booming. I only set things up with the understanding that I'd be back in a month. The point is, I'm needed out there. We bought a home that we haven't even lived in yet." John dared not mention his beloved horse, Shasta, whom John sorely missed.

Joel took a sip of his coffee, pondered what John had just said. Clearly, he hadn't anticipated being turned down. "Didn't you say that Laura's brother was running your hardware business in your absence?"

"He is, but he has plans of his own. We talked about this before I left. He's experienced a small measure of success prospecting for gold thus far, but nothing compared to his expectations. He wants to get back out there with Laura's cousin. Supposedly, there are some brand new areas they want to explore. He only agreed to take care of the store to help us out. It was never intended to be anything permanent."

"Well John," Joel said, "have you ever discussed the idea of him becoming a partner with you at the store? Invited him in at an ownership level?"

"No, it's never come up."

"Because you've never considered it before this moment, correct?"

"I suppose not. I had no intentions of doing anything other than going back and running the store myself once our honeymoon trip was over."

"There, you see? You're assuming he wouldn't relish the idea of running the store himself. Maybe now that he's had a taste of it, he might prefer it to the extremely risky venture of prospecting for gold. You said it yourself, he's not had much success with it thus far. I've been doing some reading up on this, preparing for our little chat here. I'm not sure if you been paying attention to the trends, John, but it would seem the great glory days of the gold rush might be nearing an end."

"What do you mean?" John said.

"Precisely this...five years ago, eighty-one million dollars' worth of gold had been pulled out of the ground out there. So far this year, they're on track for less than half that amount. The total yield has been going down every year. It's got to hit the bottom before too long. In fact, if I were out there, even now I'd begin to diversify my inventory. Start carrying more merchandise the average homeowners around town want to buy, not just focus on the gold miners. In a few more years, they could all be gone."

John had never thought about any of this.

"And there's something else to think about," Joel said. "Something I think you'd consider of greater importance than any business or monetary concerns."

"And what is that?"

"I have solid reasons to believe your wife, Laura, has no desire to go back home."

John sat up in his chair. "I seriously doubt that, Joel. I know for a fact Laura loves it out there. We've talked about it many times. Especially since the day we met, both of us have the fondest memories of our time there."

"I'm sorry," Joel said. "You're misunderstanding me. I'm not talking about Laura's desire to be out there in San Francisco. I'm talking about the *journey* back home. The trip itself. I've been in the room when she and Allison have discussed this. When they think I'm only paying attention to the newspaper. Laura is dreading this trip. The very thought of getting back on a sailing ship keeps her awake at night. When she sleeps, she says she has nightmares. Are you aware of this?"

"We've talked about it," John said. "Some."

"I heard Allison ask Laura just the other day — after Laura had just shared some of her fears — if she'd told you all these things. Laura said she had not. Said she didn't want to burden you, because she knew there wasn't anything that could be done. You had to get back to San Francisco. And that meant getting back on a ship."

John hated to hear this. Not because it was Joel saying it. But because he knew it was true. "I looked into trying to get back all the way on land, but in some ways, I think there's more danger in that. The trains out west just go so far. There's still huge gaps where you'd have to travel by wagon."

Joel set his fork down, leaned forward. "John, tell me you haven't seriously considered taking Laura on a wagon out west. Besides the absence of any comfortable accommodations, you could still be dealing with Indian attacks. I read about one just a few months ago in Iowa. Some thirty settlers killed by a band of Sioux Indians."

"We've talked about that, and I'm not seriously thinking about traveling there by land. We have to travel by ship a good part of the way. I've talked to Laura about this. So, what she's telling Allison is true. It's possible, I haven't been in touch with how much it bothers her. But even if I had paid more attention, I'm not sure what else I could say or do. Even after what we've been through, taking a ship is still safer."

"I've told you what you could do, John. Sell the hardware store to her brother, and stay here. Work with father and I. Even if you lost money selling the store and your new house, I guarantee you, you'd make it all back and twice more working here with us."

John sighed. He no longer had any interest in finishing his breakfast.

"Tell me you'll think about it, John. Maybe have a heart-to-heart talk with Laura, see what she says. Who knows? The outcome of that conversation might surprise you."

5

After Laura spent another ten minutes talking with Sally about this serious situation with Eli, she made her way down the staircase to find John. Halfway there, she saw John coming from the back of the house. She hoped his breakfast with Joel hadn't gone badly, but his expression looked troubling, as though deep in thought. He didn't even look up to see her coming his way.

"John?" she said softly.

He looked up, forced a smile. "Laura, I was just coming to see you."

"And I was headed downstairs to find you. How did your breakfast go?"

He met her on the same step, kissed her on the cheek. "Fine. It was good. Joel had some...interesting things to discuss. I was hoping you might have a few minutes to talk. I know we're both busy getting ready for the trip, but I think this is important. It may even have some bearing on our plans."

Laura really wanted to hear what he had to say, but she didn't think the things she'd heard from Sally could wait, either. "Let's head back to the room then. I have something pretty urgent to talk to you about, too." She turned around, and they headed up to the bedroom together.

Once inside, John closed the door. Over by a window centered in the room were two large upholstered Victorian chairs, a small ornamental table between them. John and Laura had many nice conversations in those chairs over the past month. She headed to the one that had unofficially become hers. As he sat, she glanced at his face, his eyes, trying to gauge whether she should share first or defer.

"What is it you wanted to talk to me about?" John said.

"Something very serious involving Eli that I've learned from talking with Sally. But it can wait a few minutes. What is it you wanted to say? You said it might have some bearing on our plans? You mean our future plans, or our trip back home?"

"Well, both I guess. In different ways. Before I get into sharing Joel's proposal —"

"Joel shared a proposal with you?"

"Yes, I want to go over it with you, but there's something else I want to talk about first. Something that involves you and me more than anything else."

Was she in some kind of trouble? Was John upset with her? "Okay..."

"And before I say anything else," John added, "I want you to know...I really want to hear your heart on this thing. I'm going to ask you some questions, I want you to know, I won't be upset with you no matter what your answers are. I don't want you to be thinking about saying the right thing or saying something you think I want to hear. I really want to, need to, hear what you're thinking and feeling inside."

She couldn't imagine where this was leading. "You know, John, I always try to be honest with you. When we talk, I mean."

"I know you do. I don't mean to imply otherwise. It's just...I know it's also possible for a wife to feel overpowered by her husband's influence, when she knows he feels strongly about something. I need to know if that has happened here, in the matter we're about to discuss. If it has, the fault is mine. The important thing now is, that you feel the absolute freedom to speak plainly with me, from your heart, without fear of any consequence or reaction from me."

"Okay, John. I'll do my best."

"Good, good. Okay, here's the first question. I know that both of us have apprehensions about the journey home. Understandably, because of the shipwreck. But if you could do whatever you wished, would you choose to stay here in New York, or would you rather be back in San Francisco?"

"Oh, I see. Well, I'm not sure I'm completely in touch with how I feel about that. I've known since the day you were rescued and we were reunited that, at some point, we would have to make the journey back home. The idea of staying here permanently has never been an option. So, I don't think I've ever let my heart entertain the notion."

"I can understand that," John said. "Perhaps you could allow your heart to go there now. If only for a little while. I'm not saying that I believe we should stay here. It's just the idea of going back has always been — even as you said — a certainty, not an option. But I really want to know now, if we did not have to go back to San Francisco, if that were a possibility, is that something you would prefer? Or would you prefer to return to the life we had back there?"

Laura shifted in her chair. John's questions, and the intensity in his expression, made her wonder what Joel's proposal was about? Was John having second thoughts about their plans, or was he simply succumbing to the pressures his older brother had applied? She knew firsthand how intimidating Joel could be, even when he wasn't trying. "Well, John, I'm not sure my answer will be all that satisfying. The truth is, you know I loved our life together in San Francisco. I could never have imagined anything happening to alter my desire to return. If we're talking about having my wishes fulfilled, then my wish would be to snap my finger and have us miraculously transported back home. But I know that can't happen."

John leaned forward in his chair. "So, it's merely the journey back home you dread, and that alone? You really would prefer to live there and not here?"

"I guess that's what I'm saying. I don't know, though, John. I've genuinely come to love the people here. Your family, I mean." She leaned forward and whispered. "Including Joel and your mother...although I'm not quite there with your father yet. And then there's Micah, Sally and Eli. I can hardly bear the thought of never seeing them again." *Sally and Eli.* Laura dared not forget to share with John what Sally had said.

She continued. "As a city, New York certainly has its own charm. But my desire to live here, I guess, would be more about continuing the relationships that have begun, and not wanting to see them come to an end. Because we both know, the distance between these two cities, in terms of keeping any meaningful relationships going, may as well be the distance between the earth and the moon."

John smiled. "You're certainly right about that. And it's so odd. When I moved out there two years ago, things were so bad with my family, I wondered if San Francisco was going far enough. But now, I completely understand what you're trying to say. It's one of the more challenging aspects of this for me. Not getting to continue a close relationship with my family. And I don't just mean Allison. I always missed her. But..." He leaned forward and whispered back, "with Joel and my mother, too."

John leaned back in his chair, gazing at Laura's lovely face. He so desperately wanted to make her happy but wasn't sure this conversation was closing the gap or making it wider. There really wasn't any easy answer.

"So," Laura said, "was that the reason Joel wanted to meet with you, the nature of his proposal? To get you, to get us, to consider staying here in New York?"

John nodded. "Laura, it's fair to characterize the substance of his words as... *pleading* for us to stay. And it wasn't just an emotional approach, some underhanded effort to manipulate. Though he was being as persuasive as he could be. He'd given the whole matter a great deal of thought, listing several examples for each point, articles he'd read, and research he'd done to make his case. He even said he'd run all this past our father, who completely agreed with him. Can you believe that?"

Laura shook her head in amazement. "So, what are you thinking now? In a few hours, we're supposed to be loading all these trunks on the carriage to be driven to the train station?"

"I don't know what to think," John said.

"What would we do about my brother, Michael? We told him we'd only be gone a month."

"I know, I know. I guess if this is something the Lord wants us to do — some way He's redirecting our steps — then we'd have to assume He'll have been preparing your brother's heart for this idea, as well. If we decide to stay, we have to contact him, see if he's interested in buying the store."

"We'd have to sell our house, too."

John nodded. "So much to think about. So many layers to consider."

"Then maybe we shouldn't make a decision just yet," she said. "I mean a definitive one, to either stay here permanently or leave today as planned. Perhaps, we could get word to him, see if he's open to the idea of running things for us in San Francisco a while longer."

Perhaps, John thought, Michael's response to that request would serve as a gauge regarding the bigger question of whether he'd consider buying the store. "I think that's a great idea. We won't leave today, as planned. Maybe we'll wait another week or so, give us some time to think and pray about what to do next."

Laura smiled.

"Are you relieved?"

"Maybe a little."

"So, what is it you want to talk to me about? Something about some trouble with Eli?"

Her face instantly changed.

"Laura, what's the matter?"

6

Laura looked at John, unsure of where to start. The news she had to share was so entirely different from his.

"Is Eli all right?" John asked.

"According to Sally, no, he's not. I mean, he's fine now. But if he goes through with what he's planning, she's quite certain none of us will ever see him again."

"What? Never see him again?" John repeated. "Why? What is he planning to do?"

Laura took a deep breath. She wanted to share this calmly. There had been so much emotion when she'd talked about these things with Sally. "I guess I'll begin with this... did you know Micah had another daughter, named Hannah?"

"No, I didn't. But I have heard that name mentioned occasionally over the last few weeks, mostly in conversations between Eli and Sally. I just assumed it was some acquaintance of theirs, or maybe some young lady Eli was interested in."

"Well, Sally said there is a young lady he's sweet on, as she put it, named Bella. But Hannah's their little sister. Sally explained the situation to me while you were having breakfast with Joel. It's pretty awful. I'm not sure if I'm more mad or sad about what I've heard. Just the terrible things people do to other people. It's so wrong. Being away from it for those years in San Francisco dulled my senses to the sheer horror of it."

"What did Sally say?" John said. "What is Eli going to do?"

"Well, it might help if I shared a little about their family history. Up until about four years ago, they had all been something of a family living near Fredericksburg. The first big thing that happened was, the mother had died, Micah's wife. Although she and Micah had lived on two different plantations the last few years they'd been together. Next, Eli got caught teaching other slaves to read, so he'd been sold off to a different master. He was still in Virginia but a few hours away. Before long, he escaped and went back to Fredericksburg to try and free the rest of the family. He found Micah had already been sold off to Captain Meade. And Hannah, the youngest one, was in love with this slave from another plantation, and she refused to leave. So, Eli was only able to free Sally. They made their way north with some others and eventually wound up here."

"Okay," John said. "Then a month ago Eli and Sally are reunited with their father. I'm guessing what Eli's planning has something to do with his sister Hannah?"

"Yes. He wants to head back south for Hannah, to free her. But she's not in Fredericksburg anymore. She was sold off to another master who lives near Charleston."

John shook his head, sighed. "Charleston, that's the deep South."

"That's why Sally's so afraid," Laura said. "Hannah's not in a border state anymore." She and John had learned a little bit about the Underground Railroad's activity since being in New York. Most of the successful slave escape missions happened in states just south of the Mason-Dixon line, like Virginia and Maryland. South Carolina was arguably the most pro-slavery state in the Union. Their entire economy was dependent on slavery to succeed.

"So, Eli thinks he can make it down to Charleston somehow, find her and free her?" John said.

Laura nodded.

"Do they even know which plantation Hannah's on?"

"No, just somewhere near Charleston."

"I've read there's supposed to be several hundred plantations in that area."

"Several hundred?" Laura said. "I would have guessed a dozen."

"Eli will never find her if he goes down there." John stood, began to pace behind his chair.

"Sally's afraid he won't even get close. He'll be picked up by slave catchers or bounty hunters on the journey down."

"She's probably right," John said. "Why would he even risk such a thing? It's a fool's errand to try."

"Well," Laura said, "there's more to the story. Eli learned Hannah's new master isn't just your run-of-the-mill slaveowner. This man wasn't there in Fredericksburg buying slaves to work his fields. He was only interested in buying attractive young Negro girls."

"Oh, my," John said.

"You remember that abolitionist article you read to me, about these southern slave owners who deliberately buy female slaves for their own pleasure?"

"And for breeding," John said. "To create more slaves for themselves. The hypocrisy of it galls me, not just the immorality. On the one hand, they're saying Negroes are less human than whites, but then they're perfectly capable of bearing their own offspring. It's pure evil."

"It is," Laura said. "But Sally said she knows her sister. And that Hannah will not allow herself to be used by a man that way. To quote Sally, she'd sooner drown herself in a river than put up with being treated like that. Eli knows this, too, which is why he's desperate to get down there and rescue her before this goes on too long. He doesn't, Sally says, Hannah will be dead."

For a moment, neither said a word. The full weight of Laura's news hung in the air between them.

Laura was right. It was so hard being back here routinely confronted with the horrors of slavery. Obviously, it was much better in New York than in the South, but still, everywhere you looked the evidence of this ungodly abuse was all around. Finally, John said, "Even as bad as this is, it still makes no sense for Eli to attempt to save her. He has zero chance of succeeding."

"I agree," Laura said. "So does Sally. But she says Eli's mind's made up."

"What do you want me to do?" John said.

"I don't know. But it feels like we have to do something."

"I suppose I could try talking with him."

"Would you?" Laura said. "It's obvious he admires you a great deal."

"I don't know about that, but I guess it couldn't hurt to try. Do you know where he is?"

"Sally said he left to take your father to the office for an early morning appointment. But he should be back fairly soon."

John looked at his timepiece. If that's the only place Eli went, then he should be back any minute. He could head down to the carriage house, see if he could find a way to dissuade Eli from pursuing this ridiculous idea any further. He walked to Laura, kissed her on the forehead. "Say a prayer for me. I have absolutely no idea what I'm going to say."

7

John walked downstairs and out through the back toward the carriage house. As soon as he stepped inside, he knew Eli wasn't back yet. Father always took the same carriage to the office, and it was gone. Just as well. He still wasn't sure how to approach this. He liked Eli, but it wasn't as if they'd become good friends. They hadn't spent any real time together in the four weeks since John arrived. Their only conversations had been exchanging polite pleasantries in the moments before and after Eli had given them a ride somewhere.

At one point, John had asked Eli to please consider him a friend and to stop talking to him so formally. Calling him things like *Mr. Foster*, *Mr. John*, or even just calling him *sir* all the time. Eli thanked him for the offer and said he'd do his best to consider John a friend but didn't think he should drop his formal manner of speech. "If it's all the same to you, sir," he'd said, "if I stop talking that way with you, I might forget and speak that way with your brother, or worse, your father. And then where would I be?"

John walked from one end of the carriage house to the other, then upstairs to Eli's quarters. No sign of Eli. It was a beautiful morning, so he decided to take a lap around Gramercy Park. Maybe Eli would be back by then, and it would give John some time to pray and think. Gramercy Park wasn't just the name of the upscale neighborhood where the Foster mansion was located. It was also the name of a beautiful little two-acre park surrounded by an ornamental wrought-iron fence and a locked gate. Each of the thirty-nine residents had a key.

John didn't have one, so he walked around the perimeter fence. As he did, he marveled at the beauty of the individual townhouses lining the adjacent streets. Somewhat similar in style, but each one unique. Most would not be considered mansions like his family home, but even the smallest of them dwarfed the home awaiting him and Laura back in San Francisco.

His brother, Joel, lived in one of the nicer townhomes a few blocks over. As fine as they were, John knew the possibility of owning one someday would play no role in their decision to stay, or leave.

He rounded the second corner and came to a bench across the street from a red brick townhouse. Instantly, an unpleasant memory came to mind. Was John eight or nine years old then? He couldn't remember. But it was the first time he'd ever been punched in the face. John had been running for some reason and sat briefly on the bench to catch his breath. Two older boys came by. One he didn't recognize as being from the neighborhood, but the other was Ronnie Carver, the son of a banker who lived in the red brick townhouse.

At first, the boys walked past him but then the boy he didn't know stopped, turned around and came near. "What did you call me?" he'd said to John.

"What?" John had replied. "I didn't say anything."

"No, I heard you. You said something like, *you don't belong around here.*"

"I didn't," John repeated. "I've been just sitting here. Not talking to anyone."

The boy took a step closer.

Ronnie Carver spoke up. "Leave him alone, Jay. He's just a kid."

"No, I won't leave him alone. Now, he's calling me a liar."

"I didn't call you a liar. I just said, I didn't say anything... to you, before."

The boy, now known as Jay, grabbed John by the collar, lifted him to his feet. He was easily six inches taller than John. "But I heard you. Look at the way you're dressed. Just another stinking rich kid. Think you're better than me."

John didn't know what to say. "I don't think I'm any better than you."

"There you go again, calling me a liar."

"Jay, let him go," Ronnie said.

"I'll show you," Jay said. Then he punched John right in the face, knocked him to the ground.

John let out a cry of pain, yelled, "Leave me alone."

Jay raised his fist to punch John again, when something totally unexpected happened. The only pleasant part of this wholly unpleasant memory. A hand, bigger than Jay's hand, grabbed his wrist. From the ground, John looked and saw the hand was connected to his big brother, Joel.

"Oh, no you don't," Joel said. And with his other hand, he struck Jay hard on the side of his face, just as Jay was looking up to see who grabbed him.

Jay fell to the ground next to John. John rolled to the side to get out of the way. He saw Ronnie Carver running down the street, terror on his face. Joel lifted Jay up by the collar, just as he had done with John. "How's this feel? You like how this feels?" Then he struck Jay again, just as hard. Jay fell back on the ground then quickly rolled to the other side, leaped to his feet, and ran in the same direction as Ronnie Carver.

Joel helped John to his feet. "How's that eye? Probably gonna be a shiner."

John couldn't believe it. Joel hardly ever paid any attention to him before. He was far more aware of that fact than he was the pain on the side of his face. "Thank you," he said. "I thought I was a goner."

"You're welcome. I hate bullies. But you should be okay now. Might want to go home, let Sadie take a look at that eye." Sadie had been their nanny. Then Joel had walked off toward their home.

John had followed a few steps behind.

Standing there now in that same spot, some twenty years later, John couldn't help but wonder what had happened in the months and years beyond that day to cause his and Joel's relationship to drift so far apart. But after his breakfast with Joel that morning, in some ways, it felt like John had an older brother who genuinely cared about him again. Another reason to seriously think through whether he really wanted to return to San Francisco.

Just then, he heard the familiar sound of his father's horse and carriage approaching down the street. He looked up to see Eli reining in the horses as he approached the carriage house. John walked in that direction, prayed, "Lord, please give me the right words to say."

8

John walked the last few yards under the shade of an old familiar maple tree at the corner of the Foster property, stepping on big red and brown leaves which had begun to fall with more regularity these days. Eli had already pulled the carriage inside, but the doors were still open. John watched him climb down from the driver's seat, dressed in his familiar *fancy man outfit*, as Micah liked to call it.

"Oh, hello Mr. John. I didn't see you there."

"Hey Eli, I just came in from the street. Decided to take a little walk around the park, enjoy this nice weather."

"Guess it'll be a while before you see that park again, won't it? What time do you and Miss Laura need a ride to the train station?"

John smiled. "Looks like we won't be needing that ride after all, Eli. At least not today anyway."

"Really? You decide to stay in New York?"

"For the time being anyway. We still haven't made a firm decision." John stepped closer, said quietly, "But I hear you're talking about making a trip very soon. Down south, is what I heard."

Eli looked around nervously to make sure no one was listening. He stepped further inside the carriage house. "Who told you that, Mr. John?"

"Well, actually, my wife did. She had a pretty troubling conversation with Sally this morning."

Eli shook his head. "Sally...now she had no business talking to Miss Laura about our troubles. You folks have enough going on in your own lives."

"We didn't mind. In a way, we consider you, Sally, and your father like part of our family. If you're going through a hard time, we'd like to help if we can." John looked around by the front of the carriage house, down both sides of the sidewalk. "There's no one out here at the moment. Maybe we should take a walk, so no one overhears our conversation."

"I wouldn't mind that, sir, but wouldn't be good for folks to see me out there walking around with you like I belonged. Word would get back to your family, and I'd get trouble for it, since I'm supposed to be working."

"I understand," John said. "Then let's step further inside, and I'll close this door. We'll be out of sight that way. No one from my family should bother us in here, for at least a few minutes anyway."

"I really should look to the horses," Eli said.

John could tell Eli didn't want to have this conversation. "They'll be okay for a few minutes, too. You only drove them to the office and back, right?"

Eli nodded. "Yes, sir."

John walked around the carriage to the open area behind

it, sat on a wooden bench backed up against one of the stalls. "Come on over here, let's talk for a few minutes. From what Sally told Laura, she's terribly afraid if you go forward with your plans, none of us will ever see you again."

Eli looked down as he walked over, sat next to John. "She has reason to worry, I suppose. But it has to be done. I can't sit around here doing nothing, knowing what my sister Hannah's going through. Never should've left her there in Fredericksburg in the first place. Should've forced her to come with me and Sally when we escaped three years ago."

"Just so I understand," John said. "What exactly has happened to Hannah and what do you hope to accomplish if you go down there?"

"She's been sold off to a new slaveowner," Eli said. "And the way Josiah tells it, this is an evil man. They're all evil, in my opinion, but this one's especially so."

"Who's Josiah?"

"A friend of our family, a slave from a plantation not far from us in Fredericksburg. I was checking in on another friend at the Underground Railroad meeting house here in New York, when a new group of runaway slaves arrived. Josiah and his family were with them. We got to talking, and he told me all about what happened to Hannah. He saw it all himself, so this isn't hearsay. This slaveowner from Charleston—to hear Josiah tell it—was only buying pretty young slave girls. I think you know well as I do, can only be one reason a man like that does something like that. It's not to work his fields. And Hannah's husband—the young man she wouldn't leave with Sally and me for—he was begging for them not to take her away. They beat him senseless, put her in chains and dragged her away." His face went from anguish to rage as he finished talking.

This was pretty much what John had learned from Sally's account to Laura, but he felt the need to let Eli share his version his own way. Just then, the front door to the carriage house opened slightly. John stood and looked, saw Micah come in. "It's okay, it's only your Dad." John sat down on the bench again, heard Micah's footsteps coming their way past the carriage. "Listen, Eli, I'm totally sympathetic to your concern. I can't imagine how I'd react if anything like that happened to my sister, Allison."

Eli looked up at John. "Is there anything you wouldn't do to save her?"

John shook his head no. "But Eli, I've done some reading on the Underground Railroad, news articles and essays. From what I read, most of the successful escape stories come from border states. You and Sally came up from one, Virginia. You said Hannah was brought down to a plantation near Charleston. How do you expect to make it all the way down there, find her amidst the hundreds of plantations, rescue her, and get both of you all the way back here safely?"

"I don't know. Maybe it can't be done. All I know is...I gotta try. And I don't have any time to lose. Sally and me both know Hannah. She'll do even more than her share of chores and work out in the fields if she has to, but there's no way she'd let herself be used that way. Not what this man's got in mind. She'll do herself in 'fore she'll let that happen."

John felt so helpless. "How are you planning to do this? Can't the folks at the Underground Railroad help? Maybe you can go down there with them on their next rescue mission."

Eli shook his head no. "Already asked. They said they'd like to help, but they don't have another mission going south for a few weeks. They got to get Josiah's group up to Canada. By the time they get back, my sister could be dead."

"Have you talked about this trip with Bella?" John said. "I think that's her name."

"You know about Bella?"

"Just learned about her this morning. Is she someone you care about?"

"Yes, I do. Quite a lot—"

"What does she think about this?"

"She doesn't know yet. Was gonna tell her today. But, I wasn't planning on asking her permission to go. I'm hopin' to make her family someday but, Hannah's family already. And I'm her big brother. It's my duty to take care of this."

John sighed, saw Micah standing there between the carriage and the first stall. His eyes were full of tears.

"Don't do it, son. Don't go down there," he said. "I don't wanna lose my girl Hannah, but you go, it's a fact I lose both of you for good."

9

John stood as Micah came closer, pointed toward the bench suggesting Micah take his seat. Micah walked toward where he pointed, as if obeying some order. "Please, Micah, sit."

"Okay." He nodded his thanks to John.

"Daddy, it's no use you coming here," Eli said. "You can't talk me out of this. I've been thinking of this every minute since I heard the news about Hannah. But every path my mind takes ends up at the same place. We don't rescue her, Hannah will die."

"I thought about it, too. Long and hard since Josiah first told me. Thought about the very thing you're fearing. I been praying since the day Mr. John and Miss Laura freed me that somehow, someway, Hannah could be up here with us. I gotta admit, hearing what Josiah say this mornin', about the opposite answer I been praying for. I keep thinking 'bout that verse in Isaiah somewhere, the one our preacher down in Fredericksburg always quotin'. *God's ways not our ways. His thoughts are not our thoughts. High as the heavens are above the earth, that's how much higher his thoughts and ways are higher than ours.* This got to be, most certainly, one of dem times."

"I'm sorry, Daddy. I wish I had your level of faith. Because to me, all that sounds like is you making excuses for the Almighty. Something doesn't go the way we want it to—or in this case, the exact opposite of what we want—and we say God's got something else in mind. Well, maybe he does, Daddy. Maybe his plan is for me to go down there myself and get her. Maybe he's got a miracle in mind with my name on it. And I go down there, and nobody sees me, nobody stops me. I find Hannah before it's too late, and then both of us, somehow, get all the way back up here in one piece. Couldn't God do something like that, Daddy?"

Micah didn't answer right away. He just kept looking at him, nothing but softness and caring in his eyes. John felt this wasn't a conversation he needed to be a part of, so he took a few steps back toward the carriage.

Tears welled up in Eli's eyes. He exhaled deeply, then said. "I'm sorry, Daddy. I didn't mean to say all that."

Micah gently rested his hand on Eli's shoulder. "I know, son. You just upset. You got good reason to be. Even with the Almighty. King David know'd all about that. Preacher say it says so in the Psalms. Say it does no good hiding how we really feel from him, since he knows everything we thinking or feeling every moment of the day."

Eli looked down at the ground. "I just don't know what else to do, Daddy. Can't just sit here and do nothing."

"Don't rightly know, either, son. But one thing I do know...prayin' isn't doing nothin'. Seems like it sometimes, but it ain't. Word says it's a powerful weapon. And I seen that to be true more times than I can say. Trust is another powerful thing. Folks say, put your trust in the Lord. Don't come easy for me, though, even after all this time. But it's something I can do, when it seems like nothing I do can fix a matter. I make a choice to trust him. To let the thing go and give the situation to him to handle. Lived long enough to see those situations turn right around after a while. Usually way longer than I want, but...there it is. A day like any other day and God comes through."

Eli kept looking at the ground, shaking his head. Micah kept his arm around his shoulder. He looked up at John. John smiled, nodded, mouthed the words, *I'll pray.* Then walked quietly to the front of the carriage house.

Stepping out into the cool morning air, the most profound idea popped into his head. A way he and Laura could potentially help their friends with this terrible dilemma. Before the idea formed into anything solid, he could instantly see it would be fraught with peril. And there were certainly a number of risks involved, as well as a number of ways the thing could go wrong.

But it was a way. A narrow way, mind you. But a way that could conceivably solve this crisis and reunite Hannah with the rest of her family. He had to find Laura straight away, run it by her. He'd need the rest of the family's approval, too. But there was no point taking it further if Laura thought the idea to be utter folly.

John darted across the walkway connecting the carriage house to the main home then up the veranda stairs toward the back door. He met Sally coming out of the kitchen. "Have you seen Laura?"

"Yes, sir, Mr. John. She was down here a few minutes ago but went back up to your bedroom."

10

On the way upstairs to find Laura, John met his sister Allison coming down. Her face looked terribly sad. "What's the matter?" he said.

"What do you mean, what's the matter? You're the matter. You and Laura. Leaving today." She kept heading down the steps.

"We're not leaving. At least, not today."

She stopped, turned around. "You're not? What happened?"

"I can't explain right now, have to get with Laura on something. But we've definitely postponed our trip out west." He was about to say something about another trip they might be going on soon, but held his peace.

Allison hurried up the few steps between them, hugged him around the waist. "I'm so glad."

"But I need to go," he said as he pulled away. "We'll talk soon."

He headed down the hall until he came to their room.

Opening the door, he found Laura unpacking one of the trunks. "Don't unpack everything, Darling. Not yet anyway."

She turned, gave him a confused look. "Did you change your mind?"

"Not about San Francisco," he said. "But we need to talk." He closed the door behind him, headed for his Victorian chair. As he sat, she came over and stood beside hers. "You don't seem very upset. Can I assume your talk with Eli went well? Were you able to get him to give up his rescue idea?"

"I don't think so. When I left them in the carriage house, he still seemed pretty set on going."

"Them? Who else was there?"

"Micah stopped in. Apparently, he had the same intention as I."

"Micah came by?" Laura said. "I haven't seen him in days. Do you think he's still there?"

"I don't know. They were still talking when I left. But listen Laura...you and I need to talk. Why don't you have a seat?"

"Okay." She came around the front of the chair and sat. "Does this have something to do with your time with Eli and Micah?"

"Very much so. But it didn't come up in my time with them. I haven't talked about this with anyone else yet."

"What is it?"

John was just about to blurt it out but — seeing Laura's face — he suddenly realized what an alarming idea it was. He'd been so caught up in the emotional tension within the carriage house, when this idea had surfaced it seemed like a perfect fit. "I'm not sure exactly how to begin."

"Well, take your time. We're in no hurry now. Have you told anyone else about our postponing our trip home?"

"Eli and, just now on my way up the stairs, Allison."

"How did she receive it?"

"She seemed thrilled, but I didn't give her any details, since I wanted to come up here and talk with you. I want to share with you an idea that came to me quite suddenly while finishing up with Eli and Micah. It was a very difficult conversation, as you can imagine. This whole business with his sister, Hannah, is just horrible. And after hearing Eli out, I can see full well why Sally was so upset. Eli's viewing this as a matter of life or death for Hannah, and he's convinced there is no time to waste. His courage and love for his sister are commendable, but I also don't see any way this ends well, if he follows through with his plan to go down there alone."

"Then...what is your idea, John?"

"That Eli doesn't go down there alone."

"I see," she said. "And who will go with him? Are you planning to talk with the people at the Underground Railroad?"

"Eli's already done that. He was turned down. They won't have anyone going south for a few more weeks. Eli doesn't think there's enough time to wait that long."

"Then who do you have in mind?"

John paused. Held up his hand, as if to volunteer. "Me. I will go down there with him."

"You? John, you can't be serious."

"I am. I am being totally serious." Laura's face said this was not going well.

She leaned forward. "John, you can't do this. It is much

too dangerous. You have no experience with something like this. Running through the woods in the dark, sleeping out under the stars, swimming across raging creeks and rivers."

John smiled. "You're right. I have no experience doing such things. And I have no intention of gaining any new experiences doing them now. That's not my plan."

"Then what are you thinking?"

"Of riding down there in style. Dressed in fine clothes. Staying at nice hotels. Eating at fine restaurants."

"I don't understand."

"Laura, my plan is...to go down there under the guise of a wealthy slaveowner from Maryland. Since there are few, if any, slaveowners from New York or Pennsylvania. So, we'll take a train down to Maryland, with Eli posing as my slave, as my valet."

"Why Maryland? I thought Hannah was taken down to Charleston."

"Well, you're right. We wouldn't stop in Maryland permanently. Maryland would be the place where our charade would begin. We'd stay there a few days to establish our cover identities, practice our roles as master and slave, I guess. I'd have to listen to how they talk, pay attention to any wealthy Maryland merchants I see, particularly a man who has a slave for a valet. Try to understand how they function together, how the man talks to his slave, treats him and such. When Eli and I both feel comfortable with the pretense, we would get back on the train — now as master and slave — and continue our journey south. I had planned out a route all the way to Savannah. We would stop perhaps in Columbus, South Carolina. Then get off and lease a fine carriage and horses as we begin our search for Hannah in the low country area surrounding Charleston." John looked at her face as he talked. The fearful and panicked look had given way to one of mild concern.

She sighed. "I don't know, John. It still seems so dangerous. I don't think I could bear parting with you again. A trip like that could easily take weeks, maybe more. And the South has become so tense anymore. Their hostility toward Northerners seems to grow worse every day."

"But they wouldn't view us as Northerners. We'd be from the southern border state of Maryland. I'd be traveling with a slave...and traveling south to buy another slave. I'd be just like one of them."

"So, that would be your story," Laura said. "You'd be traveling to Charleston looking for another slave to buy?"

"I suppose so, yes."

"How would you explain your reasons for looking for a young female slave, like Hannah?"

"I'm not quite sure," John said. "Haven't thought everything out just yet. That's part of the reason I wanted to talk with you first. See what you thought of the idea, and hear any practical suggestions you might have. And of course, if you think the idea has merit, we'd have to talk with Eli and Micah and even my family, too, I suppose."

She didn't say anything for a moment. John could tell she was giving everything considerable thought. "Well? What do you think?"

She sighed, again. "I don't want you leaving me all alone here in New York."

"I see," John said.

"Which is why I must come with you."

"What? Laura —"

"No, John, listen. It's not just to keep me from being alone. I think I could be a great help, especially with the pretense, as you say. We could travel down there as husband and wife. I could cultivate a strong southern accent. We could say you married a Southern Belle and brought me north to Maryland. But now that I'm with child, I wanted to return home to pick out a new nanny for our child. And that I'm looking for one specific slave girl — one that I grew up with as a child —and we've learned she's recently been sold to slaveowner near Charleston."

John could hardly believe what he'd just heard. "And you came up with all that just now? Just this moment?"

She smiled, nodded. "And one thing more... I think we need to bring Micah along on this trip. He knows the South better than any of us, including Eli. And he has an amazing depth of wisdom and insight. I think he should serve as your valet, and Eli can be our driver."

Now John smiled. "See, I knew I should come speak with you first. I think those are great ideas." He got up, stepped toward her, and reached for her hand.

"Where are we going?"

"Let's go see if Micah and Eli are still together in the carriage house."

She took his hand and arose and continued holding it as they walked toward the bedroom door.

"You don't seem very afraid of this idea," John said. "Such a trip won't be easy. In fact, it will likely be filled with risks."

"I know," she said. "But at least we'll be together, and it has nothing to do with getting back on another ship."

When John and Laura got to the carriage house they saw Micah had just left. He was down the sidewalk by their next-door neighbors headed toward the Harrison home. "Micah," John yelled, "hold up a moment."

Micah turned around. His troubled countenance changed to joy seeing John and Laura. "Here I was feeling sad that I missed my chance to say goodbye to you folks for good." He walked toward them.

"Well, it looks like instead of saying goodbye," John said, "we might be spending a good deal more time together in the days ahead. That is, if you're open to an idea we've had."

He looked understandably confused. "I'm open to anything keeps you both nearby for however long it lasts."

They exchanged hugs.

"Is Eli still in the carriage house?" Laura said.

"Just left him. Don't know if my words did any good, though. In the Lord's hands now, I guess."

"Well, that's what we want to talk about," John said. "With

both of you, if you can wait to go back to the Harrisons for a few minutes. We have an idea we'd like to discuss, a possible way to rescue your daughter without losing Eli in the process."

Micah's eyes brightened at that. "Lord, have mercy. I would surely like to hear whatever y'all have to say 'bout that."

"Let's go back to the carriage house," Laura said, "and we'll tell you both all about it. See what you think."

When they found Eli, he was just finishing up watering the horses. He seemed startled to see them walk through the front door. "Daddy, I thought you just left. Morning, Miss Laura. Nice to see you. Nice to see you...again, Mr. John, sir."

"I'm back," Micah said, "because they called me back. Said they had some idea they want to share with the both of us. A way to help get our Hannah back."

There was only enough room for two to sit on the bench. "Micah, Laura," John said, "you have a seat while I explain what we're thinking. Laura, feel free to add anything along the way."

Micah and Laura sat. Eli leaned up against a stall door, rested one foot on an upside-down bucket.

"Before I get started, we want you both to know you don't have to agree to this. It's quite a bold idea. As I stand before you now, it seems considerably more outlandish than it did when it made its first appearance in my mind. But I do believe it could work. And Laura does too, or else she'd have tried to talk me out of it rather than stand next to me now helping to explain." He looked over at her. She smiled.

"This is about getting Hannah back," Eli said, "right?"

"Yes," John said.

"And not losing you along with it," Micah said. He looked up at John. "I'm sorry, go on."

"Your father's right," John said. "With this plan, hopefully, we get Hannah back and neither of you come to any harm. And neither of us, either."

Micah and Eli now shared the same confused expression. "Neither of you?" Eli said.

"That's right. My idea involves Laura and I going with you down south. Micah, you as well. All four of us traveling together." The look on their faces was priceless.

Eli spoke first. "You want to go with me — with us — to go get Hannah? I don't understand. How would that work?"

"Well, for one thing," John began, "we'd all have to get skilled at the craft of acting, because to pull this off, we'd all have to be playing different roles. But if we could pull this off, I think it would greatly minimize the danger. Especially, compared to the risk of you going down there on your own, Eli."

"I'm not sure I understand acting," Micah said. "I want to help in any way I can, but —"

"Let me explain some more," John said. "Truly Micah, I think you'll find your role to be very suitable for you. In some ways, you just need to be who you already are. See, I'm thinking if Laura and I traveled south as a couple, say from one of the border states like Maryland, escorted by our two trusted slaves, in search of purchasing a third slave — a young woman — to serve as the nanny for our future child..."

"You having a baby, Miss Laura?" Micah said.

"No, not yet."

"But she'll be acting as though she were expecting," John said.

"And I won't talk like this, the way I do now," Laura said. "Ah'll talk like thee-is. You know, like I'm from South Caralina." She tried her best Southern accent. "I know that wasn't very good, but I have a friend not far from here who's from Georgia. I'll ask her to give me a few lessons before we go."

"We're thinking we could travel south by train — the four of us — then at some point, maybe in Columbus, we'll get off and lease a fine carriage for the actual search for Hannah."

"Eli, you would serve as our driver," Laura said, "and Micah could be John's valet."

"What a valet do?" Micah said.

"You just act like Beryl does," John said. "My father's butler. A slave version of that. I hate that your roles involve you both acting like slaves again. Especially you, Micah, after only being free a month, but—"

"No," Eli said, "we don't mind. Do we, Daddy? It's a brilliant idea. If we pose as slaves, no one will pay us any mind. We can just be ourselves, right out there in the open."

John loved the excitement on his face.

"That's what we're thinking," Laura said.

"We'll have to get some papers drawn up, some traveling papers," John said. "You know, ones made to look like you both legally belong to us. In case any authorities asked for proof along the way."

"I'm sure some of my friends with the Underground Railroad can help us with that," Eli said. "They made papers for Sally and me when we got here three years ago, to make it look like we were legally free. I'm sure they can do the same thing going the other way."

"And we'll also have to get my folks and the Harrison's to approve this," John said. "Since the two of you work for them, and we'd be gone for several weeks."

Eli and Micah both lost a little of their zeal hearing that.

"But I feel certain my family will be supportive," John said, with a good deal more confidence than he felt. "And I know the Harrison's really love you, Micah. I'm sure, if I explained the situation with your daughter, they would be sympathetic to our cause."

He certainly hoped so.

"They been very good to me," Micah said.

No one said anything for a few moments.

"So, John said, "I take it you're both on board with this idea? Do we take it to the next step?"

"I am," Eli said. "I can't believe you both came up with this plan, let alone are willing to go down there with us. I don't know how to thank you."

"It's okay," Laura said. "You're like family to us. And Micah, I literally owe you my life. We couldn't just go on our way as if nothing happened after hearing this news about Hannah."

"There is one other thing," Eli said. "If we do find, Hannah, and we break her free, the getting back part will be a lot more dangerous than the getting down there part. Because—from what I hear about this man—he will be chasing us the whole way trying to get her back."

John looked at Eli. "He won't be chasing us, Eli. Because we won't be breaking her free, or helping her escape. We'll be purchasing her freedom the same way we did for Micah. When we leave, we'll have all the right papers saying she belongs to us. And when we get back, we'll set her free for good."

Micah didn't say anything. He just leaned over and hugged Laura, then stood and hugged John. Tears filled his eyes. "The Lord been so good to me this day. When I walked down here this mornin' to speak to Eli, I didn't know what to say. Didn't know what to do. Didn't know how this situation could be made right. Still so many things I don't know. But I do know this...since he give us friends like you to help us on our way, I got hope...where just a little while ago, no hope could be found."

12

John and Laura had just left the carriage house. Eli had asked permission to go visit Bella, the young lady he was seeing. Micah was on his way back to the Harrisons. John had suggested he not tell them anything until John could be there to explain.

They walked through the back gardens up the veranda stairs and found Sally cleaning up after John's breakfast with Joel. She looked at them, forced a smile and a quick wave.

"John," Laura whispered, "can't we tell Sally about our plans? She still thinks Eli's planning to go after Hannah by himself."

"I really think we need to get my family behind this before we start talking about it to anyone else."

"I'll just tell her a little. Not the whole thing."

"I suppose that would be okay."

"Sally," Laura said, "can we speak to you a moment?"

Sally set the tray of dishes and silverware on the table and came over. "Yes, Miss Laura. You need something?"

"No, I just wanted let you know...we had a good conversation with your brother and father in the carriage house just now."

Sally's whole expression changed. "Were you able to stop him? Eli, I mean. He not going after Hannah anymore?"

"Well, he's still going after her," Laura said. "But he won't be going alone. I can't explain now, but I will in a little while. I just wanted you to know, the situation is much improved from this morning. We have something we have to do first, and then I'll come find you and explain more."

"Oh, thank you, Miss Laura. I've been praying up a storm since we last spoke."

"Actually Sally," John said, "there is something you can do for us, if you don't mind."

"Anything, sir. You just say it."

"We'd like to have a conversation with my mother and Allison. Right away. Could you go ask them to meet Laura and I in the parlor?"

"Yes, sir. I can do that. You want Mr. Joel there, too? He upstairs talking with your Mama."

"Joel's still here?" John said. "By all means, ask him to join us, too. Tell them it's urgent. We'd really appreciate it if they could join us there right away."

Sally picked up the tray and hurried into the house. John and Laura followed her and walked through the downstairs hallways until they reached the parlor. "How are you feeling about all this," Laura said, "now that we're starting to move forward? Having any second thoughts?"

"Second, third, and fourth thoughts," John said. "But I'm ignoring them. I know what we're doing is the right thing. That's all that really matters. How I feel about it is something else altogether. I'm trusting that if God is not in this, he'll close the doors and make it impossible for us to proceed. But if they keep opening as we move forward —" he opened the parlor door — "like I'm opening this one, then we'll keep walking through them."

As John and Laura sat in the only seat in the parlor that could hold two people, John gazed around the room. It had pretty much been off-limits to him growing up as a child. And because it was, he never felt comfortable here. Even now. It was exquisitely decorated with the finest furniture, draperies, wall art, and rugs. A beautiful glass and crystal chandelier hung from the ceiling. Positioned directly across from the mahogany double-doors was a magnificent fireplace with a finely-crafted mantle and dual-wooden pillars lining each side, also made of mahogany.

Of course, it was all for show. John couldn't recall ever seeing an actual fire in the fireplace all the years he'd been here.

Suddenly, the door on the right opened. In walked Joel, who held it open for Mother and Allison. After they had taken a seat across from John and Laura, Joel closed the door and sat in the middle chair between them.

"My goodness, John," Mother said, "whatever is going on? Sally said you needed to speak with us right away."

"Sally saved Joel from the last few minutes of Mother's lecture," Allison said.

"It wasn't a lecture," Mother said. "It was a...talk."

"And I was about to use Sally's interruption," Joel said, "to make my escape when she said I needed to come also. Needless to say, little brother, you have piqued our curiosity at the very least."

Laura reached over, grabbed hold of John's hand. He could feel her starting to tense up. He squeezed it gently, trying to reassure her. "Well, thank you all for coming so promptly. I'm sorry if my interruption to your day caused any undue alarm. I guess I should start by saying, nothing is wrong. That is, nothing is wrong with Laura or I. We are both fine."

"You're having a baby, aren't you?" Mother said, her face instantly alive with joy. "That's why you wanted us here altogether, to hear the news at the same time."

John smiled, looked at Laura, then back at his mother. "No, I'm sorry to disappoint you. We are not having a baby."

"Not yet," Laura added. "Someday soon, we hope."

"You decided to accept our proposal," Joel said. "You've decided to stay here in New York and not go back to San Francisco."

"Is that it?" Mother said. "You and Laura are not leaving us today?"

"Well," John said. "We will not be leaving you, not today anyway."

Joel looked confused by John's answer.

"But that's not what I need to talk about," John said. "Although I'm still seriously considering your and father's proposal. But what I have to say will, by necessity, delay any official response. Perhaps this will go more quickly if you all would stop guessing, and allow me a few minutes to explain. I assure you, that's all it will take."

Joel and Mother repositioned themselves in their chairs. Allison continued to listen with interest.

"I'm not exactly sure how to approach this issue with you all," John said. "It's a matter of great importance to us and, as you already know, some urgency." He looked at their faces, especially Joel's and Mother's, and got an idea. "I'm sure you all have a fresh appreciation of how much our family life means, to all of us, I mean. Now that we've been...reunited."

"It's been so great having all of my children together again," Mother said. "And you too, Laura. You're part of the family now."

"Exactly," John said. "Having us all together again, safe and sound is a wonderful thing. The problem is, we want Micah, Eli, and Sally to have that same blessing. And right now, they can't."

"I don't understand," Joel said. "But they are together. They've been together since you've come home."

"Yes," Laura said. "But one of their immediate family members is not here with them. Her name is Hannah. Micah's youngest daughter. She's still a slave down south, and we've just learned her life is in grave danger. John has come up with a plan, a way for us to hopefully rescue Hannah and bring her safely back here with us. With Micah, Eli, and Sally."

John spent the next ten minutes explaining everything to them. When he'd finished, most of the previously positive atmosphere had left the room.

Joel was the first to speak. "It sounds like you've thought everything through, John. At least in a preliminary way. And your willingness to help Micah's family this way is certainly commendable, but how can we be of any help to you?"

"Well," Mother said, "the whole thing sounds entirely too dangerous. If I could, I'd forbid you from even considering such a thing. Isn't there someone we could hire to go on this...rescue mission?"

"I wish there was, Mother," John said. "But there isn't anyone else who can do this. For starters, we don't have a photograph of Hannah. We need Micah and Eli just to know who she is. And we don't know a soul in Fredericksburg, which is the last place Hannah lived before she was sold off to this slaveowner in Charleston. Micah and Eli know all the right people there, people who could give us connections and clues about where to look. But they can't go by themselves, or they'll be kidnapped by slave catchers and resold as slaves. This is the only way I can think of to do this. The only safe way."

"But it's not safe," Mother said.

"Well," John said, "it's the safest way I can think of. Think about it, we'll be traveling in the South as slaveowners with slaves accompanying us, looking to buy another one. Once we find her, find Hannah, we'll buy her, legally, and bring her back here to New York."

"Well," Joel said, "that's the plan."

Yes, John thought. That's the plan.

13

Eli dreaded the conversation he was about to face. He really liked Bella, pretty sure he even loved her. If not for this terrible news about his sister Hannah, he'd likely be coming here later on to tell her so. It only took him a few moments to find an opening along the curb to park the carriage. He was on 7th Avenue near the intersection with 14th Street, where Bella worked mending clothes. This was an area where many of the freed Negroes lived and worked; where he'd probably live too except that his accommodations in the Foster's carriage house were included in his pay.

Eli nodded and smiled at the folks walking by, not often accustomed to seeing a carriage this nice or a young man dressed so fine in this part of town. Of course, Bella's boss Ella Mae had said she'd be happy if he'd park right there in front of her shop whenever he paid her a visit. "Be good for bidness," she said. He hopped down and secured the carriage. Walked over and gave both horses some affection and chopped carrots.

Looking through the glass window, he saw Ella Mae hanging dresses on a rod. A large woman, middle-aged, with a big smile and bright eyes. She hurried over to greet him as he made his way to the front door.

"Well, what do we owe the pleasure of seeing your smiling face so early in the day?"

Eli didn't know he was smiling.

"Let me guess. I don't see you holding any clothes that need fixing, so you here to see Bella. Am I right?"

"Yes, Ma'am, Miss Ella. She working today?"

"Every day but Sunday. She in the back. You can go on through. I know she be happy to see you. Talks about you all the time."

"Thank you, Ma'am. I won't keep her long. I promise." He walked past the stacks of clothes and through a curtain, found Bella leaning over a table sewing a patch on a pair of trousers. She turned when she heard him, and her face lit up.

"Eli, what a pleasant surprise." She set her project aside. "I didn't even think I was going to see you today." She hurried over and reached out for his hand.

He gave it an affectionate squeeze, but he really wanted to take her in his arms and kiss her proper. But they hadn't kissed yet. Wanted the first time to be something special. "I figured I better come today, since I have some news to share. Figured it best to get right to it."

"Oh? The look on your face is saying it's not good news. What's wrong?"

"Certainly nothing with you, Bella. Just some family news, is all. My younger sister got into some serious trouble, needs my help in a big way."

"Sally? What kind of trouble she in?"

"Not Sally. I've got another one younger than her, named Hannah. Probably didn't mention her since she lives so far away. Don't really get to see her anymore."

Bella let go of his hand. "Far away? And she needs your help? Guess that means you'll be going on a trip then?"

"Afraid so. Can't be helped."

"I see. When will you be leaving?"

"Very soon. Fact is, this might be the last time I see you till we get back."

"How long might that be?"

"At least a couple weeks. Maybe a few days more."

She looked stunned. "My goodness. Mind if I ask where she lives? Where you're needing to go to help her?"

"Just down south a ways."

She gave him a look. "Down south a ways, huh? How far south we talking?"

"Now don't you be worrying about this. I'll be just fine. I'll be there and back before you know it."

"You don't want to say. So, we're not talking south as in Pennsylvania or Maryland?"

Eli shook his head no. But he really didn't want to get into the details. "Further south than that. But seriously, you don't gotta worry. We'll be careful. Won't take any chances. Once we help her out, we'll head straight home."

"Am I allowed to ask what kinda help she needs?"

Eli sighed.

"Then it *is* something dangerous."

"There's always some sliver of danger when you head down that way. But I won't be on my own. Mr. Foster, John, I told you about him. He and his wife, Laura, gonna help us.

And my Daddy, too. He's coming. So see, I'll be in good hands."

"Still haven't said what kind of help she needs."

Eli stepped back. "Do we need to get into all this, Bella? Can't you just trust me? I'm not making any of this up."

"Trust you? Eli, I want to trust you. But you know what I said when we first started courtin,' that I wasn't ready yet after what I been through. You know how my first beau treated me. I liked you right from the start, but I said I can't be with a boy unless he's willing to be totally honest with me about everything. You said you would be."

"I am being honest, Bella. Everything I've told you is the truth."

"It may be, but it's not the whole truth. You holding somethin' back. I can tell."

She had him dead to rights. "Okay, I am, but it's only so you don't worry."

"You think being vague about your plans gonna keep me from worrying? Probably make me worry more."

"Okay then," he said. "My sister Hannah's still a slave. She was in Fredericksburg where we used to be and just got sold off to an evil man who lives near Charleston. We're gonna go down there, find her, and bring her back."

"You gonna steal her? From Charleston? That's a million miles away, Eli."

"What? No, we're not gonna steal her." He explained the rest of the plan. Didn't leave anything out but did include as many positive words in the telling as he could. When he was done, she took a step forward, took both of his hands in hers, and looked into his eyes. "Eli, please don't do this. Don't go. I got a feeling 'bout this. You walk out that door, I'll never see you again."

"Bella, listen," he said softly, "we're taking every precaution on this trip. We're going down there as slaves, with our owners right there with us. No reason for anyone to be suspicious. And when we find Hannah, we're going to buy her, all legal like. So won't be any reason for anyone to come chasing after us."

"Can't your father just go down there with them then? He's not a runaway."

"No, Bella. I've got to go. It's my duty. She's kin. And she's in trouble. Can't you see? I'll be there and back before you know it." He leaned down and kissed her on the back of the hand.

"Oh, Eli." She put her arms around his neck. "You'd better come back to me. Whatever you gotta do. You come back to me."

14

Clifton Plantation

16 miles Northwest of Charleston, SC

THE SILENCE and lack of motion woke Hannah up.

First thing she aware of were the aches and pains in her back and shoulders, her behind as well. Come from sitting in this mostly-dark cage-on-wheels, the one she and three other slave girls been riding in for days now. Had a wood roof on it and wooden sides all around. Just enough opening at the top to let a sliver of light in between the bars. A little more light come in through the bars on the door.

Kitch, a big colored man who appeared to be running this show, said riding in this thing for they own good. "You young ladies be treated way better than dis we get where you goin'," he'd said at the start. "This cage keep pryin' eyes from seeing what Massa Clifton bringin' back...a bunch-a pretty girls inside."

Whatever the reason, so far it didn't feel like they been treated any better than a load a pigs. But one thing she knew...they definitely in the south now, judgin' how much warmer it got in here once the sun come up.

Hannah looked over at the three other girls in there with her. About her same age. One's eyes were still closed. One looking down at the floor. The one closest to the back, stared up through the bars at some spot in the sky. Didn't find out much about any of them on the ride down. No more in a mood to talk than she was.

But then, what was there to talk about anyhow? Maybe how their lives been totally ripped apart by this man, Massa Clifton? How they been taken from the only place they ever knowed, ripped out of the arms of all the folks they loved? Thrown in the back of this wagon and carted hundreds of miles to some warm, humid place they never been to before. Not knowin' what to expect one moment to the next?

She thought about Lucas, her husband. The pitiful scene when they parted. How he pleaded for them not to take her away. Kept on pleading as they beat and whipped him till he couldn't plead no more. They all devils, every last one. Will she ever see Lucas again? It didn't seem so. No way she can even write him. Never learned how. Now she wished she been nicer to her big brother, Eli. Before he ran off up north, he tried to teach her to read and write, but she didn't see any point to it.

And now she wished she'd gone off with him and Sally when they come for her a few months later. But how could she leave Lucas? He just wouldn't go. But now look...she

didn't have him anymore, neither. She had no one. No
friends. No family.

Nobody.

Oh, Lord. What am I gonna do?

Suddenly, the chain on the door rattled. Then three loud
bangs on the side wall. "Wake up, ladies. Your journey has
ended. We here."

Kitch's voice.

The chain slid off the bolt. The door opened letting too
much sun in. Hannah squinted as she waited for her turn to
get out. Wasn't easy keeping her balance in this tight space,
especially with her wrists chained together. At least the
shackles weren't on tight. Kitch had said that was on
purpose, too. Didn't want their pretty little wrists — as he
put it — to get all bruised on the ride down. "You girls won't
be whipped at all," he'd said. "Unless you don't mind what
you're told. Even then, I've learned how to make it so's I don't
leave a mark. These white men don't wanna see their women
all bruised up...unless they the ones doing the bruisin.'"

Hannah didn't wanna hear none of that talk. She had no
plans of being any white man's woman.

"Well," Kitch said, "y'all don't look too much worse for the
wear. Sorry we couldn't provide finer accommodations. But
y'all line up now, let Celia get a look at you."

Hannah did as she was told. So did the others. She took a
quick glance around. Nice-looking place. The road they just
come down was lined with a row of big old oak trees, same
number on each side. Acres of green grass on either side
going way off till it ended in some woods. The heat wasn't as
bad as inside that box, even a little breeze blowing.

The two white men who made the trip down with Kitch

stood off about ten feet away holding rifles. Hannah couldn't quite understand the situation. They was white, but it seemed Kitch was in charge. And he not a free man, judging by the way he kept calling Mr. Clifton *Massa*.

"Let's see what you brung me."

Hannah turned toward the woman's voice. Saw a petite Negro lady come around from the other side of the wagon right toward them. Kitch stepped aside to let her by.

"Massa get a good bunch this time," Kitch said. "He say bring them directly to you, and you can get them all fixed up the way you do, so he can show them off when the other plantation owners come by. Know when that is?"

"No, I don't," she said. "Because I couldn't send word to give them the time, because somebody didn't get a message to me this morning telling me what time you'd be arriving."

"I tried to, Celia. Went right down to that telegraph office before we got on the road, but it wasn't working. Man said he didn't know why. Somebody must-a cut the wires, or something."

She turned her attention to Hannah and the girls. "Don't never mind. You're here now, and so are they. We'll get those gentlemen over here one way or the other." She walked by each of the girls, looked them over, up and down. "Yes, these young ladies will do just fine. Course, we couldn't get the price of a mule for how you look now. But we'll clean you up right nice. When I'm done, those men will be bidding up a storm to get you back on they plantations."

Kitch came over to Celia, whispered in her ear. "Except that one." He pointed to Hannah with a head nod. "From what he say, Massa got his eye on that one. Think he means for her to stay right here."

Celia walked over, stood in front of Hannah. Gave her a closer inspection. Felt to Hannah like this woman looking her over the same way Massa Clifton did right before he bought her. She didn't like it one bit.

"So, you gonna be Massa Clifton's new lady, that right?"

Hannah wanted to say something badly, but thought about what Kitch said about knowing how to whip so it don't leave a mark.

"I can see why he'd pick you. Specially over these others. But we'll get you all fixed up just the same, even if he don't mean to sell you tomorrow. Help him see you the way you could be, not the way you look now. And I know just what to do. See, I used to be his lady, so I know what he like. And if you listen to old Celia here, I can teach you how to play this game, so you almost get the best of everything amongst the servants and slaves. And I say *almost*, because I still get the very best. I get it, 'cause I learnt how to play this game well. And if you be nice to Celia, and do what I say, I'll teach you what I learnt."

Hannah looked at her, at Celia's eyes, for just a second. And said NO with those eyes, in that second, as loud as she could. She wasn't gonna be no white man's lady. No matter what the prize.

It just wasn't gonna happen.

15

Over the last hour, Celia saw to it that they all got cleaned up, got some better clothes to wear, and got fed. Oddest part of it, was other Negro servants were serving them. Hannah never had other slaves do things for her like that. And that was another thing that was different...Celia said the ones who worked all the chores related to the house were called servants. Only the ones worked the land were called slaves.

"Any of you ever been house servants before?" she'd asked. No one had. "Well, y'all just been promoted. You servants now. Course, the pay ain't any better, but the work is. Most the time anyway. And if you learn how to play the game right, you can make some money on the side, too."

She led them down a dirt path bordered by tall shrubs till it opened up in an area filled with little buildings with white, clapboard siding. A lot like the slave shacks they lived in back home, only those were made of brick. And the roofs on these looked like they might keep out all the rain. This plantation did have brick shacks like home. She'd already seen a whole row of them across the way. But slaves lived in these wood ones, too. She saw several going in and out of them. Maybe she was gonna get to live in one.

Celia stopped at the first of them, maybe twice as big as the rest. "This my place. I'm gonna let you in, but you remember always knock first." Then she looked at the other three girls. "What am I telling you this for? You'll be gone before too long. Even so, the plantations you going to run much the same, I expect."

The thing Hannah could hardly take in was that a place this big housed only one woman. They followed Celia up three steps. As soon as Hannah stepped inside, she could see it was very much like places back home made for two families. Only instead of a wall dividing the building by half, this wall had a doorway in the middle, so that Celia had two separate rooms. All to herself. Hannah could see a nice sized bed through the open doorway. And the wood floors were smooth, like you see in white folks' houses. On the left wall, as usual, was a big brick fireplace, but Hannah didn't see any kitchen area in the place. Where the kitchen ought to be was a passable-looking wood table with five chairs. And in the front, by the window were two comfy-looking padded chairs, the kind you see in parlors.

"Some of you probably wondering where my kitchen is," Celia said, "how I cook my food. Thing is, I don't. Haven't cooked my own food for years. Got my own girl brings it to me from the big house, made by the same chef who cooks for the Clifton family. It's like I said, things not as bad as they could be, you learn how to play the game. Now, I'm going to sit in my favorite chair over here by the window. You ladies pull up one of them chairs, sit close enough so I don't have to yell."

They did what she asked. Hannah could tell by the looks on the other girls' faces...they were starting to buy whatever Celia was selling. But none of it mattered a whit to Hannah.

After everyone sat down, Celia leaned back in her chair. "Now, I'm not saying you young ladies will be staying in a place like this. It took me years to have all this. But the thing is, you got to know, you got bought by Massa Clifton for your looks, plain and simple. Kitch and I knew when he went on that trip what he was shopping for. He told us straight out. Now he comes back with you pretty young things and calls this meeting with a bunch of his plantation-owning friends. And he tells me to get you all ready to show off to 'em when they come by. Can only mean one thing. He's done this once before. He aims to make a good deal of money off you ladies. Maybe two to three times what he paid for you."

She leaned forward in Hannah's direction. "All except you, honey. What's your name again?"

"Hannah, Ma'am."

"Kitch tells me he ain't planning to sell you. But everything else I'm gonna say is just as much for you as these other girls." She leaned back in her chair, directed her comments to the group. "And these other slaveowners be willing to pay that extra money for only one reason. Your looks. God made you pretty. And white men — guess all men for that matter — like 'em pretty. But see, these men all got wives and families and respectability in the community. So, you girls gotta have more going on than just your looks.

Since none of you been house servants before, I gotta teach you some skills that you don't have. 'Cause your new owners gotta convince they wives that they didn't buy you because you pretty. But make no mistake, that's why they going to buy you, either tomorrow or the next day, one."

"But how we gonna learn all these house-servant skills in a day?" one of the other girls asked. "I only ever picked cotton, 'cept when I was young, I babysat my Massa's chillun' sometimes. But I never worked a day in the big house."

"I expect," Celia said, "once you get bought, and your new owners find out you ain't ready to work in the house, they gonna pay extra to Massa Clifton to have me train you and get you ready."

"For how long?"

"Long as it takes," Celia said. "So, don't you go frettin' 'bout that. They ain't gonna bring you home till you got more to offer than a pretty face."

"What kinda things you gonna teach us?" another one said.

"I won't be doing all the teaching myself, but a lot of it. Some of it will depend on what you can and cannot do. If any of you good at sewing and mending clothes, even if you can pick things up quick, that's a skill we can work on. You can't do that, maybe we'll have to settle for you washing clothes and learning how to use an iron. Teach you tricks to get out stains and such. 'Sides that, all kinda work to be done in the kitchen. Any of you ever worked as a scullion?"

Everyone shook their head no.

"Well, we'll get our chef to see what you can do, lots of different jobs in a kitchen. You got a steady hand and good balance, we'll see if you can serve food when the family eats.

Can't have a servant who spills things. We'll learn you how to set a table right. How to keep all the silver polished and looking bright. Learn where everything goes, so things get put back in their proper place. But maybe one of the most important things I'll teach you is how to act around the family or when guests arrive. See, they need you around to attend to their wants and needs, but they don't really *want* you around. They want to pretend they in the rooms all by themselves and can talk and act however they please. You gotta learn how to be there, but not be there. Available but unseen. They want you to look like you're not listening to a thing, unless they ask you to do something, then they expect you to hear every word."

The more Hannah heard, the more she wished they'd let her just work in the field.

"Any more questions?" Celia said. "Well, I expect you'll have plenty in the days ahead. You do, you ask. Massa Clifton expects me to train you right, and I can't let you cause me trouble by getting things wrong 'cause you wouldn't ask." She looked at each of the girls' faces, spent a little more time looking at Hannah, for some reason. "Okay then, y'all probably tired from riding in that wagon. The little building right next to this one empty, except for four bunks. That's where you'll be sleeping tonight and for however many days I be training you. Y'all can go get some rest until lunch. Then we'll get to work after that. And we will work, mind you. You best be prepared for that. Your pretty face won't help you avoid the whip, you ain't willing to work."

One by one, they stood and walked out the front door. As they made their way to the building next door, Hannah looked back at Celia's place, thought about all she'd seen inside. Truth was, if Celia offered Hannah everything she'd gained through all them years, in a heartbeat Hannah would trade it for that damp little shack she shared with Lucas back in Fredericksburg.

16

About two hours ago, Hannah and the other three girls were abruptly awakened from their naps by a servant girl and told they best hurry up and get ready. She didn't know exactly for what, only that Miss Celia sent her over and said she wasn't to leave until she was sure all four of 'em were up and ready to go. Ten minutes later, Miss Celia came in and told them she'd heard from Massa Clifton that all them plantation owners didn't care how late it was. They were itching to get over here and check out the new stock he brung in from his trip.

"Case you didn't know," Celia then said, "you girls are the new stock."

She spent the rest of the time till now getting them ready for some kind of big showing Massa Clifton had scheduled at 4PM. In a way, the next part was somewhat enjoyable. They were led back to Celia's place where these servant girls —maybe ten to twelve years old — kept bringing in all these dresses for them to try on. All different kinds of fancy clothes in all different kinds of colors. Lots of lace, ribbons and bows. The kinda clothes Hannah had only seen white ladies wear in plantation houses or walking down fine city streets. She never expected to get close to dresses like these, let alone be allowed to try one on. But here, Celia having them try on one dress after the other, looking to find the one she thought looked the best on each girl.

When she figured she had the right outfit picked out, they spent the next twenty minutes trying on different hats. When she finally had the right hat for each girl, Celia changed her mind. Decided they shouldn't wear hats after all. Then she spent some time picking out shoes, only not as much time on this, since the dresses pretty much covered up the shoes. The trick was, finding ones that fit. All the girls, including Hannah, had never worn shoes like this. All shiny and stiff. Celia said it would take some getting used to, but they had better get used to it. Their days of going barefoot were over.

One of the girls, Hannah thought her name was Lucy, asked Celia, "I thought you said we were going to be house servants. I never been one, but I seen a good many at my old place. None of them dress like this. We look like we going to a ball."

Celia actually smiled. "I guess I can see why y'all might be confused. Any of you ever been sold before?"

Everyone shook their head no.

"Really? Not a one of you been sold at an auction before?" Again, same response. "Any of you ever *been* to an auction? You know, a place where slaves get sold."

Again, no one had.

"Really?" Celia couldn't believe it. "You girls didn't get

around much, now did you? Then how did you come to be bought by Massa Clifton?"

The girls didn't quite know what she was after, but Hannah took a guess. "We were sold, but not at some auction. In my case, I'm out working in the field like I always do when a boy who works in the main house come out to fetch me. Said I had to stop what I was doing, follow him directly. He said a man dressed in fine clothes, riding in some fancy coach had stopped by, talked with our master a while, and now the master sent this boy out after me. When I got there, I see my massa talking with Massa Clifton. Couldn't hear everything, but it seemed like they'd met earlier in town over some drinks. And Massa Clifton had come out to see the slave girl they'd been talking about. Turned out, that slave girl was me. In no time at all, after living all my life at that place, he sold me to Massa Clifton."

Each of the other girls shared a similar story that made it clear they'd also been handpicked by Massa Clifton then sold to him on the spot.

"I guess that makes sense," Celia said, "seeing as Massa Clifton weren't up there looking to buy field hands. He buying field hands, he'd have done so at auction. I been to plenty. As a rule, they are a pitiful sight."

Maybe so, Hannah thought. But the scene when she got sold off was plenty pitiful in its own right.

"In a very little while," Celia continued, "I'm gonna bring you over to a building sits right next to our stables. And we gonna have an auction, of sorts. Won't be the pitiful scene you usually see when auctions commence, because nobody's buying or selling field hands. These plantation owners coming got something else on they minds. They looking to buy a young lady — a young Negro lady like yo'selves — that they can bring home and convince they wives you make fine house servants. But for what they really want you for, I need you to be looking your finest, so you can bring my Massa the highest price."

Hannah was horrified.

She looked at the other three girls and was surprised to find no change in expression on their faces. Either they didn't understand what Celia was meaning by her words, or else they had no problem with it.

"Now, as for you, Hannah," Celia said, "since it seems Massa Clifton doesn't intend to sell you, I still wanna dress you up all pretty like, just so he could see the possibilities for the future. In case he decides to make you his lady. Or at least, one of them."

Hannah sighed. Celia singled her out like this as though it made her special, but it only made things worse. Somehow, someway, she'd have to make her understand...there were NO possibilities that in the future Hannah would become Massa Clifton's lady.

Or even one of them.

17

The time had come.

Celia led the four ladies in a procession past her place down that long, hard-packed dirt path with big bushes on either side until it opened up to a wide area. Over on the left, was the big plantation house. It was easily twice the size of the main house where she come from. To the right looked like a garden area bordered by neatly trimmed bushes. Beside that, a white painted horse fence drew a line around the stables. Celia led them past all that to a tan-colored building standing by itself. About the size of a barn but just one story. Must've had a high ceiling, though, judging by where the roof began.

"That's where we going," Celia said.

There was a commotion over by the main house. A team of horses had just brought a shiny black carriage around to the front door. An older, well-dressed black man hurried outside to meet it. He stood at attention near the carriage door. Then Hannah saw Massa Clifton himself come out through the front door, across the porch and down the steps toward the carriage. His face, all smiles.

"Jacob, my man. You're here early."

The well-dressed black man — Hannah guessed him to be the butler — opened the carriage door and out stepped a heavyset gentleman with a wide-brimmed hat. Dressed like a plantation owner, if ever there was one. Had a gray mustache and matching goatee. "Well, my place is the closest to yours, Colonel, figured I'd take my advantage, see if I could get first pick."

"Hurry girls," Celia whispered, as she shepherded them toward the tan-colored building. "They haven't seen us yet. Massa don't want anyone eyeing the merchandise too soon." After they walked past a big live oak tree, some bushes blocked their view of the main house.

Celia brought them into the building, which was just one big open space. It did have a high ceiling. The walls were all plastered but somewhat rough, not like the inside of a house. But the wood floor was nice and smooth, just like Celia's place. On the left was some kind of platform, big enough to hold four or five people, with three steps leading up to it. Looked to Hannah like a spot for someone to give a speech, if they had a mind to. But there weren't no podium. Set out in front and facing the platform, maybe fifteen feet away, were five stylish chairs. The kind you might see around the dining room table in the big house, but they were set a couple feet apart.

Celia walked them past the platform and steps to the far side of the room, but still near the front. She took a moment to position each of the girls a certain way, all facing the door.

"They gonna be here very soon. You all look very nice. Massa Clifton handpicked each one of you, now I can see why. These men gonna gobble you girls up. But see, it's very important you don't speak. And don't make eye contact with them, even if they talking about you, and you know it. You don't say a word. You may like some of the things they say, and some things you may not. But don't you go showing it on your face, either way. Just pretend they talking about something else."

"Miss Celia," one of them said, "can I ask a question?"

"Sure, child."

"That man came out of the carriage. He one of the men coming to buy us? One of the plantation owners?"

Celia's eyes and eyebrows reacted in a way that made Hannah think she didn't like the man. "Yes, he is. And judging by the chairs we asked to set up, they be three others. That man is very rich, and very influential. His place not far from here, maybe twice the size of our plantation. You want to be very nice to that man."

"Why he call Massa Clifton, Colonel?" another girl asked.

"Because he used to be one. He fought in that war with the Mexicans, back in '48. Went to West Point and everything. Got wounded, though I don't recall how." She looked toward the door. "Okay, you ladies stay put. I'm gonna check, see how much longer till they come."

Fifteen minutes later, she was back. "They coming over now. Four buyers for three girls. Should be something to see."

Hannah couldn't believe how excited she seemed by all this, as if the lives and futures of these girls were all about to be greatly improved. Not that they were about to be auctioned off like prize horses.

Hannah could hear the men outside before she saw them, laughing and talking loudly. The front door swung open. The first man in was Massa Clifton himself, followed by the heavyset man who arrived first. Behind them were three more well-dressed gentlemen. All of them wore wide-brimmed hats that matched their frock coats. And all except for Massa Clifton had mustaches and goatees, trimmed in different styles. He was clean-shaven except for his thick bushy sideburns.

"Have a seat, gentlemen," Clifton said. "No bad seats in the house tonight. As you can see, the merchandise is already here." He quickly glanced at Hannah and smiled. She turned away.

The other men were already looking the girls over before being invited to do so. They made their way to their seats. Three of them smoked cigars. One said, "Would you have an ashtray, Colonel? Or should we just drop the ashes on the floor?"

The Colonel sent a disapproving look toward Celia for the oversight. "My apologies, Edward. Go ahead and use the floor for now. We'll clean up after. But what do you think, men? In general, I mean. Was my trip north worthwhile? Did I oversell my acquisitions, or do these creatures meet your expectations?"

"Speaking for myself," Jacob, the heavyset man, said, "if anything, you underplayed your hand. They are exquisite. Every one of them is finer than any of the female slaves I currently possess."

The other men said similar things.

"Tell me," one of the other men said, "they all seem rather young. Can we assume none of them have had children yet?"

"I know for a fact," Clifton said, "none have had a child yet. But think of the possibilities for the future. With just one purchase, you will be acquiring four, five, maybe six future slaves, or more. If you're like me, and you prefer mulattos, you can sire them yourself. If not, you can take your biggest and strongest male slaves from the field and reproduce the same through these lovely creatures. All for the cost of one purchase."

Hannah couldn't bear to hear this. These men talked of them as if they were broodmares or prized heifers, beasts who couldn't understand human words. She looked over at the Colonel, her new master. *If you're like me...you can sire them yourself*...she already despised him for taking her from Lucas. But to hear him talk like this? She decided then and there she would never let this man use her that way.

No matter what it took.

18

Foster Mansion
Gramercy Park, New York City

THE FOLLOWING MORNING, John was out on the veranda having breakfast again. Joel wasn't there. John supposed he was back at his home a few blocks away. But Laura was there, and so was Allison. His father had already left for work, driven by Eli as usual. Mother still had not come down from upstairs. Sadly, there was a new underlying current of tension in the Foster home today. Fortunately, it would not be present at the breakfast table. It began during dinner when John's father decided to tell him and Laura exactly what he thought of their rescue mission idea.

Sitting there stirring his coffee, while Laura and Allison were up at the buffet getting their food, John couldn't help but replay the moment in his mind. Just prior to his father's abrupt introduction to the subject, everything seemed to be going fine. Although understandably nervous, both Joel and Allison had been totally supportive of the idea. Mother had even begun to back the plan. At least, that's what John had thought before the incident at dinner. But since John had not been able to brief his father before the meal, and earlier Joel had agreed not to say anything to him, John could only suppose that Mother had done the honors. However she had communicated things, his father was none too pleased with what he'd heard.

John was just about to put the first forkful of roast beef in his mouth, when his father set his fork and knife down on the plate. "What's this foolhardy scheme I'm hearing about?" he'd said. "Some cockamamie nonsense about you and Laura traveling down to Charleston to rescue some slave?"

John had to fight hard against the tendency to react in kind. In the month since the shipwreck, he'd almost forgotten how arrogant and condescending his father could be. "I guess I don't have to wonder what you think of the idea," he'd said calmly.

"No, I guess you don't," Father said. "So, it's true. You and your wife are not traveling back to San Francisco. Instead, you're heading down to the deep South to poke a hornet's nest."

"Not the metaphor I'd use," John said. "But we are planning a trip down there. Not sure what you've heard or how things were explained but —"

"Wouldn't matter how they were explained. It's a fool's errand. No, it's not that. It would have to graduate several notches to become a fool's errand. Your mother said you're calling it a rescue mission. It's a suicide mission, I tell you. That's what you need to call it. Plain and simple."

John looked at Laura. He was saddened that she had to see this, but maybe it might help her more fully understand why he'd left New York in the first place. "There are some dangers involved. I don't deny that. But if you've heard the entirety of the plan, you'd see that it's very far from being a suicide mission, as you call it."

"John, these Southerners, especially these plantation owners, are getting very angry about all the slaves escaping their bonds and fleeing to the north. They say it's ruining their economy, and they're not gonna stand for it. Just read an article in the Times today — in the editorial page — saying that if things don't change and change quickly, he could easily foresee a full-fledged war breaking out between the North and South. The Fugitive Slave Act was supposed to calm things down, assure Southerners we weren't trying to destroy their livelihoods. But now they're saying, because of all the abolitionists in the north, especially in places like Philadelphia and here in New York, things are about as bad now as they were before the law took effect."

"Father, I don't see how anything you just said has anything to do with our plans for this trip. We aren't going down there to help some slaves escape. Our plan is to buy Hannah's freedom, legally. We'll be coming back with papers that say so. To anyone who asks along the way, she will be our slave, and we will be her owners. And yesterday afternoon, I went down with Micah and Eli to where those Underground Railroad folks meet. They're already working on creating papers for the two of them, showing we're their rightful owners. That's how we'll be traveling the whole time. As southern slaveowners on a trip in the South to buy another slave."

His father didn't immediately reply. John could tell by the look on his face that he'd made a dent in his father's tirade. Of course, he'd never let it show. Obviously, Mother had left out this important detail.

"Even so, John," his father continued in a slightly calmer tone, "I think you're biting off way more than you can chew. If anything goes wrong with your scheme, if anyone fails to play their part convincingly — even for a few moments — and you get caught, with the level of tension going on between the North and South right now, you and Laura could be put in prison. Do you realize that? And Micah and Eli? They could get lynched. That's the kind of thing they do down there with Negroes that give them any trouble. And it's not even a crime."

John saw something in his father's eyes just then. Something unexpected. Fatherly care. That's what motivated this anger. He didn't want anything to happen to them, any of them. He was trying to stop that — the possibility of real harm — coming to any one of them. "I appreciate your concern, Father. Honestly, I do. We're going to do everything we can to make sure we don't get caught, that everyone knows their part, thoroughly. Did Mother explain we're going to spend a few days in Baltimore before going further south, just to get our parts right? To make sure we understand how we're all supposed to behave?"

"No, she didn't. But I think that's wise."

John could hardly believe he'd heard those words come out of his father's mouth.

"John? Are you okay?"

It took a moment to register where these words were coming from. He looked across the table at Laura, Allison now sitting next to her.

"You haven't touched your food," Laura said.

"I don't think he's even blinked," Allison said. "Let me guess...you were thinking about what happened at dinner last night. Am I right?"

John smiled, picked up a forkful of scrambled eggs. "You're right."

"It started off quite badly," Laura said, "but I don't think it ended poorly. He never actually said he approved —"

"And he never would," Allison said. "But I agree, he did soften to the scheme once John fully explained things. What's your plan today?"

"Yes," Laura said, "I'd like to know that, too."

"Well," John said, "I've got to meet with the Harrison's and hopefully secure their blessing to release Micah for a few weeks. Then get with Beryl and enlist his help to teach Micah how to at least act like a butler. Then bring Micah down to a tailor Joel recommended, see if we can get him some proper butler clothes. Then finally, go to the train station, see if I can exchange these two tickets to Savannah for four train tickets to Baltimore."

"Oh, that's right," Allison said. "Eli and Micah will be riding on the train with you. How's that going to work? Do they even let slaves ride in the same car as their masters?"

John sighed. "I have no idea. I've never traveled as a slave-owner before."

19

The meeting with the Harrisons could not have gone better. After John had explained Micah's dilemma about his daughter's situation, they were completely sympathetic. "We consider ourselves almost abolitionists now," Mr. Harrison had said. "The sacrifice you're asking us to make is a small thing considering what others are doing to fight against this national disgrace. Micah has such a way with the horses, we haven't had to give them a second thought since he began looking after them. But I'm sure we'll be able to find some temporary help until you get back."

The meeting with Beryl, the family Butler, went as well as could be expected. He had been in the family's employ ever since John could remember, so it wasn't likely he would refuse any request they'd asked of him. And he rarely showed any emotion that John could see, so he couldn't tell whether Beryl would embrace the task of training Micah with any enthusiasm. "A valet and a butler have very different duties," he'd said. "And considering Mr. Micah has never worked in service before...well, we will see what we can do."

In any case, Beryl had agreed to do it and that's what mattered. Laura had found it thoroughly amusing to hear Beryl use the term, Mr. Micah.

Presently, she, John, Micah and Eli were just arriving at the tailor Joel had recommended, so they could buy Micah some clothes more appropriate to his new role. John and Laura had invited Micah to sit with them inside the carriage, but he felt too uncomfortable doing so. He'd said it was because of his clothes. "They all dirty and musty from working with them horses." But he'd quickly added, "Anyway, gives me a chance to spend more time with my boy, Eli."

John heard a knock behind his head, then the little door slid over allowing Eli to communicate with those inside.

"We're here, sir," he said. "At Smith Brothers, your brother's tailor." Then Eli whispered, "Remember, Mr. John, to wait and let me open the door for you and Miss Laura. I know how you like to do it for yourselves, but we gotta start practicing doing things the way they need to be on our trip."

"You're right, Eli. But you know how much I hate it."

"I do, sir. But it's what we gotta do."

The door slid over again. John heard Eli ask Micah, "You want any help getting down, Daddy?"

"Appreciate the asking, son, but I think I can manage it."

Once everyone was out of the carriage and ready to walk into the store, John stopped them and said quietly, "Now remember, we don't know what these folks' political beliefs are. Either the tailors themselves, or their customers. So, let me do all the talking. We need to be careful from here on out talking loosely about the purpose of our trip. Everyone understand?"

They all agreed. Then Eli added, "maybe I should just stay with the carriage. That would really be proper. Not like I need any new clothes for the trip."

"That's a good idea," John said. "Say, how did that talk go with your lady friend, Bella?"

Eli smiled, for just a moment. "All right, I guess. She worried about what could happen, but I explained how we had no choice. She'll be all right after while."

"Good," John said. "I guess."

They walked into the shop with Micah, who was looking all around with a startled look on his face. "I ain't ever been inside a store sells clothes, let alone fancy ones like these."

Laura gave John a sad look.

"You just stay close to me, Micah," John said. "You have the same right to be here as we do." John looked about the store. Toward the back, an older gentleman was being fitted for a coat, standing in front of a mirror. One of the tailors was measuring the length of his sleeve. John glanced at the counter just in time to catch the look on the other tailor's face as he spotted them by the front door. His smile quickly changed to concern when he saw Micah standing behind Laura. Laura took a step forward and now the man could see how Micah was dressed. His expression grew more sour. John had to admit, his friend seemed entirely out of place in a place like this.

The man looked around the store nervously, to see if any of his customers had noticed the trio who'd just entered. John didn't see anyone else, besides the man being fitted for the coat, but he sensed the tailor's apprehension. He took the initiative and headed his way. "Hello, Mr. Smith I presume?" John held out his hand.

The man looked at John then past him at Micah. "Uh, yes, I'm Mr. Smith. Alfred, is the name. That's my brother Raymond in the back. I don't believe we've had the pleasure."

"I don't think we have. I've never been in your store before. My name's John Foster. My brother Joel recommended your fine establishment to us."

His expression instantly changed. "Joel? Yes, Mr. Foster has been here many times. He has exquisite taste." His face somewhat improved, he glanced at Micah. "Is he...with you? I don't mean to be a snob, but we only carry the finest fabrics and materials here. I could recommend a few other stores that might be better suited to —"

"No, thank you. We actually came here on purpose. Because of what you've just said. See, my friend Micah here will be...let's just say, changing jobs very soon. He's quite a wizard with horses, but his new duties will be bringing him inside, and we need to have appropriate clothing for his new role. Are you familiar with the Foster mansion? It's in Gramercy Park, just about a mile from here."

"Oh, yes. We've done lots of business for clients in Gramercy Park. It's a lovely area of the city. And I quite agree, a servant working inside any one of those homes needs to dress appropriately. How many outfits will you need and when will you need them?"

John looked at Laura.

"He'll need at least two," she said. "They can both be the same. And then another set of clothes that he can wear when he's...off-duty, let's say. But still nice clothes. Just not as fancy."

John loved the look on Micah's face. He couldn't believe what he was hearing.

"I be happy with just one suit to wear," Micah said.

"I know you will, Micah," Laura said. "But you'll need these others because of our —"

John realized, she was just about to say the word trip but caught herself. "In case something spills on one suit. This way you won't have to wait until it's cleaned and dried."

"And we'll need these outfits for Micah as soon as possible," Laura said.

"And I'm willing to pay extra for that," John added.

"Very good," Smith said. He started leading them toward the back of the store, but on the opposite side from where his brother was still working with that older gentleman. "If you don't mind, we typically do things for house servants in the back here, behind this curtain. It affords us...a little more privacy."

John and Laura instantly knew privacy wasn't the man's concern. He glanced at Micah. Either he didn't catch the shadow cast his way, or didn't care. "You lead the way," John said.

They walked behind the black curtains to another fitting area, similar to the one in plain sight.

"Can I assume your friend has never been fitted for a suit before?" Smith asked.

"You right about that," Micah said cheerfully. "I ain't ever wore nothing could rightly be called a suit. But I'll do whatever you tell me."

Smith smiled. "Very well. Could you stand over here, and step up on this little pedestal.

Micah did as he asked. Smith asked him to take off his coat, so he could get more accurate measurements. He walked Micah's coat over to a hook, holding it like he was carrying a dead rat. He came back and asked Micah to hold out his right arm perfectly straight. Micah giggled when Smith started the measurement from under his arm, which caused John and Laura to laugh.

"Always been a little ticklish there," Micah said. "But you go on. I'll try to behave."

"Do you have any idea," John said, "how long it will take to have these three outfits made and the approximate cost?"

Smith looked over at him. "If we hurry the order — for an added fee, as you said — I can have them ready in three days. And the cost will be..." He leaned over and whispered the sum into John's ear.

The money didn't bother John, but the timing did. "I'll pay you double that amount to have them ready by the end of the day tomorrow."

Smith looked shocked to hear this.

"I'm sorry," John said. "But time is of the essence for this. I can't explain why."

20

"This is the train station?" Laura asked. On the way here from the tailors, a considerable ride uptown in the carriage, all John had said was it wasn't very fancy. She had been to the train stations in Philadelphia and San Francisco and expected something similar. This was New York City, after all. But this wasn't only *not fancy*, it was incredibly small. There were no trains in sight and except for a sign that read: *New York and Harlem Railroad* on the building, she'd have never guessed this was a train station.

"I know," John said. "When we came here before to get our tickets for our trip home, Eli rode right past it. We had to ask someone for directions a few blocks down the road. When I asked the clerk at the ticket counter about it, he reminded me that New York is a seaport town. Everyone travels by boat. It's hard for trains to compete. It's almost completely surrounded by water. And there are no bridges across the Hudson to the mainland, just ferries. You should see how many different trains we have to take before we get on one that travels any great distance south."

"I'm not complaining," she said, "just a little surprised." She quickly realized how much easier their journey would be if she wasn't so deathly afraid of ships and boats. They could probably take a single ship out of the harbor here and be docking in Charleston in a matter of days. But she shuddered at the very thought of it.

"Remember to wait for Eli to open the door for us."

"You think it matters in this part of town?"

"Probably not," John said. "We just need to develop the habit. I know this part of it's going to be hard for us, but we've got to start treating Eli and Micah like slaves. Once we get to Maryland and anywhere south, one slip up could be a disaster."

"I know," she said.

She heard Eli and Micah get down from the carriage. A moment later, the door opened to Eli's smiling face.

"We've arrived, as you can see."

John got out and turned to help Laura down without tripping.

"Do you want us to come in?" Eli said.

"I don't think that'll be necessary," John said. He reached into his pocket and pulled out his billfold. "Here's a few dollars for you and your father. It's about lunchtime. See if you can find someplace to eat."

"Someplace that serves our kind," Eli said. He looked around. "Shouldn't be too hard this part of town." He stepped closer and whispered, "Not sure you and Miss Laura should go exploring when you're done. Quite a few unseemly characters around here."

"Good advice," John said. "We'll wait right here if we get done before you return."

Laura watched as Micah and Eli headed down the walkway in search of food. John reached out his arm, which Laura gladly took.

"This way, my dear. Doesn't look like we'll be standing in a line like we've had to do making our travel arrangements by ship."

They walked through the front door and into an open area that looked very much like any small railway station you find in a town a fraction the size of New York. Through two different sets of open doors along the back wall, she could now see the railroad tracks. Besides her and John, there were only three others in sight. A Negro pushing a broom just outside, another older Negro man sitting in his own chair at a shoeshine stand. No customers. And then, walled in behind a small ticket office in the far corner, a white clerk looking at them behind an opening covered by iron bars.

"Help you folks?" he said. "Next train not for two hours. Runs north, of course, seeing as we're the end of the line for the New York and Harlem."

"This was the same fellow who waited on me before," John said quietly. He led them up to the counter window. "Hello, I was in here last week buying tickets for my wife and I. We were heading for Savannah. Think we were supposed to be on that next train you just mentioned, but we've had a significant change of plans and won't be leaving after all."

"Supposing you're here for a refund then."

"Not quite," John said. "We're still taking a trip south, just not as far. And there will be four of us, instead of two. I was hoping we could exchange these tickets and use that money to help pay for the new ones."

"I suppose that can be arranged," the man said. "Thankfully, there isn't any line of people behind you, so let's see if we can figure this out. Now if you recall, I can't give you tickets from here to any place in the deep south. In fact, I can only give you tickets that get you to Philadelphia, by way of Croton Falls. That's where you'll get off and take another train that'll take you south as far as Philadelphia. Once there, you'll have to get four tickets from Philadelphia to wherever it is you're going."

"I remember something about that," John said. He looked at Laura. "It's a bit convoluted compared to traveling by ship, because there's a number of different railroads, owned by different people, between here where we need to be."

"Convoluted," the clerk repeated. "That's one way to put it. But these days we do have trains that run pretty much up and down the entire East Coast. So, if you're traveling in that general direction, it won't be too hard to figure out a route. Where you folks headed now?"

"Eventually to South Carolina, but we're going to stop a week, maybe more, in Baltimore."

"Now see, I can't sell you a ticket that far, but I know for a fact you can buy one in Philly that goes directly into Baltimore. Think it runs about a dollar a person."

"So how much for four tickets from here to Philly?" John said. "I should say, how much more, after you refund these tickets we're trading in?"

The clerk looked beyond John and Laura. "You said four, but I only see two of you. Are the other two adults or children?"

"They're adults. They went to get something to eat, but they should be back shortly."

He began writing something on a piece of paper. "Okay then, four adults from here to Philly, less the tickets you're turning in..."

Laura remembered something Allison had asked that morning, thought she better mention it. "Excuse me, sir. The other two adults traveling with us are our Negro servants. I'm not sure if that affects the price."

He looked up. "Sorry to say, but it does. Turns out though, in your favor."

"How's that?" John asked.

"Well, company's got strict policies about whites and coloreds traveling together. For starters, they gotta be on separate cars. We put our white customers in the rearmost cars, our Negro riders stay up near the front. The accommodations aren't quite as nice in those cars, but we do make it up to them by charging less. Costs almost half as much, as a matter of fact. You'll find that's pretty much how it's gonna be in all the trains you'll take on this trip, even more so when you get down south. Although, can't say for sure they'll give your colored servants a price break like we do. So, let me rework my figures here, given this new information."

Laura and John looked at each other, saddened but not surprised by this news. At least they'd be on the same train together, she thought. And at least they weren't traveling by ship.

When the clerk gave them the price difference, given the discount, John only had to pay four dollars more. He put the tickets in his lapel pocket and they started walking toward the front door.

"I get why they won't let us travel in the same car," Laura said, "even though I believe it's wrong. But why do they have the train cars with white people toward the back, and the ones with Negroes in the front?"

"Three reasons," the Negro shoeshine man said. "Sorry for speaking up. Hope you don't mind, but I overheard your conversation."

"I don't mind at all," John said.

"Like I said, three reasons. The stink, the noise, and the smoke. The cars closest to the front get all that coming from the train engine. So, that's where they put us. Most of that gone after the first few cars, so that's where they put the white folk."

"Why does that not surprise me?" Laura said. "So sorry for that," she said to the man. "If my husband and I were in charge, everyone would sit together and no one would be treated any better or any worse than anyone else."

The shoeshine man smiled. "Nice of you to say that, Ma'am. In this city at least, a good number of white folk think like you. Y'all have a nice day."

Laura looked down at the little handwritten sign announcing the price of his services. She reached into her purse, pulled out double that amount and gave it to him. "I don't need my shoes shined, but I can see this is the slow time of the day, thought you could use a little help."

"Thank you kindly. You right about that."

As John opened the front door, they all heard a great commotion across the street on the opposite corner. Two men who looked like cowboys had just grabbed a third man — a Negro about Eli's age — right off the sidewalk and started dragging him in the dirt.

Close by Laura heard, "No, Eli. You stay put, son."
It was Micah's voice.

21

John heard Micah's voice, too. He looked for and found them amidst a small gathering on the sidewalk about fifty yards away. Everyone else was still looking at the scene with the three men.

Eli was trying to pull away from his father. "We've got to go help him, Daddy. Don't you see what's going on? They slave catchers. They kidnapping that man."

"I see, son. But it ain't your job to fix it. Not today."

"We can't just let them take him away."

John noticed people listening to this conversation, their attention divided between the two events. He looked back toward the slave catchers.

"You got the wrong man," the captured man yelled. "I ain't Henry Johnson. Now, let me go."

"Shut up, Henry," the bigger of the two said. "Course you're gonna say that. But we know it's you. One of your own pointed you out to us." They appeared to be headed for a wagon parked two stores down the sidewalk.

"That don't mean nothing," said the man being dragged. "People say anything for money."

"Thing is," his captor said. "We didn't have to pay them a dime. They give you up just because it was their civic duty."

"Then it's gotta be somebody out to get me. You can't trust people like that. I'm telling you, I ain't no Henry Johnson." They got within ten feet of the wagon.

John heard Eli again. "Daddy, I just can't stand here and let this happen. We both know what they'll do to him."

"John," Laura said, "you better do something. If Eli gets in the middle of this, it could ruin our plans."

"I know. Stay here." He hurried over to Eli and Micah, leaned toward both of them. "Come with me." He had to get them away from the crowd. They stepped into an alleyway by the next building. "Let's talk down here." Micah was paying attention but Eli was distracted, mostly focused on what was happening across the street.

"Eli," John said. "Listen. You need to let this go. Your father's right."

"I hear you, Mr. John. But you don't know what they do to men like that. I do. We only got this one chance to save him."

"Boy," Micah said, "you do that, and you'll get arrested for trying, or maybe worse, then where your sister be they take you away? We can't do this trip down south without you."

That got Eli's attention.

"I'll tell you what," John said. "I'll go talk to the men, see if there's anything I can do."

"Thank you," Micah said.

"I am grateful, sir," Eli said. "But I'm afraid there's only one kind of language men like that understand. Maybe two. Force and money. I know you mean well, but you don't likely have the money to buy the freedom of every slave here in New York City. And I don't think you got it in you to use force to stop these men." He looked back at the scene around the corner. "They're chaining him up in the wagon now."

"Okay," John said, "stay here." He rushed across the street toward the scene, ignoring Laura's pleas to come back. Some among the crowd of onlookers had already begun to circle the wagon, yelling for the men to let the Negro go.

"Y'all better back off now," the big man said, standing up in the wagon. "Law's on our side, dead to rights. You inter- fere, we can have you arrested. Any of you ready to go to jail for this man?" People backed away. "Didn't think so."

John came around to the front to gain a little separation from the crowd. The second slave catcher had just finished chaining up the black man then hopped into the front seat of the wagon. His partner was still standing in the back, one hand on a six-shooter by his side.

"Excuse me, gentlemen," John yelled. "Could I have a word?"

"What you want, Mr. Fancy-dressed man?" said the man in the front. "You best stay out of this."

John ignored him, directed his attention toward the bigger man. "I'm aware of the Fugitive Slave Act. A ridiculous law, you ask me, but that's beside the point."

"Law's the law," the bigger man said. "And this here's a *federal* law. We got every right to—"

"I'm not trying to argue the law with you. But you heard this man. He's saying he's not the man you're looking for. What if he's not? What if you're wrong? You have any proof he is who you say he is?"

"We got all the proof we need. The colored man who

pointed him out knows Henry Johnson firsthand. They from the same town, one plantation over. And this man here matches the height, weight, and description given to us by the owner himself. He even wearing the same color shirt he wore when he run away a week ago."

"But that's not proof," John said. "It's circumstantial evidence at best, based on hearsay. What if this man here is right, and the man who tipped you off holds some ill will toward him? And you bring him all the way down to wherever it is you came from, only to find you got the wrong man?"

"You some kind of lawyer?" the man said.

"No."

"What's this fellow to you anyway?"

"Just a fellow human being," John said.

"Well, if we do have the wrong man — but I know we don't — we'll still get paid a tidy sum when we sell him at auction. Either way, we make out all right."

"But what about him?" a man in the crowd yelled. "He's back to being a slave again. And that's just wrong. You gotta know how wrong that is."

"I don't know how wrong it is," the man said, "and I don't care. And I'm not gonna stand around here anymore talking with y'all. I don't need your permission." He looked straight at John. "But just to settle your mind some, about us having the right man and all, I'll give you the proof you require." He yanked the colored man to his feet. "Owner tells me his Henry Johnson got three scars on the left side of his back. Three big 'X's' he called them." He grabbed hold of the man's shirt and ripped the back apart.

Everyone gasped, including John at the horrific sight.

Just like he'd said, they could plainly see three big 'X's" etched into the man's skin on the left side, blending in with dozens of similar scars across his back, all evidence of a lifetime of cruelty and abuse at the hand of some southern master's whip.

"See, just like I told you. This is Henry Johnson, the runaway slave we been chasing. He was lying, just like we said. They'll say anything to avoid going back where they belong and to whom they belong."

"Nobody belongs to anyone else," John said.

"Maybe not up here," the man in the front said, "but they do in the South. By the thousands. And this owner Johnson belongs to willing to pay us several hundred dollars to get his property back."

"Property," John repeated. "How would you like to be someone else's property?"

The man smiled. "Can't happen. God made me white."

"That's right," John said. "God made you white. None of us has any control over the circumstances of our birth. Which is why no one should be treated any different than anyone else. We're all made in his image and likeness, regardless of the color of our skin."

"Mister," the bigger man said, "you can keep the sermon to yourself." He hopped into the driver seat, took hold of the reins. "We're done here. Now, kindly get out of the way."

John stepped aside. The man snapped the reins and yelled for the horses to go, and they did. He looked over at Laura, then at Micah and Eli, who had come out from behind the alleyway and were now walking down the sidewalk toward Laura.

John sighed, more convinced than ever that slavery was just pure evil. And that he and Laura must do everything they could to rescue Hannah.

Before it was too late.

22

Thirty minutes later, they were back at the house.

Everyone was still upset by the scene with the slave catchers outside the train station. Eli and Micah had ridden together in the front of the carriage while John and Laura sat inside. After talking things out with Laura, John had decided the four of them needed to have a serious discussion before this trip plan went any further.

Out in the backyard beyond the veranda stood a large, shady tree. It had been there ever since John could remember. Some years ago, his father had built a brick patio below it. At its center, sat a wrought-iron table with six matching chairs. Before they'd left the carriage, John had asked Micah and Eli to meet them there before returning to their daily duties.

John and Laura were already there. Sally had just left after bringing them fresh cups of tea. Laura could tell she was a little nervous when she learned her father and brother had been asked to attend a meeting there with John and

Laura and were expected at any moment. Laura had assured her the meeting had nothing to do with canceling the trip to rescue Hannah.

Once Sally was beyond earshot, John quietly said to Laura, "I'm not sure you should have given Sally such firm assurance on that point."

Laura was stunned to hear him say this. "You're thinking of canceling the trip?"

"I didn't say that. But after what we just experienced, I'm not ruling it out entirely."

"What is making you reconsider? The scene with the slave hunters? We've seen things like that before."

"It's not the slave hunters that concerns me," he said. "It's the way Eli reacted to them."

Just then, Eli and Micah arrived. They walked across the short span of grass from the carriage house. John stood and waved them over. "Right here, gentlemen."

Laura could see the apprehension on their faces. John hadn't explained the reason for the meeting, just the urgent need to have it. She stood next to him and smiled. "Can we get you anything to drink?"

"I'm just fine, Miss Laura," Micah said. Eli said something similar.

"Well, have a seat," John said. "I know you both have to get back to work." He sat back in his chair. "But after what happened this morning at the train station, I realized, there are some very important things we need to talk through."

Laura had a feeling she knew what John intended to say, and she agreed with it. She just hoped he'd be gentle in his demeanor, especially with Eli.

"Look, Mr. John," Eli said as he sat in the chair. "Daddy

talked with me on the way home. And I want to apologize. I know we had to let that poor man get taken away. I don't blame you for that."

"That's good, Eli, but there's more to talk about than just that. I was able to get the train tickets, at least for the first part of the trip. As well as some information about what to expect for the rest of the way down. But this slave catcher incident — if I'm being honest — has given me reason to pause. We may have the tickets, and soon your father will have the proper clothes and even some training from Beryl about how to act as a valet. But that doesn't mean we're ready to face what we're all likely to face once we leave this place. Especially, once we get south of Pennsylvania. More so when we head into the deep south."

Laura looked at Micah. He was nodding and glanced over at his son. Made her think he may have said similar things to Eli already.

"To be fair," John said, "I'm mostly concerned about you, Eli, not your father. Before I say anything else, please understand, I totally sympathize with your desire to help that young man today. It grieves me beyond belief thinking he's headed back into slavery after such a brief taste of freedom."

"Especially back into the hands of the wicked people who put those stripes on his back," Laura added. She remembered seeing similar scars on Micah's back when they were on the ship.

"See," John said, "I've never been in the south before. We didn't have slavery in San Francisco. And before that, I lived here. I've seen plenty of prejudice and various other forms of racism before today. But it's been all words. Harsh, abusive words. But just words. I've never seen a man treated as badly as that man at the station. Dragged through the street like that, publicly humiliated and then chained to a wagon. And when the slave catcher ripped open his shirt exposing all those terrible scars, I...I could barely look at it. I've seen a picture like that once, a slave who'd been whipped, but to see it in person. And to think of the suffering that man must have endured, the amount of lashes he must have received..." John shuddered. "I don't see how a man can do that to a fellow human being."

Laura looked at Micah. He returned the glance in a way that suggested he knew she remembered his own scars.

"But here's the problem," John said, "think of how upset we all were by this scene, here in New York. I have to imagine we're going to witness things far worse than that the further south we go. Would you agree, Micah?"

"Oh, yes sir. We most certainly will. Many times a day, I expect. Far worse things. That boy today didn't get beat. He just got dragged through the dirt some. When you're in the South, you see colored folks getting slapped, kicked, beat with whips and canes. Called all sorts of names. All day long. Happen so much, most folks don't even stop to look, let alone try to stop it, the way those folks did today. The way you did. Because they know if they tried, they'd get beat too. You and Miss Laura may have never seen this, but Eli surely has. Haven't you, son?"

Eli nodded. Looked down at the ground. Like he knew what was coming.

No one said anything for a moment. In the silence, Laura felt her stomach tense up. Hearing Micah say this, coupled with the scene they just witnessed made her question whether she herself was ready to face all this.

"See Eli," John said, "we just can't have you reacting to any of the scenes we will most definitely face on this trip, the way you did today. It can't happen. You behaving that way shows you're still thinking like a free man, not a slave. I know it's been several years since you've been a slave, and you hated it so much — understandably so — that you ran away from it at great risk to your very life. I'm not sure you can set aside all that pent-up hatred you feel for this heinous practice, and the people involved with it. But set it aside, you must. You've got to be able to act like you're still a slave. And not just a slave, but one who lives without the hope of being freed at any time in his future."

"I understand some of what you say," Eli said. "But maybe not the last part. What do you mean, I've got to act like a slave who has no hope of ever being freed?"

"I get exactly what he means," Micah said. "It's how I lived every day for all them years, once I gave up running. Right up until my last day on the ship, when you and Miss Laura pay for me to be a free man. I never saw it coming. I thought my only hope of being free come the day I see Jesus face-to-face."

Eli looked at his father, still trying to grasp what was being said.

Laura thought she could help. "Eli, a person who has no hope for their situation to change, doesn't try to change it. They accept things as they are. Even something as awful as the injustice of slavery."

"That's the kind of mindset, the kind of attitude," John said, "we need you to have if our trip has any chance of success. So that any time — no, every time – you see a fellow slave being mistreated, you won't even think about getting involved or trying to stop it. The way you did this morning. Because if you do, I suspect men like the kind of men we dealt with today, wouldn't show the kind of restraint they did with us."

"Not in the South, they won't," Micah said. "Son, you know everything he's saying is true."

Eli released a deep sigh, looked down again. "I know. I know."

"Eli," John said a little softer, "I can't even get involved the way I did. Not once we leave this place. If I am going to pull off my role, I've got to be okay with it. Seeing people of your race treated terribly by people of mine. But I'm not okay with it, and I never will be. But that's how I have to act the whole time we're on this trip together. Otherwise, we'll have no chance of ever rescuing your sister."

"Okay, Mr. John," Eli said. "I hear you. I really do. You too, Daddy. And Miss Laura. I'll do whatever I gotta do to save Hannah. Even this."

23

Four Days Later
Baltimore, MD

OVER THE LAST SEVERAL DAYS, things had gone relatively smooth and mostly according to plan. Eli seemed to have taken to heart all that was said and was clearly trying to be more subdued and submissive in his demeanor. He reminded John of Eli's father, Micah, who behaved that way toward all people all the time. Yesterday, Micah's new clothes had arrived from the tailors and, after trying them on for everyone, he said they made him look like Frederick Douglass. He couldn't get over how shiny his shoes were and wondered how he'd ever keep them so clean.

Beryl had finished giving Micah his best advice on how to serve as John's valet. John felt like he'd unintentionally gone a bit overboard. Since the trip south began, John was routinely having to curb Micah's zeal to serve in that capacity. John simply didn't need or want that much personal attention. He hoped that now that they were here in Baltimore they might observe a wealthy gentleman or two interacting with their valets, so Micah could get a clearer picture of his role. John had at least gotten a break from the overdose of attention during the train ride here.

It turned out to be true: Negroes were forced to ride in separate cars, the ones closest to the front near the train engine. And, of course, when they had stayed overnight in a hotel in Philadelphia, Micah and Eli had to find separate hotel accommodations. Negroes weren't allowed where John and Laura stayed, regardless of whether they were slave or free. It was clear this was going to be the way of things throughout the remainder of their trip.

Neither Micah nor Eli seemed offended by this. They were simply grateful John was willing to cover their expenses. He'd given the cash to Eli, since Micah had little experience handling money; enough for Eli to secure the best food and lodging they could find, given the limitations.

Presently, John and Laura were waiting for Micah and Eli as they sat on a bench at the far end of the train station, next to their trunks and suitcases. John was reading the morning edition of *The Baltimore Sun*. Thirty minutes ago, after they'd exited the train and reunited, Eli told John he'd gotten a tip from one of the men unloading luggage regarding the rental of an upscale carriage and team of horses.

John pointed out an ad in the paper to Laura. "This might suit us. The Giles European Hotel. It says it's only a few blocks from the train station. And it's got a restaurant and bakery right on the premises. Look, even lists some of the menu items. You know, Baltimore's known for its seafood. They've got fresh perch, halibut, pike or mackerel, fried or broiled. Only twenty-five-cents each. If you're in the mood for something roasted, you could have a nice roast beef dinner, roast veal or lamb. Also for twenty-five-cents. If you're looking for something a little more exotic, they have stewed rabbit. Of course, it's also twenty-five-cents."

"Stewed rabbit?" Laura repeated. "I don't think so. Roast beef sounds nice, though. How long do you expect us to stay in Baltimore?"

"You don't sound like a southern belle to me," John said, smiling. "We're supposed to be practicing."

"Well, excuse me kind sir," she said, now in character. "I'm just curious about the length of time we'll be staying in this fine city."

John looked down the road, had his eye on a carriage he hoped was theirs. "Maybe two or three days. Wish we could stay longer, but I know Eli and Micah are very concerned about their sister's safety. We're just here to get a little more acclimated to the roles we'll be playing before heading further south."

"Our next stop is Fredericksburg, isn't it?" she said. "Where Micah and Eli are from?"

"Yes, and where Hannah was last seen before being sold to her new owner. But I'm not sure we can get a train all the way into Fredericksburg. Might have to stop in Richmond, then do like we're doing here. Lease ourselves a horse and carriage, then have Eli take us the rest of the way."

"But John, aren't you forgetting something?"

"Possibly, though I'm not sure what."

"Eli is a runaway...from Fredericksburg. He can't just ride us into town. Someone might recognize him."

John sighed. "I did forget. I guess Micah will have to be our driver when we get close. We'll talk to them about it, see what they think." He looked down the road again at that carriage and could clearly see Eli holding the reins, Micah right beside him. He stood, folded his newspaper and offered Laura his hand. "Our ride has arrived, my dear."

"Why, thank you kind sir." She took his hand. "Much obliged."

John waved at Eli and Micah. They slowly maneuvered their way through the traffic toward the curb. "Not a bad looking carriage," John said. "Did you have to pay an arm and a leg?"

"No, sir," Eli said as he got down. "Got it close to the daily rate you gave me. Had to promise them we'd keep it for three days, though. Hope that's all right."

"That'll be fine," John said. "Laura and I were just talking about that, how long we'll be staying." Micah started to get down. "You can stay up there, Micah. Eli and I can handle the suitcases and trunks."

Micah got a startled look on his face and continued his descent. "Oh, no, Mr. John. You forgetting where we is. You can't be doing any more chores, especially with me and Eli close by. Not now, and not for the rest of our trip."

"You're right, you're right. I'm sorry. This just feels so wrong."

Eli opened the carriage door. "How about you and Mrs. Foster have a seat inside? Daddy and me will see to the luggage. They built a rack on the back, so we won't have to load it on the roof."

"Well, that's clever," Laura said, stepping into the carriage.

"Have an idea where I'm going to take you both?" Eli said, walking the biggest trunk around to the back. "I asked the man who ran the carriage place about some nice hotels nearby, and other ones Daddy and me could stay at. Said there were plenty of suitable hotels just north of the harbor a few blocks down Baltimore Street. Got the names to a few boarding houses okay for Negroes to lodge in several blocks further."

John held up the newspaper ad he'd shown Laura a moment ago. "Coincidentally, I found what sounds like a nice hotel in here, which also happens to be on Baltimore Street."

"Good, I got directions on how to get there from here. I hope you don't mind, but I took the liberty to ask him a few questions about this area. See, he's like us but not a slave. He runs the carriage place, and all the workers we saw were like us. The owner's a white man, but he hardly comes down to the place anymore."

"The man say," Micah added, "every one of his workers were free. In fact, he said Baltimore is filled with thousands of freed colored folk. Said there probably more freed Negroes than slaves. Maybe more than in Philadelphia and New York City."

"Really?" Laura said. "That's encouraging to hear."

"Maybe so, Ma'am," Eli said. "But he also said this place is plenty dangerous just the same. Lots of slave catchers roaming the streets on the lookout for runaways. Mostly coming from Virginia."

"Did you tell him about...our situation?" John said.

"No, sir. But I was tempted to. Seemed like a man I could trust. But I decided to play it safe. Told him we were slaves but that our masters treated us very well, almost like we were free."

"He does sound like a reliable soul," John said. "But I think it's still wise to be safe. There's a lot of money being made in the slave-catching business, and I've heard that, sadly, quite a few of your people are involved in turning in their own kind to these predators for a finder's fee." He held up the paper again. "Even here, right next to the hotel ad, there's a reward ad for help to catch a runaway slave they think is right here in Baltimore. Pays two-hundred-dollars."

"Two hundred dollars," Laura repeated. "That's a lot of money."

"Yes, it is. And a huge incentive for people to turn in other people for some quick cash."

"But we got them papers now," Micah said, "that say we belong to you."

"I know. And for law-abiding people, that should be enough. But with the kind of money being made in this terrible business, some have branched out into kidnapping freedmen like yourselves. They could care less about what's on a piece of paper. The point is, let's stay close together while we're here in this town, and don't share our business with strangers."

Both Eli and Micah agreed. They finished loading up the luggage, got back into the front seat of the carriage. "Next stop," Eli said, "The Gates Hotel."

24

The next morning, just a little after 8AM, Laura sat at the vanity in their hotel room putting the finishing touches on her hair and hat, so she could accompany John to breakfast downstairs. Of course, he had been ready to go for the last twenty minutes but had been such a dear, choosing to read his Bible by the window seat rather than hover behind her hoping to rush her along. She had slept fairly well, though it was nothing like the bed she and John had enjoyed at the Foster mansion during the last month. But the accommodations at the Gates Hotel were proving most satisfactory.

She hoped the breakfast turned out to be half as good as the dinner last night, which was exceptional. When they finished, John had said, "Best fifty cents I've spent in quite a while." She only hoped Micah and Eli were able to find decent lodging and food. John had asked them to rendezvous at the hotel at nine.

She stood up and walked toward the front door. "I'm

ready whenever you can pull yourself away from your comfy chair."

John looked up, smiled, still enjoying her best efforts at crafting a southern accent. At some point, he must have finished reading his Bible and picked up the morning paper. He stood and folded it, put it under his arm. "Good, I'm actually quite hungry." He looked her over, said, "It would appear the extra time devoted to your appearance was well spent. You look lovely, my dear."

"Oh? And how did I look before?"

He smiled, shook his head. "The trap has sprung. But I'll not fall into it. You start the day a beauty from the moment you awake. Thereafter, your looks only improve."

She laughed. "A terrible fib, love. But I appreciate the effort. Anything interesting in the newspaper?"

"Just reading the local section, trying to understand the area a little better. I was thinking about what Eli and Micah said after talking with that man who runs the carriage place. The primary reason for our stop here was to be able to observe the interactions of slaveowners with their slaves. But that task is made more challenging by the very great number of freed Negroes."

"Maybe we need to go a little further south," she said. "Like Virginia. I'm sure the ratio of slaves to free men works the other way there."

"We may have to do that, but I did get one possible opportunity here," he said, holding up the newspaper. "There's a slave mart about a half-mile from here on the other side of the harbor. There's an auction there this morning, starts at eleven. We could go there posing as potential buyers. I'm sure we'd see all kinds of interesting things at an event like that."

Laura sighed. "Yes, I'm sure you're right."

John walked over to her, took her hand. "I'm sure it's going to prove dreadful, in every respect. But it has to be done. If we're to be believed once we're in the deep south, we need to understand how these people think and interact with other slaveowners and especially with their slaves. An auction like this would give us plenty of insight into that world." He opened the front door of their hotel room, stepped out into the hall.

"I know. It's just going to be so hard to see such a thing... in person."

"I'm sure it will be," he said. "We'll be tempted to spend everything we have just to set a few of them free."

Micah heard a knock on the door. Gotta be Eli coming back from using the outhouse. The two of them shared the same room at the boardinghouse they'd found yesterday afternoon after dropping off the Fosters at their hotel. Before going on this trip, Micah couldn't remember the last time he and Eli had slept under the same roof, let alone in the same room. And here they'd done it two nights in a row. "No need to knock, Eli. This your room, too."

The door opened. Eli walked in, all dressed except for his coat. "Didn't want to catch you with your drawers down, Daddy. Not a sight I care to see this early in the morning."

They both laughed.

"Well, as you can see I'm all dressed, except for this fancy tie thing I'm supposed to wear around my neck. You help me with it?"

"I will, but Daddy you gotta remember what I teach you this time. What are you going to do some morning down south if we wake up in different places? I can't help you then. Folks aren't gonna understand why a valet don't know how to tie a tie."

"You right, you right. I'll pay better attention this time."

Micah watched and listened closely to Eli's instructions. Had him repeat the last step twice, but he figured he had it now. They both put their coats on and stood in front of the mirror. "My, oh my," Micah said. "Would you take a look at the two of us? Who'd ever thought me and my boy be standing here side-by-side wearing these fancy clothes?"

Eli put his arm around his father, gave a squeeze. "They look good on you, Daddy. Maybe after this trip, you learning all you have about being a valet, maybe you can try to get a job doing that or being someone's butler. Then you could dress like this every day."

"Nah. Good of you to say. But I'd miss my horses too much. And I wouldn't get to see Crabby all day long. Already miss her so much being on this trip. Couldn't take it every day."

Eli opened the door and they headed into the narrow hallway. "Can still smell breakfast coming up the stairs. Can you believe a colored woman owns this place? It's nowhere near as nice as the hotels white folks stay at, but it's nice enough. She said when I paid her the money yesterday she only had this one room left."

"Nicest place I ever stayed on a trip," Micah said. Then he realized, that wasn't saying much. Hadn't been on too many trips in his life, except maybe all those times he'd tried to run away when he was Eli's age. Most nights then, what sleep he got would be out under the stars.

Twenty minutes later, they were finishing up their breakfast at the boardinghouse.

"I did enjoy that," Micah said. "Scrambled eggs, pork sausage, and grits. Been too long since I had grits, and these cooked just right."

Eli set his fork down on the plate, looked around at the other folks in the room. He leaned forward, "Guess these folks not used to seeing men so dressed up 'round here. People been staring at us ever since we came downstairs."

Micah hadn't noticed and wouldn't have cared if he had. He took a quick glance around the room, smiled and nodded at a few of them. "Don't think they mean us any harm." They hadn't seen any white folks, since they crossed a certain street a few blocks back. "Everyone in here dressed in regular clothes. I'm sure that's all it is."

Eli sighed, checked his watch. "We should leave in five minutes, give us enough breathing room to get to the Fosters' hotel on time."

"I just got two more bites," Micah said. "You gonna let me eat 'em in peace, or you gonna rush me?"

"No, you go ahead and eat. I wish I could be as relaxed as you are. Not just now, but in general. I don't know how you do it. You always stay so calm, no matter what's going on. Like today, we've got to stay here in Baltimore, pretty much doing nothing. Tomorrow too. Maybe even a third day. So, the Fosters can figure out how to act like slaveowners. Meanwhile, Hannah's down there in Charleston suffering who knows what. Were up to me, we'd be on the road right now riding hard till we get there."

Micah was just about to eat his last bite, but he paused, looked up at his boy. "I know it may feel like we're wasting time here, son. And I may look like I don't care as much about our Hannah as you do."

"I'm sorry, Daddy. I don't mean to —"

Micah held up his hand. "That's all right. I ain't mad at you. I'm glad you care so much about your sister. I care just as much, though it may not seem so. It's just you and me caring isn't all there is to this. The Bible talks about a thing somewhere, called zeal without wisdom. Talks somewhere else about a man feeling strongly about a matter, not knowing all the while if he does what he thinks it ends up in death. Only difference between you and me is...I've lived long enough to make both these mistakes myself, and seen others make them more times than I can count. The reason I can be so calm is not because I don't care, it's because I know my Shepherd is in this thing we doing. And I'm following where he leads. And I know he cares about Hannah more than both of us do. See, we going right smack dab through the valley of the shadow of death here, and we gonna need his help every step of the way. That's why it ain't wise to rush on ahead doing whatever feels right at the moment. We gotta go at the pace the Shepherd goes, follow the path he takes us down, wherever it leads."

25

John happily paid his tab at the restaurant, which took up most of the first floor of the Gates European Hotel. They were now standing out by the sidewalk of a bustling street waiting for Eli and Micah to appear. "If it's possible," John said, "I enjoyed that breakfast even more than the dinner last night."

"Seeing your sheer delight with every bite," Laura said, "made me wonder if I'd made the wrong choice. But I've never heard of eating crabmeat with eggs."

"If we have breakfast here tomorrow, you'll have to try it. The poached eggs and toast blended perfectly with the crab-meat. I'll have to sneak back to the kitchen sometime and ask the cook for the recipe of that sauce they poured over it."

"Maybe it was something European," she said, pointing at the hotel sign above their heads.

"Look, here comes Eli and Micah with our carriage." John offered his arm and walked Laura to the open spot in the sidewalk where the carriage was heading.

"I still can't get used to seeing Micah so dressed up," Laura said.

Micah saw them, waved and pointed them out to Eli. When the carriage stopped, Eli jumped down, greeted them, then opened the carriage doors.

"Thank you, Eli," Laura said in her southern drawl as she stepped into the carriage.

"You're welcome, Miss Laura." He smiled. "Begging your pardon, Ma'am, but you're going to have to stop thanking me. Remember? A few days from now we'll be in the deep south. A slave doesn't get thanked by his mistress for doing what he's supposed to do."

"Do you know for a fact that all southern women are rude and ungrateful?"

Eli laughed. "No, Ma'am. I don't. Not all, maybe. They were plenty kind and polite to other white folks, just not to slaves." He looked up to Micah. "Daddy, you ever know a white mistress who thanked her slaves for doing what they were supposed to do?"

Micah shook his head. "Can't say as I do. Knew some that weren't always mean to they slaves. But didn't know any anywhere near as nice Miss Laura."

"Okay," she said. "I stand corrected. From now on, I'll refrain. You'll just have to assume I thanked you, because I'll be saying it on the inside."

"Yes, Ma'am." He continued to hold the door open for John who didn't get in.

"Thought maybe we should get our plans together first. Find it easier than talking through that little door inside the carriage. Did you two manage to sleep all right? Were you able to find adequate accommodations?"

"Oh, yes sir, Mr. John," Micah said. "Eli found us a nice boardinghouse. Bed was nicer than the one I have back at the house. Food was good, too. Much obliged you paying our way like this."

"Happy to do it," John said. "Well, I've been thinking about what you said, Eli, about how many freed Negroes live here and thought of a way to make sure we cross paths with some slaveowners, so we can better see how Laura and I are supposed to behave. Read in the morning paper they're holding a slave auction at eleven just a few blocks from here on Platt Street. It's part of that big market area we drove by on the way to the hotel, but at the other end."

Both Micah and Eli's expressions instantly soured.

"I know," John said. "We're dreading the task. But I know how much you want to get south as quickly as we can. If we did this, we might learn all we need to learn in one sitting."

"No, I understand," Eli said. "Sounds like a good idea. And I think I know where Platt Street is. We passed by it at some point. I'm sure once we get in the vicinity, it won't be hard to figure out where the actual auction's taking place."

"I'm so sorry we have to do this," Laura said. "But you won't have to wait there for us, right John? They can just drop us off, and we'll pick a place and time for them to come back later and get us."

"Yes, that's fine," John said. "It's going to be unpleasant enough for us to have to sit through it. I can't imagine what it would be like if I were...well, you know."

"Appreciate your concern, sir," Eli said. "I'm sure Daddy and I can find some worthwhile way to occupy our time. But you said this auction takes place at eleven. There someplace else you want to go between now and then? We got some time."

"As a matter of fact, there is."

"While Laura was getting ready this morning, I read a very interesting article in the newspaper. The first stop for this morning is just a few blocks down this same street as our hotel, where it intersects with South Street. It's actually the building where the newspaper offices are located."

"And why did you find this interesting?" Laura said.

"It's about architecture, my dear. Apparently, here in Baltimore they've developed a new kind of construction technique, called the cast-iron building. The very first one, built just six years ago, is the Sun Iron Building, as in the Baltimore Sun. It's supposed to be the latest craze in architecture. In just the last few years over twenty more downtown buildings have been constructed using the same technique. The article lists several addresses of the better ones. I'd like to view them."

"Okay," Laura said. "But I've never known you to take such an interest in architecture before."

He laughed. "And I'm only mildly interested in it still."

"Then why the —"

"Sudden interest? I am somewhat curious after reading the article, to see what all the fuss is about. But I'm more interested in its potential to provide us with a solid cover story for our trip down south. We're going down there as a wealthy couple from Baltimore looking to buy a specific slave girl for our household. Well, according to this article, this particular style of architecture started here and is slowly spreading to some other northern cities. But it hasn't yet begun to show up in the South. I thought I'd familiarize myself with it, as much as possible. And we could say—if asked what I did for a living—I build cast-iron office buildings."

"Oh," Laura said, "why, that sounds quite clever. So, I'm to be the wife of an architect now."

"I like how you think, Mr. Foster," Eli said.

"You do go on," Micah said, smiling. "See what I tell you, Eli? We's in good hands on this trip."

"Thank you, gentlemen," John said, handing the newspaper to Eli. "I'd like to stop first at this Sun Iron Building, maybe get out and walk around it a bit, see if they'll let me tour the lobby. Then as time permits, we'll visit some of the other addresses in the article. Work things out so that we arrive back at the slave mart by around ten forty-five."

"Will do, sir."

John got into the carriage. Eli closed the door and hopped up beside his father and took hold of the reins. "Next stop, the Sun Iron Building."

26

It appeared John was really taken with this cast-iron construction idea. Laura had to admit the buildings were quite lovely, if such a thing could be said about downtown commercial buildings. Clearly, there was a lot of craftsmanship at work, especially around the windows, but John said beyond their aesthetic appeal, this new method offered greater protection against fires and even made the buildings stronger. He'd spent a full thirty minutes touring the first one while she'd waited in the carriage chatting with Micah and Eli.

They had enough time to drive slowly by four other similar buildings, but John only got out at one, a bank. As he headed inside, Eli had to remind him they only had fifteen minutes left to make it to the slave mart at his specified time. John nodded, went inside and came out five minutes later, all smiles.

He got into the carriage before Eli could get down to

open it. "I've definitely found my cover story," John announced as he sat beside Laura. "Spoke with the loan officer about my interest in these cast-iron buildings. A very polite gent. Turns out, he served as the liaison between the bank and the main contractor. A virtual wealth of information on the process. He's agreed to meet with me this afternoon and will answer any other questions I have." He leaned toward the little door and yelled to Micah, "All set to go. Head directly for the slave mart."

"Will do, sir," Micah said.

John begged Laura's pardon, saying he had to capture a bunch of these thoughts and ideas on paper while they were fresh. So, she spent the time looking out the window taking in the sights. For the most part, Baltimore seemed similar to New York City. Lots of hustle and bustle. A wide variety of people going about their day, some dressed in the finest clothes; others poor as church mice. About the same amount of street noise in both cities. A constant din of chatter occasionally broken by loud shouts of street vendors announcing the virtues of their wares. Fine carriages like theirs rode beside old wooden wagons loaded with crates and barrels. Soon, the strong smell of fish told her they'd come within range of the market.

"I think we're getting close John."

He looked up from his notepad. "What? Oh." And looked out the window. "Yes, there's the sign for Pratt Street. Oh, my." A moment later his countenance fell, and he sighed. "This is going to be hard going."

She looked out following his gaze. A white, bearded street worker in a straw hat was leading a line of four male slaves down the sidewalk, all in chains and ragged clothes.

They were staring at the ground, hopeless looks on their faces. "Oh, John. How are we supposed to do this? Everything in me wants to scream at that man holding those chains. Or do worse. How are we supposed to sit with these people a few moments from now, acting as if we're excited at the possibility of buying some brand-new slaves to work our fields, or do our chores?"

"I don't know, love," John said. "I was thinking something very similar. Everyone else at this auction will have woken up this morning in a fine bed, put on fine clothes and ate a delicious breakfast, anticipating an opportunity to pick up a great deal today. Not feeling a bit of guilt that they're bargaining over the lives of fellow human beings. People made in the same image of God as they are themselves."

"Maybe there's another way to educate ourselves," she said. "Maybe we should tell Eli and Micah to keep driving past the market."

John looked at her. "I can't see any other way, Laura. This has to be done. We could spend weeks here in Baltimore and not see as many slaveowners interacting with slaves as we will at this auction. You know what Eli has said about Hannah. Time is of the essence. We won't have to make friends with anyone or engage in trivial conversation. We can just sit in the back row, watch and listen, keep to ourselves until it's over."

A few minutes later, Eli and Micah had dropped them off near the front of the auction area. John had been to a horse auction before, which had taken place in something of a small warehouse building, like this one. A sidewalk led to a front door, which is where all the potential buyers were headed. Over on the right was a large opening where the slaves to be sold were being gathered inside. Like the four male slaves seen earlier, all were in chains and shabbily dressed. All were barefoot. None of the men wore hats, whereas all the white men wore shiny top hats, or brown bowler hats which were much in fashion.

John noticed the crowd of buyers was predominantly male; only a handful of ladies in attendance. Laura quietly pointed that out but John reminded her of their mission and asked her to please pay close attention to the conduct of the women who were there.

It wasn't as crowded as John had expected, maybe thirty people in all. Three rows of chairs were set up in front of a platform. On the right side, a series of steps connected the platform to the ground, which also happened to be the side where the slaves had been told to stand, side-by-side in a line, facing the crowd. Eight Negro men, four women, and two children. The men looked to be between twenty and forty years of age. All the women were younger, late teens or early twenties. The children, a boy and girl, maybe seven to ten years old. The adults mostly looked down, but the children's eyes took in everything. They appeared to have no idea of what was to come.

On either end of the line of slaves stood some rough-looking white handlers. Both held what looked like riding crops in their hands. Obviously, the means to intimidate the slaves into compliance should the need arise. John realized the fellow on the right side had been the same man he'd seen earlier leading the group of four male slaves down the sidewalk.

Finally, a man came in from somewhere on the right and took center stage. He was short, wore a top hat and light brown frock coat. But that was the only part of his ensemble of decent quality. He wore no tie. His shirt was wrinkled. And his pants were too baggy for his stature. "Good morning gentlemen, and I see we have a few ladies, as well. Before we get started, lest I be wasting anyone's time...including my own, you should know that while this is indeed an auction, I only present the finest slave stock in my establishment. So, the price range for the adults you see before you will range, on the low-end, from eight hundred dollars to over fifteen hundred dollars, or even more, depending upon how the bidding goes. Of course, we are prepared to take much less for the children. If you are not prepared to bid within those dollar ranges, please feel free to slip out the back door."

"Can we go?" Laura whispered.

John patted her hand. Both knew she was joking.

"No takers?" the man said. "Very well. Then we'll get this show on the road. As is my custom, before we start the actual bidding, I know you men will want to examine the merchandise more closely. That's perfectly understandable. We know you're making a significant investment here, and we have nothing to hide. So, feel free to come up and check things out for yourselves. Examine their teeth. Look at their hands. Check out their muscle structure, although I should mention the oldest male in the middle will likely fail that inspection. He hasn't worked in the fields since the age of twenty, but he's an outstanding house servant with a whole variety of skills to offer."

"If he's so outstanding, why is he not still serving his master?" a man in the front row asked.

"A fair question, with a fair answer. His owner died recently, and his heir had his own man, so this slave's services were no longer required. But I assure you, he is worth a great deal of money. In fact, the bidding for him starts at eleven hundred. Any more questions? No? Okay then, come on up and check out the rest for yourselves."

John leaned toward Laura. "I should go up, so I can hear what's being said."

She sighed. "I understand. Try not to hit anyone. You'll give us away."

He smiled, kissed her on the forehead and went forward. What he saw as he drew near was hard to take. All these finely dressed gentlemen, like himself, manhandling these poor souls as though they were a pack of plow horses. Literally, opening their mouths, examining their teeth, checking their scalps, feeling their arms and shoulders. Asking them to lift up their feet. At one point, the man who'd gone first stopped and asked, "All this is well and good, but I'm not making an offer until I see their backs. Could you ask them to take off their shirts and turn around?"

"Certainly," the emcee said. He directed the handlers to make this happen.

Suddenly a woman in the front row stood up and said, "You will do no such thing. The male slaves can, but it's inappropriate to ask the females to do the same."

"Then how can we check the level of scarring on their backs?" the interested buyer asked. "Only way to know whether you're buying a troublemaker, or not."

"You can do it with the men," she said. "Have them take off their shirts. I have no problem with that. But you can see all you need to see with the ladies if you just lift their shirts slightly from the back." She turned to the other ladies in the audience. "You agree with me, right?" All the other women nodded.

"Okay, okay," said the emcee. "We have our compromise. Men? Off with your shirts and turn around, with your backs to the crowd. Ladies, turn around, too. If you men are interested in any of the ladies' level of scarring, do it carefully. But I can tell you all this...before we go any further. I've examined them all myself. Of course, their backs have scarring. Some more than others. Using the lash on a slave, as we all know, is commonplace. Often the only way to get them to behave. But observe with each of the slaves I'm offering today, all the scarring is old and well-healed. Not a fresh wound on anyone's back. Why is this important you ask? Because, it tells you...with certainty, that they have learned their lessons, that they are obedient now, and that their troublemaking days are well behind them."

John could stand it no more. He stood there in shock as each man's back was uncovered. The little man in the top hat hadn't lied. He didn't see any fresh stripes. But the level of scarring, and what he knew it meant, disturbed him beyond measure. And to hear these men talk about these people with so little regard for them — as people — was appalling. Perhaps, this had been a mistake. Was he really learning anything of any value here? He quickly and carefully sidestepped around the other men examining the slaves up close then walked down the side aisle and around the back toward Laura's seat.

"Don't see any to your liking?" the emcee yelled to John.

"Uh, no. Not today," he said.

"Well, come back again. We'll have a new batch come Friday."

He reached Laura and whispered in her ear, "I think I've seen enough."

"Thank you," she said and stood. The two of them made their way to the front door, then down the walkway toward the street.

27

John and Laura crossed the street carefully to reach a bench they had designated as the rendezvous point with Eli and Micah. Laura could tell, John was still fuming inside.

"I don't know what I was thinking," he said. "We did get to be around a good number of slaveowners, so I suppose there was some benefit in that. But none of them had their slaves with them, so there was no chance to see them interact. Watching how they talked about these poor people in chains, though, and the way they handled them...it seems pretty clear, they have no regard for them as fellow humans at all. They treat them like cattle. But it's so much worse... cattle don't understand what men are saying about them. These slaves can understand every word. Such utter humiliation. Such cruelty."

"I know," Laura said. "In a way, maybe that is the lesson we were supposed to learn. Maybe it's not more complicated than that."

"What do you mean?"

"Well, that's the mindset we need to have, if we're to appear as proper slaveowners. We need to treat them as cattle. As mere animals, to be bought, sold, or used however we see fit." She could hardly believe she was saying this.

"Animals who can talk and think," John said. "Who have emotions and can be hurt emotionally, not just physically, when they're mistreated."

"Yes, that's part of it," Laura said.

"Animals who — if given the chance — can be taught to read and write."

"I know. It's absurd, John."

"But animals can't bear the offspring of their owners. Did you see that little girl on the end? Undoubtedly, her mother was a slave. Her father a white man. Most likely, her former master. Yet again, a tragic reality that flies in the face of this whole pretentious hypocrisy."

"I totally agree with you," Laura said. "But somehow, someway, these people —" she looked around, aware of the danger they'd be in if overheard and lowered her voice — "these people's minds have been given over to this great folly. They actually think this way and talk this way, and in every manner that matters to them, live like it is true. I don't know how such a thing happens. But it has. You can see it here in Baltimore, people who think like us are few and far between. The further south we go, the more true it will be. Likely, where Hannah's been taken, to the Charleston area, we may be the only two people who see through the absurdity of this false teaching. I'm told even the preachers down there have found ways to justify it in their sermons."

A finely dressed couple walked by, nodded and smiled. John and Laura returned the gesture. John reached for

Laura's hand, squeezed. Then leaned forward on the bench and kissed her.

"What's that for?" she asked. "I'm not complaining, just curious."

"Just so glad to have you here, by my side. So glad to have someone to talk to who completely understands my frustration."

"I feel exactly the same. But you know, there is someone else who understands what we're thinking. Really, two people."

"Who's that?" John said.

"Micah and Eli. They can't tell you how a slaveowner thinks, but they've spent years around them. Maybe we're going about this the wrong way. Maybe we just need to let them inform us about the kinds of things they've observed. Could be very insightful."

John leaned back on the bench. "Hmmm, an interesting idea. Certainly couldn't hurt to try."

John and Laura were riding inside the carriage. Micah sat across from them, the shades of his windows pulled down as a precaution. It wasn't illegal to have a Negro riding with whites in a carriage. There were thousands of freed Negroes living in Baltimore and Micah was certainly wearing the proper attire. But generally, the races didn't mingle socially, so they decided not to draw any undue attention to themselves.

The idea was to afford a time for them to talk with Micah in an undistracted manner. They explained things to both of them before setting out on this little ride. They would talk with Micah first while Eli drove the carriage around the outskirts of town. Then they could switch places and talk with Eli on the ride back to the hotel.

"As I mentioned, Micah, before we got in," John said, "our time at the auction was quite unpleasant and unfruitful."

"I can imagine that being so," Micah said. "'Specially for the ones being bought and sold."

Laura laughed then apologized. "I'm sorry. What you said wasn't funny. It just made me realize how dull we still are, even though we're on the same side."

"Guess I was fortunate that way," Micah said. "Was only sold a few times. It was plenty unpleasant, but least it wasn't at no auction."

"Yes," John said, trying to keep his train of thought. "What I meant by unfruitful was that we weren't able to learn very much about how slaves interacted with their masters. Specifically, how masters treated their slaves. I don't mean the obvious cruelty that takes place when they're mistreating them. I mean the *attitudes* of the slaveowners. Like, how would they treat a slave they might genuinely care for versus how they'd treat a slave working out in the field?"

"Did you ever have any masters who treated you well?" Laura asked. "Not that John and I would ever own a slave, but we need to behave as slaveowners the rest of this trip, so we'd like to act as ones who would at least be a little bit kind. Does that make sense?"

"I think so, Miss Laura," Micah said. "My first master, seem like he was just mean through and through. He was the one I kept trying to run away from. Wouldn't do any good calling to mind anything about him. Second one was still mean, but he could at times be almost decent. I say almost, cause I never saw him treat a slave as well as he would a white man, even one he hardly knew. But some of the slaves on the plantation, a few that worked in the main house, I could see times when he'd speak to them rather kindly. Sometimes I'd be sweeping one end of the porch, and I hear them talking on the other end. One of the house slaves come out to serve them tea or some kind of food. Next thing, I hear master say something to the slave and everyone laughing and smiling. I look up and see, the slave smiling too. Something like that happened on more than one occasion. Truth is, some of us were jealous about how some of the house servants got treated compared to the rest of us. But we didn't hold it against them. Expect if we got the chance to work indoors, we'd jump at it, too."

"Well, that's helpful," John said. "You've seen how our family treats Beryl. Of course, he's white and never been a slave. Would you say you ever saw your master treat the house servants as well as that?"

"Oh, no," Micah said. "Nothing so nice as that. Y'all and Beryl be almost like family, seems to me. Of course, that's about how you treat Eli, Sally, and me. I never been treated that nice when I was a slave. I don't think I ever saw any of the house slaves treated quite so well, either. Now mind you, I didn't get to be up close at those plantations very often. They usually call me in to help when someone get sick. Once they better, I'm back out in the fields. Now my third master, the one before I got sold to Captain Meade, he's the one got me working with horses for the first time. Not quite as nice as working at the main house, but I did get to hear the master and some family members talking a good bit whenever they came in to see the horses. They were nice enough to me, but nothing like you and Miss Laura."

"Can you think of any ways that were different?" John said. "Than the way Laura and I treat you?"

"Well, for one thing, you talk to me like I matter to you. Never felt like that with any of my masters, or see them treat even the house slaves like that. Or like this here, you asking me what I think about something. Never had that happen before. Never saw that happen before. We just there to work, to make life easy for the white folk. They not caring about what we think. Usually, a slave tells them what he or she thinks, they spend some time on the whipping post."

Laura sighed. "How awful."

"Yeah," Micah said. "But see, didn't think of it that way then. That's just...how it was. Didn't ever expect much more. We know they don't see us as too much more than the horses who pull their wagons, or the cows that give them milk. Only difference is, we could talk. Long as we don't talk back. And we had hands that can do all kinds of work animals can't do. We do what they say, and we get fed, get someplace to sleep, maybe a roof over our head. And we don't get beat."

John shook his head. "And that's how it was, even with the masters who were nicer?"

"Afraid so," Micah said. "Don't know if that helps any. But that's mostly how it was."

"Sadly, it does help," John said. "But I wish we didn't have to even pretend to treat you and Eli like this. You know that's not how we feel, about you, Eli, or Sally."

"Oh, I know," Micah said. "Y'all been so good to us. I know you only doin' what's gotta be done to save Hannah."

28

Hannah lay in her bed staring up at the knots in the planks of her ceiling. The sun had started to come up maybe a half-hour ago. Over the last few days, her sadness had lingered as a constant presence, just below the surface. She'd been too busy to let it take hold of too much or for too long. The auction had gone as Celia predicted. The three other girls had been paraded before the hungry eyes of the four plantation owners Massa Clifton had invited. Everyone complained loudly when they'd learned Hannah wasn't part of the sale.

The Colonel had explained he'd handpicked her for himself. "You gentlemen should be able to understand that," he'd said, as he looked Hannah over every which way. "After all, I'm the one who made that arduous journey north to acquire these fine specimens. I'm the one who took all the risks."

They laughed as he redirected their attention back to the bidding of the other three. Hannah could clearly see why he'd invited four owners to bid on three girls. No one wanted to go home empty-handed, so it caused something of a bidding frenzy between them. The prices kept going up and up until at the end, even the lowest price girl sold for more than twice any of them had ever paid for a slave before. At least that's what they'd said.

When it was over, Massa Clifton let them know none of the girls had ever served indoors before. None of the men seemed to mind — just as Celia had predicted — and had agreed to pay extra for her to train them here at the Clifton plantation until they were good and ready.

The other three girls began to awaken. They seemed to get along with each other fairly well, like they were even becoming friends. Hannah kept mostly to herself. Not only was she not in the mood for chit chat, but she just didn't see any point to it. In a week or so, when they were done being trained, they'd be whisked off to their new master's house, forced to do whatever chores and deeds he demanded.

"Well ladies," Nadine, the girl next to Hannah said, "we sure working hard learning all these new chores, but I gotta say, it's way better than working out in them fields back home."

"Yes, Ma'am, it is," one said.

"I know that's right," said the other. "Anyone know what Miss Celia got us doing today?"

No one answered.

"Heard her talking to Kitch," Hannah said, "when we finishing up last night. Think we'll be polishing up all the silver in the house. At least, in the morning."

"You can speak?" Nadine said. "I was beginning to wonder."

The other two laughed.

"Polishing silver? You don't say. What must that be like? Just once I'd like to see what food tastes like eating from a silver spoon."

"Maybe you can sneak a taste when no one's looking," Nadine said. "Tell the rest of us."

They all looked at each other and laughed. No chance any of them would dare try such a thing.

Listening to them go on about such silly things made Hannah wonder if they even understood what was happening to them, where all this training was leading. Maybe they did understand, and they just didn't care. Or maybe this was their way of dealing with circumstances none of them had any control over.

Over the next thirty minutes, they got cleaned up, changed into their working clothes, and headed over to some wooden table set up just outside the kitchen. That's where they ate breakfast, weather permitting. The same young girl who'd served them all their meals brought out some fresh bread and scrambled eggs. Or, if they wanted, there was grits to eat. The weather was pleasant, the nicest morning so far. Plenty of sunshine, a nice cool breeze blew through the trees. Hannah could hear at least three different birds singing different songs.

About then, Miss Celia showed up. "Okay, ladies, time to finish up and get started on this day. You might have heard me say yesterday that this morning we'd be learning all about taking care of the silver. You three ladies will be doing that, as planned. But Hannah, today you be working with Josephine changing out all the linens and lace throughout the house. She's a girl about your age, but you listen to her and what she teaches you. She was born at this place, knows almost all there is to know about working in the main house."

"I'm done eating, Miss Celia," Hannah said. "I could get started now if you show me where to go."

"Fine, girl. Glad you so eager to get started. You know where the pantry is?" Hannah nodded that she did. "Just go inside the door at the far end. Josephine already in there working. She'll show you what needs doing. The rest of you girls, finish up now."

Hannah got up from the table and was just about to bring her cup and dish inside, when she remembered she was supposed to leave it for the servant girl. "Everybody got their job," she'd been told. She walked across the brick walkway around some bushes, up the back porch steps and through the kitchen door. It was a busy place most of the time. This morning was no exception. The chef had his back to her, cutting up some big side of beef, which was just fine since he mostly made Hannah nervous, the way he always stared at her.

The kitchen staff were all doing their various jobs. Each one looked at her as she passed, but just for a moment then paid her no mind. She hadn't worked in here yet and hoped she wouldn't have to. Although she had to admit, she'd never eaten as well as she had since being brought to this place. She stepped through the pantry door, nodded to a young servant girl filling a bowl with potatoes from a sack, then continued through to the next door.

She opened it to find a woman about her age trying to fold a large white linen tablecloth.

"You mind giving me a hand?" the girl said. "Grab that other end? Trying to fold this in half, but it's just too big. This one goes to the dining room table. Don't know why these folks need such a long table when most days only five people eat at it."

"I don't mind," Hannah said, quickly grabbing the corner of the tablecloth dangling near the floor. "I'm guessing you're Josephine?"

"That's me. And you're Hannah. Don't have to guess. Everyone at the house knows who you are." After folding the tablecloth in two more halves, Josephine told Hannah, "I'll do it the rest of the way. Everything in this room got to be folded just so. I'll teach you all of it eventually. Miss Celia wants me to. But we'll start with simpler things first."

Hannah looked the room over more closely. It was almost as big as the pantry but one whole wall was filled with cabinets and drawers. "What's in all these?"

"More of the same," Josephine said, sliding out one of the lower drawers and neatly tucking the tablecloth in place. "You can't believe how much cloth be in this room. In all these drawers. Probably took all the cotton from three fields to make 'em. But the Missus loves her fancy linens and every single one got a specific place and purpose, and a certain way they gotta be folded." She leaned closer, "that is, if you want to avoid a whipping."

Hannah, matched her volume, said, "You get whipped you don't fold them just right?"

"Not anymore. Because I learned. And it's not just folding

them matters. They each got to be put in they correct drawer. Don't ask me why, but I'll show you that, too."

"I appreciate it. Sure don't want to get whipped. A moment ago, you said everyone knows who I am. How come?"

"Because," Josephine said, "you special."

"What? Why you say I'm special?"

"Just look at you. And look at me. We had a mirror, you could see why, plain as day."

"I don't understand," Hannah said.

"You really don't?"

Hannah shook her head no.

"It's simple. You beautiful to look at. I'm ugly as they come."

Josephine's answer shocked her. She didn't know how to reply. "You're not ugly," she said, although if Hannah was being honest, she might describe her as plain.

"I am, too. Ugly, that is. But it's okay. Truth is, I'd rather look like me than look like you."

"Why?"

"Because...men leave me alone. That suits me fine. But everyone knows why you brought here. You and them other girls. But you especially. Word is, Massa Clifton keeping you all to hisself. That's why he didn't sell you off. You being groomed to be his lady, just like Celia was. I got no problem with that. Suits me just fine. Massa Clifton walks by, he don't even see me. The cook in the kitchen? He don't see me, neither. But he can't keep his eyes off you. Course, you don't gotta worry about him. He knows you belong to the Colonel. So, all he gonna ever do is look. Maybe say something he shouldn't be sayin'."

Hannah didn't plan it, but hearing this, her eyes filled with tears.

Josephine's face completely changed. "I'm sorry. Didn't mean to make you cry. Don't pay me no mind. I'm just trying to help, not make you sad."

Hannah wiped her tears on her sleeve. "Josephine, I don't want any of these men to look at me. Not the Colonel and not the cook. Or any of the other men on this plantation. I got a husband back home in Fredericksburg. He's the only man I want looking at me that way. Before I came here, I was just a worker out in the field. I don't know how this happened, that the Colonel brung me here. Why he's paying me all this special attention. I want none of it. I just want to go home." The tears started coming again. "You gotta help me. Please."

"You poor thing." Josephine took out a washcloth from her pocket and gave it to Hannah. "I don't know how I can help you Hannah. But if God show me a way, and it don't get me a beating, I'll do it. Whatever it is, you just ask."

29

Hannah didn't know why she was getting so emotional. It was just so hard to understand why all these things were happening to her. Her life back in Fredericksburg was just fine. Her and Lucas were getting along good. She was a hard worker, always making her quota out in the field. Get along with most of the other slaves most the time. Then out of the blue, Massa Clifton, looking for some pretty young slave girls to buy and somehow she become a part of it. Hannah didn't even think she was that pretty. Lucas say she was. Sometimes other men say things to her when she going to town on some errand. But nothing worth all this fuss.

She handed the washcloth back to Josephine. "Thank you. I'm sorry for getting like this. Don't know what come over me."

"That's all right," Josephine said. "Guess I figured wrong, that someone look like you always getting it easy in life. I would never think you ever worked a day in the field."

"You should've seen the way I looked the morning they

brought me here, when I crawled out of that dirty wagon with them other girls. Took Miss Celia half a day to get rid of the stink and try to clean us up."

"Looks like she got you cleaned up good. You even look good in that work dress you got on." She bent down, opened another long drawer just below where they'd stored the tablecloth. "We best keep working in case someone open that door and see us talking with empty hands." She pulled out another thickly folded linen cloth with frilly laces around the edges. "This is the one we using on the big table for the fall weather. Don't ask me why. Looks pretty much like the one we just put in that drawer, you ask me. Even so, this is what the Missus wants, so that's what she gets."

Josephine unfolded it until she needed Hannah's help to keep it going. Then they set it down on a worktable. "We'll leave this here for the moment, and I'll show you how to fold up the linen napkins, and where they go."

"Miss Celia said you were born here on this plantation, lived your whole life here."

"That's true. I been lucky in one kind a way. Someone plain as me should probably be out picking cotton. But I got told to watch Massa Clifton's two little girls when they were little. I wasn't much older than they were. But I guess they liked me well enough, or just got used to me being in the house. When I got old enough to work outside, the girls spoke up for me to they Mama, and she found me indoor work. Been working inside ever since."

Hannah backed up to the door, opened it just a crack, enough to see no one in the pantry to overhear them. She closed it again and stepped close to Josephine. "If you been working indoors all these years, you probably heard pretty much everything the Colonel and his wife talk about, when they discussing things I mean."

"Yeah, I guess," Josephine said. "If I'm in the room or close by. But we not allowed to discuss the things they say to each other amongst ourselves. Miss Celia find out we do, and we get in big trouble. Lose all our privileges indoors. So, we best change the subject here pretty quick."

"I don't want to get you in trouble. Don't want any trouble for me neither. I wasn't gonna ask you to share anything the Colonel and the Missus say to each other. I just want to know if you ever hear talk of any slaves on this plantation ever running away. I know back where I live, a slave runs away and it's the biggest news going 'round for days."

Josephine thought a moment. "I suppose me saying something 'bout that not the same as telling family secrets. It's the same here. A slave tries to run away, and it's a very big situation."

"It happen very often?" Hannah said.

Josephine shook her head no. "Almost never do." She picked up one of the linen napkins, started folding it a certain way.

Hannah was too focused on what she was saying to pay attention to her method. "Why is that, you think? That because the Cliftons treat their slaves right?"

"Sometimes they treat their slaves proper. But sometimes they can be as bad as any other owner. Specially when it comes to buying and selling time. They let folks get married, let them have chillun'. But then won't think twice about selling them off, if they have a mind to. Just tear them families up, don't give it a second thought. Other times, a slave get accused of doing something wrong, even if they had no part in it. Get tied up to the post just the same and whipped till they bleed."

"That goes on back where I come from," Hannah said. "Is that when slaves run away from here? That what you've seen?"

Josephine nodded. "But only happened a handful of times, and always ends the same way."

"What way is–"

They heard footsteps coming from the doorway. Josephine tossed Hannah one of the linen napkins. Took another one for herself and spread it open across her chest. "First, you take it like this."

The door opened. In walked Celia. "You girls getting along all right?"

"We doin' fine, Miss Celia," Josephine said.

"You showing her everything she needs to know?"

"I am, Ma'am. We got a long way to go yet, but she listening good."

"Glad to hear it," Celia said. "Because you know how the Missus want everything just so."

"I do, Miss Celia."

"All right, then." She left the room the way she came.

Hannah waited a moment, then hurried to the door and opened it a crack. Celia had left the pantry room, too. "You were talking about how few slaves have run away from here and how it always ends."

"I think we need to stop talking about this. That was too close."

"Just answer these two things, then I'll stop asking. I promise."

"One reason so few have tried is how far away we are

from the nearest free state. We in South Carolina. This ain't Virginia. And all the states between here and Pennsylvania all slave states. But the main reason is what Massa Clifton do when a slave run away. No one ever made it more than two days, 'cept Amos Johnson, and he only gone for three. The Colonel do whatever he gotta do, spend whatever he gotta spend to bring 'em back. And when they back, they get tied to the post and whipped till they bleed. Then he leaves them there two full days, so everyone see what happens if they try the same."

"You say a fella named Amos got away the farthest?"

"Don't know how far he got, but he was gone the longest."

"He still here, on this plantation...this Amos fella?"

"He is. But he not gonna be any help to ya. The last time he tried four or five years ago, and he got beat so bad, he gave up trying altogether."

"I still wanna talk to him. Where he at?"

"He works mainly in the barnyard, looks after the livestock. But see, Massa just started him doing that a few months ago. Used to be out in the fields. Colonel say he rewarding him, since he now such a better worker. Stopped all his running, always make his quota. Amos really like what he doing now. Don't think he'll do anything might make the Colonel unhappy."

"I just wanna talk to him," Hannah said, "Won't cause him any trouble. But I gotta get out of this place. I ain't gonna let them make me the Colonel's woman. Ain't right before God or man, since I'm already married."

"But it can't be a sin on you, they take you against your will. I heard one of the older ladies say so."

"Maybe so, but I won't let it happen to me. And you don't have to worry about what they do to me if they catch me and bring me back."

"How come?" Josephine said.

"Because I won't let 'em catch me. I'll drown myself in a river first."

30

Hannah kept her promise to Josephine for the rest of the day and didn't bring up any more troubling questions. She did her best to care about the task at hand, but how white folks wanted their linens and lace folded just so failed to keep her interest very long. Seemed to Hannah, this whole big house filled with a thousand useless things, considering her people managed to get through they whole lives without ever owning a single one. Course, it was the same situation back at the big house back in Fredericksburg. She expected it to be the same in most plantations. Rich white folk spending all they money to impress other rich white folk they invited over to their parties and dinners. Then they all go home in they fancy carriages talking about how they need to buy even more things.

After sundown and dinner, the girls were allowed a little freedom to do as they pleased. The other three lay in their beds exchanging stories about the day. Hannah excused herself, said she'd like to get a little night air. The moon hadn't come up yet, so it was already pretty dark, which suited her plans just fine. She had it in her mind to find this fellow Amos, see if she couldn't get him talking about his last attempt to get free. She knew where the barn was and you could easily see all the fencing around it marking off the various pens.

What she didn't know was where Amos might be about now. She didn't know if any of the livestock on this plantation needed tending to after sundown. Some did back in Fredericksburg, so the men looking after them lived right there in the back of the barn. She might have to give up on this idea if Amos lived in that row of shacks she passed on the way here.

She kept to the shadows. Once she reached the area around the barn, didn't see any people. She got nervous for a moment when she saw a dog lying beside an open side door. She bent down, reached out her open palms and spoke kindly to him. His tail started wagging, and he hurried over and started licking her. She scratched behind his ears, patted him on the head and said some other kind things. That went on for a few minutes longer than she'd planned, because she realized she might be getting more out of the exchange.

"See you met Betsy."

The deep voice came from out of the darkness of the barn and almost reminded Hannah of her father. "Didn't realize it was a girl," she said.

"You could tell she was easy if it was daytime." He stepped out into the same twilight she and the dog were in. "Even without looking underneath. She got the sweet face of a girl dog." Then he looked at Hannah and his expression changed. "Oh, it's you. I'm sorry. What I said about Betsy's sweet face. Didn't mean nothing by it."

Hannah wasn't sure what he meant, but he seemed suddenly intimidated by her presence.

"You the Colonel's new girl, right?"

It felt like a punch in the gut. "I'm one of the new ones here, but I am —" she looked around to make sure no one could hear. "I am *not* the Colonel's new girl."

"My apologies then. That's what I hear everyone saying, all the workers I mean. You look like the girl they pointed out to me earlier today. Dressed like her. Said you were the prettiest in the bunch the Colonel brought back from his trip. Seeing you up close, I just figured —"

"That may be what everyone's saying, but it don't make it so. You're not wrong, though, thinking that's what the Colonel has in mind for me. But that don't make me his girl. That's not who I'm gonna be. In fact, that's why I came out here. Looking to talk to someone named Amos Johnson. Supposed to work in this area, but we never met."

"We have now." He reached down, held out his hand. "I'm Amos. And you must be Hannah."

She shook his hand. "She really is a sweet dog." Betsy had now rolled onto her back to get her stomach scratched.

"So, you say you come out here looking for me? How you know my name?"

"I was working with one of the girls works inside. Won't say who. Don't want to get her in any trouble. But I asked her if anyone had ever run away and got free. She said no, but you got away the longest. Three days she say."

Amos was no longer happy with this conversation. He looked around nervously, making sure they were completely alone. "Those days be long gone for me. Many years now. I give up on that altogether...for one reason and one reason only."

"Why is that?"

"Simple. It can't be done."

"But my friends say you were gone three days. You must've got pretty far in three days."

"Not far enough, let me tell you. The thing can't be done. I know so first-hand."

"But why? There has to be a way. Hasn't there been something you wish you did different since you been back? Something you think, if you tried that, maybe you would-a got away for good?"

Amos squatted down, came a little closer. Betsy quickly moved over to him to get some more attention. "I'm sorry, Hannah. For us to be having this conversation, for you to be coming out here at night to talk with me about it... you gotta be hurting something awful inside. But I'm afraid I ain't the one to ease your pain. The truth is, the longer I been back, the more I see how big a fool I was to ever try and run away in the first place."

"Why would you say that?"

"Because now I know better what's out there. The hundred or more things standing in the way of me and freedom. I might as well have been yelling at the wall of Jericho by myself. All I'd be doing was making noise. The wall wouldn't budge an inch."

"I know that story," she said.

"Then you know, it took a mighty miracle of God to bring that wall down. And the whole army of Israel doing everything they told. But a man like me, running by hisself through the woods at night, with over a thousand miles to go till I'm free? It was never gonna happen. For starters, how well you swim?"

Hannah looked down toward the ground. "I can't swim." Yet another thing she wouldn't let her brother, Eli, teach her to do.

"You can't swim," Amos repeated. "Then you worse off than I was. Because where we are, this here plantation? You don't go too far till you come to the Ashley River. You gotta be a strong swimmer, you have any hope of getting across. You make it past there, keep going north, you come to the Cooper River. Even wider than the Ashley. You get past those, keep going north a bit more, and you hit the Santee. That's three rivers, and we not even close to being out of South Carolina yet. Not to mention the mosquitoes, the spiders and snakes you run across, and even wild dogs in some places. Besides all of nature being against you, you got the posse Massa Clifton put on your tail, with some of the best trackers and hound dogs money can buy. And if you somehow get past all of them, you find out that every single soul between you and freedom is eager to turn you in for that hefty cash reward the Colonel has put on your head."

Hannah's heart sank hearing all this.

"I'm sorry to be the one crushing what little hope you probably had. But you came looking for me, and I gotta be honest with you. You need to give it up, Hannah. The thing just can't be done. But I'll tell you where I put my hope. Our preacher talked about how God's people were slaves in Egypt for four hundred years. That's a whole lotta years. A whole lotta generations came and went who never saw the end of slavery coming. But there was one that did. The one

Moses was born in. God appointed Moses and Aaron to come after ole Pharaoh and force his hand, made him let God's people go. My hope is, we are that generation, like the one Moses born in. The one who sees God move, that forces Pharaoh's hand. Every morning and every night I'm praying this is true. You ask me? That's where I'd tell you to put your hope. Not in any foolish notions of running away. It just can't be done."

31

It was early in the afternoon when John and Laura, along with Micah and Eli in separate carriages, arrived at the B&O Depot in Washington City. After interviewing Micah then Eli, John, and Laura decided they really didn't need to spend any more time researching their roles as slaveowners in Baltimore. They felt confident they could pull this off, especially since Micah and Eli would be traveling with them the entire time, furthering their education. That late in the day, there wasn't a train going all the way from Baltimore to Fredericksburg, but there was one leaving Baltimore for Washington.

As they had done in Baltimore, John decided they should lease a nice carriage, but this time he had Micah stay with Laura while he and Eli secured the transportation. Eli had talked with some of the Negroes loading and unloading luggage and found out that a nice carriage could be had from a stable just a few blocks away on C Street.

"We can go whenever you're ready, Mr. John," Eli said.

Laura looked down one of the main roads and pointed. "Look John, that huge building under construction on that hill. Is that the—"

"Capitol Building? Yes, I believe it is. In fact, I'm sure it is. What else could it be? They're still working on the extensions and the dome section in the center. I've seen a sketch of it in the newspaper. It'll really be something to see by the time they're finished."

Laura looked around at what else could be seen from the deck of the train station. "Have to say, this is a little disappointing. I thought Washington City would be...more impressive. Even this, the train stations in Baltimore and Philadelphia were so much nicer. And all the roads are still dirt. Nice and wide, but just hard-packed dirt."

"I think there are some better roads closer to the White House," John said, "and quite a few more impressive buildings. We'll drive by them in a little while. You'll see. Still, lots of dirt. And lots of wide-open spaces. They've got all kinds of big plans for this city. Okay, you and Micah sit tight. Hopefully, Eli and I will be back with a nice carriage in the next thirty minutes or so."

The train depot was situated on New Jersey Avenue. Eli led John west on C Street. "Supposed to be just four or five blocks down this road."

"I'll follow you," John said.

"You could've stayed with your wife if you wanted. Daddy and me could have gotten this carriage taken care of for you, like we did in Baltimore."

"Oh, I'm sure you could. I thought I should come though, seeing as our plans for the carriage this time are a little more complicated."

"Oh, how so? If you don't mind me asking?"

"Not at all," John said.

They kept a brisk pace as they talked. But John couldn't help looking around. "I think I mentioned when we got on the train. Laura and I are pretty eager to take at least a brief tour of the city. Since the next train for Fredericksburg doesn't leave till mid-morning, I thought maybe we should skip the train ride from here to there and take a carriage there instead."

"Why is that? Not trying to argue with you, sir. Just curious."

"I know you want to get there as quickly as possible, Eli. I talked with the conductor. He said Fredericksburg is only fifty-five miles south of here, and there are good roads all the way. It would be a long ride, but we could get there in a day."

"Fifty-five miles? Yes, sir. We could do that."

"Because it leaves late, the train would only get us there a couple hours sooner. But my real concern is...you ran away from there a few years back. Might not be a good thing for you to be taking a train right into the center of town, risk getting recognized by someone."

That got Eli's attention. "Hadn't thought of that, Mr. John. But you right, that could be very bad."

"This way, we can lease the carriage for both purposes. To tour Washington City for the balance of the day, then ride it down to Fredericksburg tomorrow. I want to talk to the proprietor of the carriage company, see if he will — for the right price — allow me to prepay him to send one of his workers down to Fredericksburg by train when we're done with the carriage, so he can drive it back."

A calming smile came over Eli's face. "Mr. John, I like how you think."

"The other part of the idea is, well before we get near the center of town tomorrow, you exit the carriage and, that night, meet with some of your former slave friends at the plantation where Hannah used to work. See if you can find out any more details about where she's been taken."

"Yes, sir. I was thinking the same thing. Somebody has to know more than what we been told. Something that'll help us narrow down the search around Charleston."

"Laura, Micah and I will visit Fredericksburg," John said, "And then we'll rendezvous with you the next day on the train and continue our journey south."

"I'll wait till the last minute to get on," Eli said. "Maybe come in near the back, make my way up to the Negro section in front once we out of Fredericksburg."

"That's the idea," John said.

Two hours later, John and Laura were waiting out front of the National Hotel for Eli and Micah to pick them up and start their brief tour of Washington City. John had discovered the hotel when he and Eli had walked into the stable to lease a carriage. It turned out to be quite a find. It was diagonally across the street and quite impressive, taking up the entire street corner and half a block more, and five stories tall. John hoped it might improve Laura's opinion of the city.

It did that...and a good bit more.

John had unwittingly chosen the very same hotel where a great scandal had taken place sixteen years ago in 1841. Laura had been reading all about this very thing in a book she purchased for the trip, called *Twelve Years a Slave*, written by *Solomon Northrup*. The book had just come out two years ago and was causing quite a stir. Laura hadn't finished it yet, but she had read the parts where Northrup — a renowned Negro violinist, and a freed man — had stayed at this very hotel in 1841. There he had been tricked by some unscrupulous fellows, kidnapped, drugged and then sold as a slave. He'd spent the next twelve years in Louisiana, before being freed and returned to his family in New York. How Northrup had been rescued and freed, John didn't know. Laura hadn't read that far in the book.

"John, do you realize," Laura said, "we could have eaten our dinner at the very same table where Solomon Northrup sat the night he was kidnapped."

John looked down the street, searching for the carriage. "I guess it's possible. We could have asked the waiter. He probably would have known if the hotel is mentioned plainly in the book."

"Actually, it's not. Back when the kidnapping happened, it was known as Gadsby's Hotel, named after the original proprietor. I almost didn't make the connection till I saw an old painting of the hotel in the lobby and saw the name Gadsby's on the sign. I asked the clerk, and he said that's what it used to be called years ago. After reading about it in the book, I was hoping I might see it on our tour, and here we are staying at the very place."

"I'm glad it worked out," John said. "Oh look, here they come."

"What are we going to see first?" she said.

"That's why I wanted to eat an early dinner. We only have an hour or two before it starts getting dark. Fortunately, most of the things I wanted to see aren't very far from here."

"Like the White House," Laura said. "Can we see that?"

"Yes, it's only about a mile away."

"I'm ashamed to say, I didn't even pay attention to the last election," said Laura. "I don't know anything about President Buchanan."

"I voted for him," John said. "But I'm already wondering why. He doesn't seem to be doing anything about this slavery situation at all. If possible, things have gotten worse since he took office. Nevertheless, it is the White House. If only for its historical significance, I'd still want to see it. And it's also right next to the US Treasury Building. Now, that is an impressive looking place. I've seen a photograph. Wait till you see it."

The carriage pulled up.

"How did you gentlemen make out?" John said. "How are your accommodations? I was surprised to learn the hotel at least had some rooms available for Negroes."

"Even though they were way in the back and on the ground floor," Laura said.

"That's okay," Eli said. "The rooms are quite nice. Daddy and me will do just fine. But I wasn't surprised about the rooms. I actually expected the hotel to have them. Read about it in a book recently. Of course, the book said they had rooms for coloreds back in 1841."

John looked at Laura. Her eyes lit up. "This book?" She pulled it out from her bag.

"*Twelve Years a Slave*," Eli read aloud. "Yes, Ma'am. The very one."

"Did you finish it?"

"Yes'm, about a month ago."

"Don't tell me a thing. I'm only halfway through."

"I won't. But you know…it's gonna be some tough reading after he gets kidnapped."

"I know," she said. "It's already started."

"A book written by a slave?" Micah said. "For twelve years, you say? Too bad I can't write. I been a slave over fifty."

32

The next morning, bright and early, the four travelers started their journey south to Fredericksburg, but not before making some quick stops for some essential provisions. Besides the obvious things like extra food and water, they were advised by the stable manager to visit a local gun store and purchase a shotgun and two rifles, as well as sufficient ammunition.

He said he'd made runs down to Fredericksburg on a number of occasions. It was generally a safe route, and he'd written up a map for Eli to follow. But he'd also said, "These days, can't play it too safe." He explained that since more people were traveling by train these days, there were less carriages on the roads between towns. Bums and freeloaders sometimes hung out in the woods waiting for an easy target to come by. He'd found if you kept the guys in the front of the carriage well-armed you were more likely to be left alone.

The only other groups they might encounter were slave hunters chasing down runaways, but they'd probably leave

John's party alone seeing how well-dressed Eli and Micah were, how nice the carriage was, and that they had papers proving they were John's slaves. Besides that, runaway slaves don't hide in wagons heading *south.*

After traveling for an hour, they were now well south of Washington City. The sun was shining, though the road was mostly covered by shady trees. A cool breeze blew through the carriage windows. Laura was just about to get her book out of her bag, when John asked, "So, what did you think of our tour of the city yesterday afternoon?"

"I enjoyed much of it," she said. "But I was glad to have you in the carriage explaining things. At least right now, it's one of the oddest looking cities I've ever seen. There were a few magnificent buildings. Like the White House and the Treasury Building, and way across the way from those, I loved that Smithsonian Museum building. The one that looked like a castle. But it was very strange to see all these huge sections of land in the center of town with nothing on them. And all those roads going off in different directions — some very wide —with hardly any buildings on them. And those I did see were hardly anything befitting our nation's capitol. Of course, you can see the Capitol Building will be an amazing place one day."

"Washington's definitely a work in progress," John said. "But the whole city's been laid out already. From what I hear, when it's all done all those big empty spaces will be occupied by buildings as magnificent as the few already finished."

"Will we even be alive to see it?" Laura said.

John laughed. "I should hope so. But then, while you were getting ready this morning I went down to the café to get another cup of coffee and overheard a congressman and senator talking. I don't remember their names, only that the congressman had a southern accent and the senator was clearly from New England. To hear the southern gentleman talk, it sounds like a big showdown is on the horizon. He said the plantation owners in his district were starting to entertain talks of secession."

"What is that?"

"It means pulling out of the Union. No longer being a part of this country."

Laura's face registered the shock John felt inside. "Can they do that?"

"I suppose they can try. I don't know how it could work. The idea seems preposterous to me."

"It's because of slavery," she said. "Isn't it?"

"Mostly, yes," John said. "I don't think the southern states will ever give it up. The congressman said their entire economy is dependent on it, and the northern states won't leave it alone. They've already done away with slavery, and they keep pressuring the South to do the same. He said it'll never happen. The southern states would leave the Union first. And they're arguing over the new territories about whether they'll be slave or free."

"I can't believe they'd do something so drastic as leave the union, just to keep slavery intact," Laura said.

"I'm afraid I can," John said. "After seeing the things we've already seen with these slaveowners. Yes, I definitely can. Between growing up in New York then living in San Francisco, I never had to confront the issue like we've had to this past month. Feels like there's some mental deficiency at work, a kind of collective madness. It's been going on for so long now, especially in the South, most have been born and raised with it as perfectly normal. They've been taught from their earliest days that people with a different skin color are inherently inferior to them in every way. So, they all live and talk as if it's true. They won't allow them to read or write, and then convince themselves this is one of the reasons coloreds are inferior...because they can't read or write. But look at Eli. He reads and writes wonderfully. You and he are even chatting about the same book. Even now, I'm certain Micah could learn if he wanted to and someone took the time to teach him."

"I know," Laura said. "It is hard to fathom. And even though he's illiterate, he's not only *not* inferior to me, I find his wisdom about life superior to mine in almost every way. Not only his wisdom, but his capacity for joy. He has suffered so much in this life, yet I've never known anyone more content and more able to bounce back so quickly whenever unsettling circumstances confront him. And then there's his capacity for mercy toward others. I'm sure you've seen a measure of this, but I saw it all the time on that ship. Most of those sailors treated him abysmally. Sometimes, the captain, too. But he never reacted in anger or ever spoke a harsh word to anyone who wronged him."

"I believe it," John said. "And yet, these southern slavery folks would see Micah as having no more worth than a horse or a cow. Maybe even less now that he's too old to work out in the fields." He took off his hat and rubbed his temples.

"Does your head ache?" Laura said.

"It's just the frustration of this subject, I think. I don't know how I'm going to be around them the next several days as one who thinks and believes as they do. It still makes absolutely no sense to me."

"Well, maybe if we get to a stretch of road far between any towns, you should sit up there with Micah a bit and chat with him. He might have some insights that could ease your troubled mind."

The carriage abruptly slowed. Eli yelled "Whoa" to the horses and pulled in the reins. The little wooden door between them slid open.

"We got a situation goin' on here," Micah said. "In the woods just up ahead."

John heard one of them cock a rifle.

33

"Should I just ride up through it?" Eli asked.

"What did you see?" said John.

"Woods are pretty thick out here, been so for a while now. But I definitely saw some bushes moving in a big way off to the right, maybe fifty yards ahead. Looked at it more closely, happened again. Same place. Only moving further into the woods."

"Seems like we're pretty far from any nearby towns," John said. "Could it just be a big animal?"

"Could be," Micah said. "But don't think so. No animals in these woods likely to attack a carriage. They'd keep moving deeper into the woods till they got away."

"But the moving's stopped," Eli said. "Not like an animal to stop and stay put. More like a person, who got spooked by us coming near. Question is, they staying put because they're scared or setting up an ambush?"

John looked at Laura. "I've got to get up there and help them."

"Don't you think they can handle it?" she whispered.

"Probably, but we don't know what we're facing. You just say a quick prayer." He reached for the second rifle and exited the carriage on Micah's side. "Micah, why don't you take the reins. Just ride the horse slowly forward. Eli, you slide across the roof and get in position in the back on that footboard by the luggage. I'll get up there next to your father."

"Yes sir, Mr. John." He scrambled across the roof with the rifle, as John climbed up and took his place. Micah had the shotgun leaning beside him, both hands still on the reins.

"Okay Micah, ease the horses forward. Did you see where the bushes moved?"

"Yes, sir." He pointed to the spot.

"Okay, got my eyes on it. You keep riding, slowly."

John looked back at Eli. He had the rifle pointing to the same place. John turned back around, made sure his own rifle was ready to fire, then focused his gaze at the same spot. For the next few minutes, things remained calm. Then the bush moved just to the right of where John had been looking. Micah saw it too, motioned with his eyes. John nodded. "Stop the carriage," he whispered, "when we get about another fifteen yards ahead."

Micah did.

When it stopped, John pointed his rifle toward the place in question. Micah wrapped the reins around a hook and picked up the shotgun.

"We know you're out there," John yelled. "We got two Winchesters and a shotgun aimed right at you. Way too close to miss. If you're armed, toss your guns out to the road and step away from the bushes with your hands up. We don't want any trouble, but we won't take any, either."

Nothing happened for close to a minute.

"Okay then. Looks like you're not giving me any choice. When I count to three gentlemen, fire away, right where you saw the bushes move." John looked, still no movement.

Micah raised his shotgun and pointed.

"One," John yelled. "Two!"

Suddenly, one of the bushes moved. Then a man stepped out into the open with his hands up. A large, colored man with ragged clothes. Clearly, a slave. "Please, suh, don't shoot. We not armed. And we mean you no harm."

Micah lowered his shotgun but John kept his straight and level. He wanted to be sure this was as it seemed.

When the man saw Micah lower his shotgun, some of the fear left his face. Then he noticed Eli at the back of the carriage. Eli had raised his rifle up toward the trees.

"You said we," John said. "Who else is with you? I want to see them all, just to make sure no one's armed. We've been told bandits and robbers frequent these woods."

"No, suh. We not bandits, nor robbers. We just trying to get free, is all. Mostly travel at night, so we don't be seen. But we haven't seen any water fit to drink since yesterday, so we taking a chance and moving during the day, hoping to find some." The man turned toward the bushes on his left. "Joseph, Bertie...y'all come out now. Let the man see you. They not going to hurt us."

When John saw a younger man and a girl in her early teens step out from the bushes, his heart melted. These poor people. Instantly, his gun came down. They were dressed just like the man. None wore shoes. "Micah, you stay here.

Keep an eye on the horses. Eli and I can take care of this." He started getting down from the carriage.

"You okay now, folks," Micah said. "Me and my boy Eli former slaves, too. The Lord been good to you, letting you bump into Mr. John here. He and his wife in the carriage, best folks I know."

Laura came out from the carriage then holding a big basket. "We've got food for you. Good food, too, and plenty of it. Come on over and have some."

Eli came from the back of the carriage holding one of the large water jugs. "Plenty of water, too. Expect you might want some of this first."

Tears filled the big man's eyes. He came forward, reached out his hand. "The name's Elijah. These two here are my young-uns, Joseph and Bertie. We ran away three nights ago, hoping to link up with some folks from the Underground Railroad. Haven't seen any yet. You the first people we met who haven't been chasing us."

All three of them quickly took long drinks from the water jug.

"So you're being chased?" John said.

"Our massa got a posse together, " Joseph said. "Think we lost 'em last night. But can't be sure. Even so, they won't give up that easy."

"My boy's right," Elijah said. "We worth too much money. We'd love to spend more time with you kind folks, but we should keep moving. Still got a very long way to go."

"We understand," Laura said. "If we could, we'd take you back north with us in the carriage. But we're on a rescue mission ourselves, trying to get Micah's daughter freed from a bad situation near Charleston. But one thing we can do..."

She looked at John, who nodded. "Here, you take this jug of water with you. And this basket of food."

"We can't take your provisions," Elijah said.

"Sure you can," Micah said. "If we give 'em to you."

"We'll be in Fredericksburg this evening," John said. "We can replenish our supplies there." He looked down at their feet. "I've packed an extra pair of shoes for traveling. Laura? Eli? How about you two?"

"I have an extra pair," Laura said.

"Me, too," Eli said. "Might fit you, Elijah. You taller than me, but I got feet way too big for my size."

"I don't know what to say." Elijah got teary-eyed again. "No one ever been this nice to us."

"I think mine will fit you, Joseph," John said. "Let me get them."

"If they don't," said Micah. "He can have a pair of mine."

For the next ten minutes, they helped Elijah and his two children get set for the next leg of their journey. Before departing, everyone traded hugs and Micah asked if he could pray a blessing for the rest of their journey.

After that, Eli mentioned they had crossed a decent-looking creek a few hours back that looked like fresh water to him. Then John asked Elijah whether they'd seen any suspicious looking people in the woods between here and Fredericksburg.

Elijah said they had not, but added, "You see a group of five angry white men with rifles on horses, heading this way and asking about us, could you—"

"Your secret is safe with us, my friend. Godspeed."

34

Everyone stood outside the carriage and watched as the three runaway slaves disappeared into the woods. John walked over to Laura and whispered, "Think I might have that chat with Micah you suggested."

"Excellent idea," she said. "Looks like we're in a nice long stretch of woods."

He opened the carriage door and helped her back inside. "Hey Eli, would you be okay sitting there in the back a while longer? I'd like to chat with your dad upfront."

"Be happy to, sir."

Micah walked around the front, gave the horses some attention before climbing into the driver's seat. John handed him his shotgun, then climbed up and sat in the seat beside him. Micah got the horses back on the road. Now that the threat of danger had passed for the moment, John was able to take in the view from the front seat. The road stretched out before them as far as the eye could see, almost in a straight line. About the same number of trees on either side.

The way they arched and met in the center gave the appearance of riding through a tunnel.

"Beautiful day for a ride, isn't it, sir?" Micah said. "That sure was a mighty fine thing you did for those folks."

"We were happy to do it," John said. "Wish we could've done more. I just pray they make it all the way to freedom without getting caught."

"Yes, sir. You and me both. So, something you want to talk about, Mr. John?"

"As a matter of fact, yes. Nothing you've done wrong, or Eli either. Really, just hoping maybe you can give me some advice. Over the next few days, we'll be doing some serious mingling with a number of southern slaveowners. I feel a little more equipped than I did about the role I'm to play, but there's one area — a big area, I'm afraid — that I can't get a handle on at all."

"What's that, sir?"

"See? Even that — you having to call me sir, or Mr. John. I know in one sense it's practice for the roles we're playing on this trip. But in another way, it's not. Micah, you've had to spend your entire life talking this way to people like me. White folks. Talking as if you're the inferior one, and we are superior to you in every way."

"Ah, but Mr. John...see, I don't see myself as inferior on the inside. For a long time I did. A very long time. But when the Lord set me free from my own sins, from all the hatred and bitterness I felt toward my oppressors, he filled that place with his love and opened my eyes to see how things really are. The way he sees them. Then I knew...some white folks may talk to me like I'm inferior to them, and they do. But that's because *they* broken on the inside, not because I am. How can I be inferior to them when the God who made them, and me, say we all made in his image and likeness? The preacher say, one day every race and tribe and people and tongue gonna stand before the throne — as one — giving all the glory to him, to the one who made us fit to stand there all together in his presence."

What could John say? He just sat there and smiled. "You're right, Micah. You're right. You are by no means an inferior being."

"And neither are you, Mr. John. The only superior one is the God who made us, and his son, Jesus. The rest of us? Well, we all in the same boat." He looked around. "Maybe better to say, we all on the same *road*."

They continued on a few moments in silence, then Micah said, "See, take this road here. We been on it all day, almost look like the same scene. Like we on the longest road on earth. Just riding straight ahead, trees on both sides, hour after hour. But the truth is, we are making progress. Eventually, we gonna get where we going. But the longest road in a man's life, not some earthly road like this. It's the one that separates him from God. Sad thing is, no matter how long a man travel down that road, he no closer to God than when he started. Don't matter he riding in the fanciest carriage or an ole broke down wagon. If God don't show that man mercy, open his eyes to see how blind he is, he'll never see it himself. Just keep riding down that long road till the day he die. That's why I can show mercy to others, cause I didn't open up my own eyes. God did. Just like he stopped Paul on that long road to Damascus. A little while later, he took them scales from his eyes...and he did the same thing for me. Does that help any?"

"It certainly helps some," John said. "But, I'm still struggling a bit. I'm not even sure I can explain it well enough to
make sense. See, the problem is, I'm white. That's how I was
born. It's not really a problem, it's that...I could have just as
easily been born a Negro. Or be from China. Or some other
race. And I was born to a wealthy family. I could just as
easily have been born to a poor one. And instead of having
so much, I could have grown up with very little of this
world's goods."

"No man has any control over the circumstances of his
birth," Micah said.

"That's right. That's exactly right. And I believe that. But
so many of my own race don't. Really, for the rest of this trip,
every white person we see most likely believes they are superior to you and every one of your people. Even if they themselves are poor and could never own a slave, just because
they're white. I don't understand that. Why they don't see
that the color of a man's skin matters nothing to God at all?
And — as you said — none of us have any control over the
circumstances of our birth. If they believed *that* was true,
then why don't they believe as I do? That being white doesn't
make one superior or inferior to anyone else? But they don't
see it. They don't believe it. And it makes me despise them.
And yet, I'm supposed to be around them for the next several
days, acting as if I'm one of them. As if I think the same way
they do. But I find it utterly abhorrent and revolting."

"You asking me why they don't see things as you see
them," Micah said, "or believe what you believe?"

"Yes, I guess I am. You must have something at work
inside of you that I don't. Even though we both believe in
Christ, there's something else in your outlook that I clearly

don't possess. Because...if *I* find them revolting and despise them—being white—then *you* should hate them all the more, since you're the recipient of their abuse. But you don't hate them. You seem to have a sense of mercy about you toward these racist people. Laura said she saw this at work all the time when the two of you were aboard that ship."

Micah snapped the reins to give the horses a little boost, then said, "Well, them other white folk don't see what you see or believe what you believe, because...they *believe something else*. That's why a man got to be very careful what he chooses to believe. A belief is a powerful thing. Starts off as a thought or an idea, maybe someone's opinion on a matter. If that's all it is, it can still be changed, maybe when a better idea or better opinion come along. But if it don't get changed, after a while a man's pride latches hold of it, and it becomes a belief. Once that happens, he better hope what he believes is the truth, as God sees it. Because once a man *believes* something, he will live like it is true, whether it be true or not. When someone believes in a lie — like the one that say one man superior to another because of the color of his skin — he gonna live like that lie is true, maybe the rest of his born days. And he gonna keep saying things and doing things because of that belief, and all the while, he has no idea he's believing a lie."

"It's like the man's blind," John said. "If he's believing a lie."

"Yes, sir. He sees something to be one way, and it's not that way at all. May even be the opposite way. But he can't see it. You or me can talk to that man all night and through the next day, won't make no difference. It's like that longest road we talked about. He believing a lie, he gonna keep on believing it just the same, no matter how far down that road he travels. Yes, sir…once a man believe something, gonna take some powerful circumstances—powerful *bad* circumstances—to open them eyes. Or else, a miracle of God's mercy…like I was saying…what happened to the apostle Paul on the road to Damascus."

"This is really quite profound, Micah," John said. "Thank you, so much."

"Not sure what profound is, but it sounds like a good thing."

John laughed. "Yes, it is. And this is why you are able to have mercy inside when you're around ignorant people, like…slaveowners."

"Yes, sir. 'Cause I know they blind. Just as blind as they can be."

John leaned back, looked down that long, beautiful tunnel of trees ahead and felt like, in some ways, his frustration had completely lifted. A moment later, he saw something else. Something unsettling. In the center of that tunnel, where the road seemed to meet the trees, a small cloud of dust appeared.

As he continued looking, the cloud grew larger.

"Daddy, you see that up ahead?" Eli yelled from the back.

"I see it, son," Micah said.

35

"You want me to stop?" Micah asked John.

"No, just keep going like you're going. Hopefully, it's just another carriage or some riders heading in the opposite direction. It's not likely robbers, since they tend to hide out in the woods, not ride down the middle of the road."

"Protect us, Lord," Micah whispered and snapped the reins again.

John double-checked his rifle, made sure it was ready to fire.

A few minutes later, Eli said, "Definitely got men on horses coming toward us. White men. Four, maybe five. Can't tell yet."

"My boy got eyes like an eagle," Micah said.

John slid the little wooden door over. "Laura, we've got some men on horses coming our way. Probably nothing, but maybe you should lower the shades on the windows? And if you hear us talking, don't say a word."

It wasn't long before John could see five riders coming

their way. All dressed in typical clothes for a long day's ride. Moving at a good clip but not a full gallop. John rested his Winchester across his lap, his right hand close to the trigger. He looked back, saw Eli lying on the roof of the carriage with his rifle pointing toward the approaching men. "Try not to look so threatening, Eli. Be ready in case something happens, but we don't want to look like we're anxious for trouble."

"Okay, Mr. John. I understand."

John reminded himself he was supposed to be from Baltimore, just a man riding toward Fredericksburg with his two slaves. The men were real close now. One was leading the pack. He appeared to be in his forties. The other four looked to be in their mid to late twenties. None were clean-shaven. The two in the back pulled their rifles out once the older man started slowing the horses down.

"You men put those guns away," the older man said. "What's wrong with you?"

John was relieved to hear that but still kept his hands on his rifle. "Howdy," he said. A greeting he'd never used before. Now he saw that all five men were wearing sidearms. "Wondered if we had this road all to ourselves."

"The name's Maddock," the older man said. "The lad next to me's my boy, Jason. Guess you don't need to hear about the rest. Not like we're gonna sit down for a chat."

"My name's Foster, John Foster. These are my two slaves. This here's Micah and in the back, his boy Eli."

"Slaves you say? Where you folks coming from?"

"Baltimore," John said. "On our way to Fredericksburg. Hoping this is the right road. Only ever been there by train before."

"This road'll get you there," Maddock said. "At a carriage pace, maybe two more hours to go." He looked at Micah then back at Eli. "You always give your slaves weapons when you travel? None of us own any, but...doesn't seem like a smart thing to do."

"I'm sure for some it might be plain old stupid," John said. "But Micah and Eli been in our family for ages. Trust them like my own kin. Besides, the man who leased this carriage to us said robbers and thieves sometimes travel these parts, looking for easy people to ambush. Seemed a safer bet to do it this way. Eli back there's a crack shot. You throw a nickel in the air, he'll hit it three times 'fore it hits the ground. Be a waste not to arm a man like that."

"Guess you folks in Baltimore way more trusting than we are in North Carolina," the son Jason said. "I'd be more afraid that boy back there shoot me in the back of the head, take off with this fine wagon, he that good a shot."

"Oh no," Micah said with a big grin. "Massa John treat us real good. We'd never do anything to —"

"Was I talking to you...*boy*?" Jason said.

"No, suh. You wasn't." The smile left Micah's face, and he instantly looked down.

John felt his blood rise, but he kept his cool. "Micah meant no disrespect. Perhaps we been chatting a bit too much, being out here on the road so long. He forgot his place for a moment, didn't you?"

"Yessuh, Massa John. Won't happen ag'in."

"Speaking of a slave forgetting his place, that's why we out here," Maddock said. "You said a moment ago you wondered if you had the whole road to yourself. I take it that means you ain't seen anyone else for quite a spell."

John nodded. "Not a wagon nor a single rider on horse-back since before we ate lunch, maybe three hours ago."

"How about three runaway slaves on foot?" Maddock said. "We been tracking them for days. Lost 'em sometime last night, but we know they headed this way. You sure you haven't seen any sign of 'em? Maybe crossing the road up ahead or behind you? Heard noises in the bushes just off the road? Maybe you thought it was an animal?"

"Wish I could help you men," John said. "Know how much money some owner's lost if you can't find them in time."

"Oh, we'll find 'em in time," the son said. "My Daddy the best tracker there is in both Carolinas."

"That's right, we hopin' to bring 'em back alive," one of the younger men said. "Only get half the money we bring 'em back dead."

"Why would the owner make a deal like that?" John said to Maddock. "He loses everything if you shoot them."

"Maybe so," Maddock said, "but he stands to lose a lot more any of his eighty-five other slaves get it in their heads these three got away. But we'll find 'em, and bring 'em back...*alive*." He stressed that last word to the three nameless young men in the back.

"Well, hope you do," John said, sounding as sincerely as he could.

"Say Pa, shouldn't we take a look inside that carriage, just to make sure they ain't hidin' the slaves in there?"

Maddock looked almost angry hearing this. "Guess you ain't been paying attention, boy. How you gonna lead your own posse someday, you don't use your head more often than your mouth?" He looked at John. "Apologize for my son's stupidity." He looked back at Jason. "Did you see the dust cloud from this wagon way back yonder when I first pointed it out to you?" Jason nodded that he did. "That was likely the same moment they saw us. From that point till now, did you see that dust cloud veer off to the right, or the left, like a carriage turning around?"

"No, sir."

"No, you didn't. What's that mean?"

"It didn't turn around."

"Right. So, they been riding the same direction then they going in now, correct?"

"Yes, sir."

"Which is?"

"Uh, south."

"That's right, south. And which way do slaves run when they trying to get free?"

"The north, Daddy." Jason understood.

"Ever heard of a slave who been running north for three days hitch a ride on a carriage taking them in the *opposite* direction they goin'?"

"No, sir. But why they got the shades all pulled down, like they hiding something?"

One of the shades rolled open. Laura leaned her head out the window. "Hey there, gentlemen?" she said in her Southern Belle voice. "Sorry for not being more neighborly. I've been in here trying to get some rest. All this traveling's given me a doozy of a headache."

"No problem, Ma'am," Maddock said. "We're sorry to bother you. We'll just be on our way."

"Say, Mr. Maddock," John said. "Since you're such a skilled tracker, I imagine if there were any thieves or robbers hiding in the woods between here and Fredericksburg, you'd be able to spot them, correct?"

"Definitely," Maddock said, "no matter how good they were hiding. I'd say you got safe travels all the way from here."

"Great, that's good to know. And it's about two more hours ahead?"

"Bout that, yeah. Well, y'all have a good afternoon. What's left of it anyhow." He turned to his men. "Okay, let's get a move on. Afraid we gonna have to split up and go deeper into the woods, if these folks haven't seen 'em anywhere near the road all day."

36

Thankfully, the next two hours were uneventful. Passed just one carriage and one wagon, occupied by harmless-looking folks coming from Fredericksburg. Both just nodded and waved, didn't even stop. The woods were still pretty thick on both sides but occasionally opened up at the intersections of a dirt road, some to the left, others to the right. John, Micah, and Eli stayed in their same seats and stayed armed, just as a precaution.

"This starting to look familiar," Micah said. "I think those roads, if I'm recalling correctly, connect to some of the smaller farms just north of the city. Eli, this area look familiar to you?"

Eli crawled across the roof from the back, sat closer to John and Micah. "I think you're right, Daddy. They not plantations but private farms, with only a handful of slaves. The plantations we worked on ran along the Rappahannock. Just down this road maybe twenty minutes more, we'll come to a little place called Falmouth. It's just upriver from Fredericks-

burg, maybe a mile and a half. But it's best I get off this
carriage before then. Some folks in Falmouth might recognize me. If it's still there, should be a small church on the
right-hand side, three or four blocks from the center of town.
You could let me off there. I know my way through the
woods to the plantation where Hannah used to be at. I'll wait
till it gets dark then head there, see if I can find her husband
or at least some of the other colored folks we used to know.
See if they can tell us anything more about where she is."

"Get all the details you can, Eli," John said. "We've got to
narrow down the search area if we have any hope of finding
her."

"I will."

"You think you should go with him, Micah? Any concerns
about people recognizing you in town?"

"No concerns at all," he said. "See, I wasn't a runaway. The
captain bought me fair and square. Anybody sees me won't
be hard to believe you and Miss Laura bought me from him.
Truth is, that's what happened. We'll just leave off the part
about you giving me my freedom right after that. Besides, if I
go off with Eli, who's gonna ride this carriage into town?
Won't make sense for you to do it, dressed all nice like you
are, Miss Laura being in the carriage all by herself."

"You're right," John said.

"Matter of fact," said Micah, "you might as well go be
with her now. Don't expect any trouble from robbers this
close to town."

"Who you fooling, Daddy? I know why you don't want to
come with me. You don't wanna get your fancy clothes all
dirty running through the woods."

Micah laughed. "You right 'bout that."

. . .

THEY REACHED the little church just like Eli had said. Micah pulled the carriage off to the side. John and Laura got out to stretch their legs.

"Looks pretty run down," John said. "Wonder if they stopped using it."

"Looks about as bad as it did last I saw it," Eli said. "This church for the poor white folks live out away from town. Not enough of them to afford a preacher, or someone to take care of it. Used to come out every few Sundays to preach." He looked around. "We good now. I'll just change into those slave clothes we bought, so I blend in better."

"You mean, so you don't get them dirty traipsing through the woods," Micah said with a smile.

"That too, Daddy."

"Why don't you change in the carriage, Eli? Just pull those shades down."

"I'll be glad to get a few more minutes off this carriage," John said, doing some stretches for his back.

"Here," Laura said, "let me rub those shoulders."

"I won't say no to that."

A few minutes later, Eli stepped out from the carriage looking very much like a field hand. "I sure don't miss looking like this."

John looked up at the remains of the sun, already beginning to drop below the tree line. Micah had watered the horses and gave them each an apple, then got back in the driver's seat. "Son, before you go, I want to make sure I'm remembering this right. I stay on this road through that little town of Falmouth, then keep going south on that road comes out the other side."

"That's right, Daddy. Stay on that road just over a mile or so. It runs along the Rappahannock, but you hardly know it because all the trees. Eventually, you see Fredericksburg across the river and a bridge coming up on the right."

"I know what to do then," Micah said. "Now you come over here let me pray a moment on you."

John and Laura came behind Eli and prayed silently, too.

Micah reached down his hand. Eli took hold of it. "You be extra careful, son. God go with you." Micah squeezed hard on Eli's hand.

"I will, Daddy. Hannah's life depends on it."

"I checked the schedule before we left Washington," John said. "The train station's on the south end of Fredericksburg. We need to be on that train by 10AM tomorrow morning to start heading down to Columbus. To be safe, we'll be back here at this church to pick you up an hour before that."

Eli thought a moment. "No sense in you folks backtracking for my sake. I'll get down to the train station by 9:30. When I'm sure there's no one there who knows me, I'll make my way to the Negro car up front."

"Okay then," John said, "I'll give your ticket to your dad, and your nicer set of clothes. You sure you don't want to bring one of the rifles?"

"I want to, but I can't bring it. Gotta go in there quiet as a mouse. I fire that rifle, it'll start a whirlwind of trouble."

They shook hands and Eli ran off toward the woods behind the church.

37

Eli decided to make use of whatever sunlight remained and do all his running through the woods now. He knew this entire area like the back of his hand, since he'd spent all but the last years of his life here.

Eventually, he found the road that folks from the nearby plantations used to get back and forth to town. He traveled alongside it maybe twenty yards inside the woods. It was thick enough and dark enough that he'd be nearly invisible to anyone who came by.

For the next forty minutes, he might just as well have strolled right down the center of the road, because he hadn't seen a soul. Kind of what he'd expected, given how dark it was outside. Most of the plantation business for the day had already been done, the horses put up for the night. Wasn't a weekend night, either, so there wouldn't be anyone traveling into town for a party or some other kind of entertainment.

He reached the turn-off road for his old plantation, but Hannah and Lucas worked for another slaveowner. Folks called him old man Nicholson when he wasn't around. Eli used the think Nicholson was a more decent fellow and wondered if he'd been Eli's owner, he might have never run away. But now look what he'd gone and done to Hannah and Lucas? Let them finally get together on the same plantation, let 'em get married, then go and sell Hannah off to some Charleston man who came by with enough money. No regard for his sister's welfare, at all. She just property, proving he just like every other slaveowner.

Eli kept running another fifteen minutes or so until he reached the back fence to the livestock area of Nicholson's plantation. He remembered the row of slave shacks where Hannah and Lucas lived and kept in the shadows, running until he reached them. But there were too many people still walking around the common areas to feel safe enough to approach anyone. So, he sat in the dark biding his time until things settled down, or until he saw someone come by he recognized and could trust.

Turned out, sitting there wasn't so good for his soul.

He'd been close enough on the carriage to hear most of the conversation between his father and John, the one where they talked about God. He respected his dad and admired him so much but couldn't find half the faith inside his own heart that clearly lived inside his dad's. Oddly enough, listening in on that conversation, Eli found he had far more in common with John's struggle with white men. Which was strangely comforting, seeing that John was white, too. And many of the abolitionists Eli had met since running away were also white.

That by itself made it impossible for Eli to hate all whites. Considering all the white people who'd been so kind to him. Like John and Laura. Their hopes and dreams for Eli's people seemed to match his own in almost every way. This very trip owed its entire existence to their kindness and generosity. Eli had no misgivings about it now. Had he come down here on his own, like he planned, he'd have already been captured and forced back into slavery, or else shot dead.

The whole thing was so confusing.

He'd listened intently to what his father said to John, trying to grab hold of its meaning and actually envied his father's measure of faith, because it did him so much good. Eli could only be happy, truly happy, on those rare occasions when everything went his way. But his dad seemed to be able to find joy regardless of how good or how bad a day went.

How much was that worth?

This thing about showing mercy to others, even those who did you wrong... Eli just couldn't lay hold of it. Like now. Here he was sitting in the dark on a plantation. On his left, a long row of shacks way too small for the dozens of people crammed into them. Folks who looked like him, worked from sunrise to sundown for no pay. So that one single family, on his right, could live in this huge mansion all their days, never lifting a finger, while they grew richer every day. And these rich white folk treat all these people who serve them every day like they weren't nothing. Like they don't matter, at all. Hardly fed them. Barely clothed them. And sold them to the highest bidder the first chance they get.

How could Eli show such people mercy? He didn't understand. They just... didn't deserve it.

Eli took stock of the situation again and realized things had calmed down some. In fact, he didn't see anyone walking around by the slave shacks anymore. The only light at this point came from what the stars and half a moon provided. When he came to the third shack from the end, he snuck up to the lone window and whispered loudly, "Lucas, Lucas, you in there? It's me, Eli." He waited a few seconds. No reply, so he said it again. Same thing. No one answered.

"Anyone else in there? It's me, Eli." This time he knocked gently on the wood beside the window.

Finally, a woman's voice whispered back. "You shush out there, now. You hear? Whoever you is, you shush. You trying to get us in trouble?"

"I'm sorry, Ma'am. Don't want anyone to get in trouble. I'm looking for a big man, named Lucas. Be married to my sister, Hannah. They used to live in here." He heard someone shuffling, then approach the window. It was a girl about Hannah's age, but someone he'd never seen before.

"I remember Hannah. She real nice. They came and took her away a short while ago. Next day, Massa say Lucas can't live here no more by hisself, so he make him move to another cabin across the way. Not sure which one, though. Not that it really matters anyway."

"Why you say that?" Eli said.

"Because Lucas not there, either. Least ways not tonight."

"Where's he at?"

"He hanging by his hands in the barn, all night Massa say. Whipped him but good. He so depressed ever since they took Hannah away, he not making his quota out in the field. Massa finally had enough of it today, say he get the lashes to snap him out of it. Don't think it'll help none. But there it is. So, Lucas still over there in the barn, hanging by his hands."

Eli sighed. Not exactly helping with his mercy problem.

"So, you Hannah's brother? Never seen you before."

"I've never seen you before, either. I work on another plantation pretty far from here. Had to come give Lucas a message. So, you were here the day that other slaveowner came and took Hannah away?"

"I was here. But I didn't see nothin.' None of us did. We all out in the field. Even Hannah. They call her in, and we didn't find out till later she was gone."

This wasn't good.

"But Lucas might know somethin'. Somehow, he found out what Massa up to and ran off to try and stop it. Course, they beat him bad for all the fuss he make."

"Okay then," Eli said. "I'll leave you be, see if I can find him in the barn." Eli decided not to tell her what his real intentions were. He'd learned the hard way...you couldn't always trust those from your own race, either. Way too many times he'd watched Negroes betray their own kind if the white man made it worth their while. "Thanks for your time," he said, "sorry to bother you."

He ran off before hearing her reply.

38

Eli continued to make his way toward the barn — still keeping to the shadows — but steered well clear of the live-stock, not wanting to set any of them off. He reached the broad side of the barn, thanking God they didn't have a dog, or else God had put him in a deep sleep. He was able to peek through a broken board. Good, no lights on, and the only sound was a deep moaning just out of his view on the right.

Had to be poor Lucas.

Imagine someone takes your wife away, sells her to another man. Right before your eyes. And you're not supposed to do a thing about it. Just stand there and take it. Course, Lucas had to try and stop it. Any man would. For that, he gets beat senseless. Probably the very next day, he supposed to go back out in the field, as though nothing happened. Work just as hard as he did every other day. Gotta get that quota for Massa. But he can't do it. His heart's too sad. So what do they do? Let's beat him some more. That'll show him. Then we'll hang him by his hands in a barn all night, just for good measure.

Lord, how you put up with these people? How long we supposed to?

He found the side door toward the back of that same wall. Tried it, and it opened right up. Took a few moments for his eyes to adjust to the lower level of light. When they came around, he saw the silhouette of Lucas hanging not ten yards ahead, between him and the open barn door. He came near, grateful the dark made it so he couldn't see the welts and slash marks across Lucas' back. But he'd seen enough over the years to easily imagine what they looked like. Eli snooped around, found a small stool tucked under a workbench. He brought it with him toward Lucas.

"Lucas, Lucas," he whispered, "can you hear me?"

Lucas moaned and his head moved slightly.

"Lucas, it's me, Eli. Hannah's brother." He came around to the front, looked up at Lucas. "Open your eyes. It's really me. I gotta talk to you, 'bout Hannah."

Hearing his wife's name, got his attention. His eyes flickered. He looked down.

"It's me, Lucas. Eli, Hannah's brother."

"Eli? That really you?" He moaned again. "What you doing here? We heard you run away, years ago."

"I did, but we're back. We come to rescue Hannah. Heard about her being sold to that fellow in Charleston. Listen, I got this stool here. Going to put it under your feet, so at least you can stand a little, if you want."

"Thank you, Eli. Feels like my arms gonna pull out of they sockets."

"Well, hold on. Let me put this under you. Okay, can you

feel it?" Eli could barely see, but it felt like the stool was maybe an inch too short.

"I can touch it with my toes, but can't really put no weight on it."

"Let me fix it." He walked around, found a small stack of lumber, pulled out a board that would work. "Here, try this."

Instantly, Lucas released a sigh of relief. "My, that does feel better. Least a little. Thank you, Eli. But why don't you just cut me down? I wasn't ready to go with you years ago, but when you go back, I sure is ready now. Especially, if you're going after Hannah. I wanna help."

"Can't do that, Lucas. Wish I could, but I can't. Plans are all made, already in motion. Would take too long to explain, but you can't be a part of this rescue mission."

"Rescue mission? Who you got on this besides yourself?"

"My daddy's here as well as some rich white friends who hate slavery 'bout as much as we do. They agreed to help us. Look, better you don't know the details. But if we can free up Hannah, I promise you...we'll come back for you, and take you with us back to New York. But you gonna have to behave and sacrifice yourself a little longer. I'm gonna have to leave you hanging here, just like I found you. Can't nobody know I was here. They'd set the law on us and ruin everything."

"What will I tell 'em when they come back here in the morning, see me standing on this stool? They got to know somebody helped me."

"Just tell 'em you don't know who it was. It was dark. Someone came in, put a stool on your feet and left. That's actually the truth, except the part you don't know who it is. Now, listen. The main reason I'm here...all we know is they took Hannah to a plantation somewhere in Charleston. But it would take us months to go through 'em all trying to find her. I talked to the girl staying in the shack you and Hannah used to stay. She said no one knows where she went. You're the only one that came out of the field when it happened."

"That's right. Word spread fast in the field. I ran quick as I could, just in time to see them throw her in the back of some dark wagon. Mostly this big old colored man, way bigger than me. His master was just paying my master the money up on the porch. I ran to the wagon, fast as I could, yelling out for Hannah, begging Massa not to do this thing. Over and over, I'm pleading for them to stop. He yells for the slave drivers standing nearby to grab me, take me away. Says I'm embarrassing him with this display. Those his words...*this display.*" Tears began to slide down Lucas' face. "The men begin to beat me and drag me away."

"I'm so sorry, Lucas. For you and my sister. It's a horrible thing. But listen. This is real important. I need to know...do you remember who this man was? The slaveowner from Charleston? You ever hear his name mentioned? Or maybe this big colored fellow, the one put her in the wagon. Remember anything about him, anything at all?"

Lucas thought a moment. "Clifton. That's the slaveowner's name. Don't know the first part. But I heard the big colored man say, as they drag me away, *Anything else you need me to do, Massa Clifton?* Then I hear this Massa Clifton say back, *That'll do, Mr. Kitchen. That'll do.*"

"He called the man Kitchen?"

"Sound like it to me."

"Clifton and Kitchen," Eli repeated it three times. "That should help us, Lucas. That should help a lot. You done good."

"Doesn't feel like I done much. You sure you can't take me with you?"

He shook his head no. "But after we got Hannah safely out of harm's way, we will come back. I promise."

"How am I going to know when that be?"

"Can't know for sure," Eli said. "We taking the train most the way. Figure two days down to Charleston, two days back. Maybe two days once we there to find her. How about, starting in five days, you start showing up by that last shack on the right side of the plantation house, soon as it gets totally dark, looking for me? Wait there as long as you can. But don't do anything to get in trouble, either then or during the day. You get that quota back up, too, so they leave you alone. Hopefully, in less than a week, I'll be back. This time, with Hannah, too."

"God, be praised," Lucas said. "I'll be praying up a storm till then. And I'll get everyone else to —"

"No, Lucas. You can't tell any of this to a soul. Not a living soul."

"Okay then. You better get out of here now. Had a couple runaways a week ago. So, Massa got guards on foot patrol. The one out there tonight same one who whipped me, tied me up here. Mean as a badger."

"Good to know. I'll keep an eye out as I head back to the woods. You take care. Won't be long now, brother." Eli started back toward the side door.

"Wait, Eli. You better come back a second. Go ahead put this stool back where you found it."

"And leave you hanging there the rest of the night?"

Lucas sighed. "Gotta do it. Otherwise, they'll come after

one of the other slaves, start punishing them all till they find out who helped me."

"Okay then." Eli did as he asked. Heard the creak in the rafters as they took on the full weight of Lucas' body.

"Gotta do it for Hannah," Lucas said as Eli headed out of the barn.

39

"Clifton, Kitchen. Clifton, Kitchen. Clifton, Kitchen."

As Eli ran toward the woods, he kept repeating these two names. They the most important two words on earth right now. He forget them, and the whole mission was ruined. He wished he had asked Mr. John for a piece of paper and pencil before he'd left the wagon. He stopped running for a moment to think. He couldn't keep saying these words all night. Had to think of another way to keep hold of them. Didn't think he'd have much trouble remembering Kitchen. Never heard of a man named that before. He just put the image in his mind of that big old kitchen at the Foster mansion.

The harder one was Clifton. What image could he conjure up and attach to it? The closest thing he came up with was a cliff, the kind you fall off of and you die. The slaveowner and a cliff. Then he smiled as an image appeared in his mind of him pushing the slaveowner over a cliff. But he had to come up with something for the second part...*ton*.

How about a big old two-ton boulder rolling down the hill, hits the slaveowner, knocks him off a cliff.

That should do it. *Clif-ton.* A cliff and a two-ton boulder.

He started back through the woods but going a little slower, realizing he only had a few miles to travel between here and the train station, and nothing but time in between. He came to a fence that he didn't recognize. Must've been put up since the last time he'd been here. Tracing where it headed in his mind, he figured it must be some kind of property marker, since it was several yards into the woods at this point. It temporarily threw off his bearings. He followed it back out toward the direction of the barn, to see if he was at the place he imagined himself to be.

As soon as he broke free of the woods and looked across a wide pasture, he saw the barn off in the distance, right where it should be. He was just about to head back into the woods when he heard a loud cracking sound on his left. Maybe a large animal.

"Hold it right there, boy." A deep, southern male voice. Then the cocking of a rifle. "Where do you think you're going this time of night?"

Eli turned and saw the image of a man about his same size emerging from the shadows. "Just heading home, sir."

"Heading home through the woods, eh? Running away from home is more like it."

As the man came a few steps closer, Eli could now see the rifle aimed at his chest.

"Step further into the pasture, into the moonlight. Let me get a better look at you."

For a second, Eli thought about running. Figured he had a fifty-fifty chance of getting away. It was dark. He was a fast runner. But the other half of that fifty, had him shot dead in the back. He backed up into the moonlight.

The man came forward. Eli judged him to be about forty, scraggly beard, straw hat. "You ain't one of ours," he said. "Where you from, boy? What plantation I mean. They'll probably pay a decent reward for me bringing you back. You look like a strong, healthy field hand."

"I'm not from around here," Eli said.

"Don't lie to me, boy. You obviously a runaway slave. Not ours but somebody else's. Well, hope you enjoyed your brief taste of freedom, 'cause here's where your trip ends. You turn around, start walking toward that barn. Too late to do anything with you tonight. I'll tie you up in there till mornin.' Get any ideas about taking off, I can put three bullets in your back before you get twenty yards. Won't get as much for your corpse, but hey, somethin's better than nothin."

It was now or never.

Eli pretended to start turning around but instead he quickly grabbed the end of the man's rifle barrel and smashed it upwards into his face, as hard as he could. The man howled in pain and fell back, tripping over his own feet. As he fell, Eli held fast to the gun barrel and grabbed another part of it with his other hand.

When the man hit the ground, Eli was holding the rifle. The man was holding his bloody face.

"You busted my nose," the man yelled. "My lip, too."

Eli plunged the rifle butt into the man's stomach. "Shut your mouth, old man. You say another word above a whisper, and I'll beat you to death with this thing. Do you hear me?"

"I hear you," the man said quietly, doubled over after the second blow.

Eli turned the gun around and pointed it at the man's head. He wanted so bad to pull the trigger. Undoubtedly, this was the mean-as-a-badger fellow Lucas told him about. The one who'd whipped him and tied him up in the barn.

"You shoot me," the man whispered, "you'll have posses from the three plantations 'round here chasing after you."

"I know that. That's the only reason I haven't pulled the trigger already. But there's nothing saying I can't do this." He jammed the rifle butt into the man's right knee. He screamed out in pain. "You scream out again like that, and I will bury this rifle butt into your head over and over until you're dead. Won't hardly make any noise at all."

"Why you doing this to me?"

"Why? Are you seriously asking me why? You say that, as if you never done anything to me before."

"I haven't. We only just met."

"*Met?* We haven't met. We didn't bump into each other out here and have a pleasant conversation. You put this gun to my chest and told me to head over to that barn over there, where you were going to tie me up — all night — just leave me hanging there like —" Eli was about to say Lucas' name, but realized since he wasn't going to kill the man, it would be a serious mistake.

"You followed that up by threatening to shoot me in the back three times if I tried to run. So, the way I see it, I got every right to treat you like this, and a whole lot worse. I get it, you one of the big boss men at this plantation. Which means, you been routinely whipping and beating the slaves around here as often as you please."

Eli slammed the rifle butt down on his left kneecap. The man began to yell but caught himself this time. Eli figured, since he was gonna teach the man a lesson, might as well make sure he couldn't run and get help once Eli took off. "You gonna lie to me again? I was born on a plantation, spent my first twenty years on one." He was dying to tell him that plantation was less than a mile from here. "Never met one of you slave handlers who only beat a slave when ordered to by the owner. Every single one, without exception, whipped and beat us for everything and for nothing."

A picture of the pitiful sight of his brother-in-law, Lucas, hanging up there in that barn not two hundred yards away, flashed into his mind. This was the man did that to him. "How's it feel to be on the receiving end of a beating? And this ain't even half the pain you inflict on the backs of these poor people, who never did a thing against you. Not one thing. Work hard out in the field, in the hot sun all day, for no pay. Always living in fear of their next whipping." Eli smashed the rifle butt into the man's shoulder. "You like how that feels?"

"Please stop," the man pleaded. "I'll do better...by your people, I mean. I'll treat them better from now on. I swear it."

"Oh, how I wish that were true," Eli said. "But if I let you live, first chance you get, you'll go sound the alarm, have a posse come after me. And you'll still treat the poor slaves in this place as bad as you ever did."

"I won't. Honest. I swear it. You don't gotta kill me. Here, I got some rope looped around my belt, in case I found one-a-you and had to tie you up. Use it to tie me up to this fence-post. You can use my bandanna here to gag my mouth. I'll be stuck here till dawn or later 'fore someone finds me. You can be twenty miles further north by then."

Eli had no plans of killing the man, but realized, what he'd just said wasn't a bad ending to this dilemma. The only problem was...he knew the man would start screaming bloody murder—through the gag—the moment Eli was far enough away. "All right," he said. "That's what we'll do. But first, I gotta do this." He gave the man a measured smack across the side of the head with the flat end of the rifle, knocking him out cold.

Then he dragged the man up against the fence post, used his rope to tie him up good, gagged him, tossed the rifle as far into the woods as he could, then started back on his journey.

Since the man thought Eli was a runaway, as he said, he'd expect Eli to flee toward the north. Instead, Eli headed south and would run all the way along the Rappahannock past Fredericksburg, until the train station was in sight. Only then would he stop, maybe grab a few hours' sleep in the nearby woods before dawn.

40

John and Laura were sitting at the train station on Lafayette Blvd. in Fredericksburg, anxiously awaiting the rendezvous with Micah and Eli. John looked at his timepiece. It was 9:25 in the morning. Last evening, Micah had dropped them off at a nice little hotel on Caroline Street. They didn't have rooms for Negroes, but the clerk had told Micah how to get to the part of town where the colored folks lived. Said he shouldn't have too much trouble finding a room to let at a boardinghouse.

Micah didn't seem too concerned. Said he'd stop by a stable nearest the train station, so they could store the carriage there until the man from Washington City arrived to drive it back, as they had prearranged. Eli was supposed to show up also at any minute, hopefully with enough information gained at Hannah's old plantation, to lessen their search time for the slaveowner down in Charleston.

"Well, this seems like a quaint little town," Laura said. "That hotel was the smallest one we've slept in so far, but it was clean and the bed was fairly comfortable. How did you sleep?"

John was pacing back and forth along the wood decking beside the track. "What? How'd I sleep? Pretty well. The breakfast wasn't too bad, either. Nothing like the one in Baltimore." He looked again at his timepiece.

"They'll be here, John. The train doesn't come for thirty more minutes."

"I know, I know. There's just so much riding on this. Especially with Eli. So many things could've gone wrong. I wish there was some other way to get that information besides having him sneak around at night at a slaveholding plantation. What if he —" John looked through a small gathering of people at the other end of the station. "Good, there's Micah. And look, he's smiling."

"He smiles all the time, John."

"That's true." John walked toward him, waving.

Micah saw him, waved back, grinning even more.

John was about to shake his hand then remembered he was supposed to be a slaveowner. "Relieved to see you. Have any trouble with the carriage situation?"

"None, at all. Eli here yet?"

"Not yet." John looked up at a wall clock. "It's just a few minutes after 9:30. Hopefully, he'll be here any minute. Before I forget, here are your train tickets." He pulled them out of his lapel pocket. "One is for you, and one for Eli. And you already have his suitcase, I see." They started walking back toward Laura.

"We all set, Mr. John. All we need now is my boy, and that train."

"Hope he's all right."

"I'm sure he'll be fine."

They reached Laura. "Did you find anywhere decent to sleep?" she said.

"Passable," Micah said. "Got me spoiled after Washington and Baltimore. But I was thankful I wasn't on a moving ship, and if they any rats in the place, they let me be."

"Aww," Laura said. "I'm sorry, Micah."

"It's all right. My poor boy likely had to sleep out in the open. I was praying for him a good bit 'fore I fell asleep."

"Micah? Is that you?"

All three of them turned toward the voice. John felt a moment of panic, till he remembered Micah wasn't a runaway. A white man about ten years older than John, dressed like a cowboy, was headed their way. He looked at Micah, relieved that no alarm registered on his face.

"It is you," the man said. "As I live and breathe...never thought our paths would ever cross again."

"How you doing, Mister Joe?" Micah said.

"Same as I ever was," Joe said. "But look at you...you certainly doing better than when I last saw you. Didn't the boss man sell you to that old sea captain? What was that, three, four years ago?"

"Yes, sir. He sure did. And I was on that ship till just a few months ago when I..." He looked over at John and Laura. "... when I met Miss Laura and Mr. John here. They my new massas now. Miss Laura sailing on our ship, and we got to talking. Turns out, they needed someone to look after their horses in... Baltimore." Micah looked at John Laura again. "Mr. Joe here the one who taught me everything I know about horses."

John held out his hand. "The name's John Foster. This is

my wife Laura. So, we have you to thank for all the good things Micah has done with our horses?"

Joe shook his hand, tipped his hat to Laura. "Possibly, but I have to say, Micah had a real sense about horses. Before long, they liked him better than they liked me. But look at you now, Micah. All dressed in these fancy clothes. That's why I didn't recognize you at first. We don't generally see colored folk 'round here dressed so fine. Maybe the butlers in the plantation houses, but they don't come into town much. What brings you back to Fredericksburg anyhow?"

"We've just been here for one day," John said. "Actually, waiting for the 10 o'clock train heading south."

"Me, too," Joe said. "But I ain't going nowhere. Here to pick up some shipment the boss man's wife ordered from up north. Guess it's on the same train. In the mail car or somethin'. I was gonna ask if you got to see your kids while you're here, but then I realized...ain't any left in these parts no more. You probably heard Eli and Sally run off not too long after you got sold to that captain. Guess they're gone for good." He leaned a little closer to Micah and said, "I was real sorry to see what old man Nicholson done to your girl, Hannah. You heard 'bout that, right?"

"I did," Micah said, then looked down. "Broke our hearts." He quickly realized what he'd said. "Me and my new massas' here, I mean."

John knew the *our* that Micah had in mind was Eli and Sally. "My wife and I were thinking of buying Hannah ourselves," John said, "so she and Micah could at least see each other sometimes. You don't happen to know who bought her, do you?"

Joe shook his head. "Nope, sorry. Was out making a

delivery when it all happened. Only thing I heard when I got back was he's from South Carolina. Didn't even catch the city."

Just about then they all heard the whistle of a steam engine sounding off from across the river. Joe looked up at the clock. "9:45, right on time. Well, guess I better get over to where that mail car's gonna end up, so I can get that package soon as they open the door. Don't know what it is, but the Boss Man's wife been talking about it comin' for days. Good to see you again, Micah. Nice to meet you both." He nodded and headed down the wooden walkway.

Micah looked exhausted. "I'm sorry, suh. I almost went and said too much. Just surprised me so, seeing Mr. Joe like that."

"It's okay, Micah. No harm done." After the whistle sounded, more people came out from the train station. The area suddenly became crowded. John looked all around. "I still don't see any sign of Eli."

Micah was looking in every direction, too. "Me neither. Lord, he better get here soon. These trains leave right on the hour."

Everyone watched as the train engine and cars started making their way over the bridge crossing the Rappahannock River.

"What are we going to do if Eli doesn't show up in time?" Laura said.

"We can't go on without him," John said. "We'd be scouring the low country around Charleston for weeks looking for Hannah without—"

"There he is!" Micah yelled over the growing noise. "There my boy!"

"Where?" John and Laura said in unison.

Walking through a crowd of passengers, came Eli, his eyes darting all about. He'd seen them but acted almost as if he hadn't. The train finally slowed to a crawl as it pulled into the station and continued past them. It kept rolling until they were standing right in front of the passenger cars. The car for Negro passengers and the mail car were up toward the front.

Finally, Eli reached them. He looked tired, dirty, and nervous.

"You made it, son," Micah said. "Gave us all a fright."

"I'd hug you, Daddy, but I got dirt all over me. Sorry to make y'all worried like that. I was actually here over twenty minutes ago. Right over there in those woods. Then I saw old Joe there walking right toward you folks. Saw him stop and talk to you. He knows me well. I know he's a friend of yours, Daddy, but I couldn't take the chance of him seeing me and turning me in."

"That's okay, Eli," John said. "You're here. That's all that matters. Your Dad has your tickets and luggage. Your nice clothes are in there. Afraid you'll have to change on the train."

"I figured so," Eli said. "We best go get on our car, Daddy. Not much time left." He and Micah turned and started to walk away.

"Wait," John said, "How did your mission go? Did you get the information we needed?"

Eli stopped and turned. "The two-ton boulder knocked the slaveowner off the cliff," he muttered. "*Clifton*. The slaveowner's name is Clifton."

41

For the next few days, life on the Clifton plantation wasn't as bad for Hannah as it could've been. Mostly since the Colonel had been off the property working in town. Celia had said the Colonel didn't care if Hannah learned a number of different jobs indoors. One that she could do well was sufficient. Celia then reminded Hannah of her real purpose here at the plantation, to be one of "the Colonel's ladies." The indoor job was to throw off any suspicion the Colonel's wife might have.

Since she and Josephine got along so well, and Josephine seemed happy enough with Hannah's abilities, Celia was prepared to inform the Colonel upon his arrival that Hannah's training could be considered complete. This was not good news to Hannah. She had been told this during breakfast that morning and her heart had filled with dread ever since.

Yesterday afternoon, Celia had decided the other three slave girls had also been adequately trained, so Kitch escorted them by carriage to their new homes and new owners. Hannah couldn't quite understand the happy look on their faces as they'd left.

Now alone in the cabin she had shared with the other girls, she pondered her fate. As more and more days had passed since she'd last seen Lucas, she had pretty much given up any hope of seeing him or her old life ever again. That door had closed. But a new door had not opened. She could invest no hope in the future.

For the simple reason that...she had none.

A knock on the door. It opened. Celia walked in. "Just saw Josephine. Working by herself. Thought I had made it clear that today you be working with her on a regular basis. Did I not make that clear?"

"You did, Miss Celia. I'll go over there directly." She stood but was unexpectedly ambushed by a flood of tears. She wiped them on her sleeve and walked past Celia, but Celia grabbed hold of her arm.

"What's going on with you, child? You still sad about losing your man? That what this is?"

Hannah nodded. "I know what you gonna say, that I just have to let it go. I keep trying. Every day I be trying. But it just don't want to let me go."

Surprisingly, Celia didn't get angry. "Sit down here, child. Lemme talk to ya' a minute. You know this can't do you any good."

Hannah sat back down on the edge of the bed.

"There are forces at work we got no control over. Not just you. But you, me, every slave on this plantation. Every slave on every plantation. Things are what they are. Been this way over a hunnert years. Maybe more. You can choose to be sad and melancholy, but it ain't gonna change a thing. You still wake up in that same bed tomorrow like you did today. You still be in this same place, facing the same situation. For some reason, don't know why, you used to be there with your man, now you here. You didn't want it to happen, it still did. But since it can't be changed, it just don't make no sense to waste time asking why, or staying sad."

She lifted Hannah's face, so she was looking right at her. "You should just do what I do. What I been doing since I first became the Colonel's lady. I was about your age and just as pretty. Did I love him? Did I want to be is lady? No, Ma'am. I didn't even like him. Still don't. But I knew I couldn't change it, so I decided to play the game. Play pretend, you could say, like the chillun sometimes do. And because I could do that, all kinds of good things come my way. Things I'd get to do I could never have done before. Get to own things I'd never have owned, or could even dream of ever having. Can you see what I'm saying? Can you see I'm trying to help you, child?"

"I know that's all you're doing, Miss Celia. But can I ask you a question?"

Celia nodded yes.

"When you got took and made the Colonel's lady, did you get taken from the man you loved?"

"Well, no..."

"You even met a man you loved by then? Loved with all you got, more than you loved anything else before?"

"No, Hannah. I never met that man then, and haven't met him since."

"Well, see, that's my main reason for being sad. I did meet that man. And I waited a long time for us to finally be together. During that time, I had a chance to run free. My brother and sister were leaving, escaping to the north, and wanted to take me. I only didn't go, because of that man. He meant more to me than my own freedom." The tears returned. "And now he's gone. Not because he died, because I got taken from him. And brought here. To be the Colonel's lady, as you say. Maybe I never met my man, I could bear all of this better."

Celia thought a moment. "Maybe so, child. Maybe so. But...it still don't change anything I said. Whether you met that man, or like me, never had the privilege. You still here. And the situation is still the very same." She took a step toward the door. "It's just something you gonna have to face. And face real soon. The Colonel's coming back this morning. And I'm about certain he'll be having you on his mind." She opened the door. "You better head on over there to Josephine, see how you can help her with whatever she's doing."

Celia went out, closed the door. But just a few seconds later, she hurried back inside. "Spoke too soon. Just saw the Colonel ride up to the front of the house. He got off his horse, and he's headed this way."

Hannah's heart began to race. A cold fear took hold.

Celia opened the door again to face the Colonel, who Hannah could now see walking this way through the window. She stepped back, so she could not be seen through either opening.

"Celia," Clifton said boldly, "just the person I'm looking for. The other three girls have been delivered to their new owners, correct?"

"Yes, sir, Colonel. Kitch got them all brought to their rightful place yesterday afternoon."

"So, that means this cabin is now empty, correct?"

"Except for Hannah," Celia said.

"And her training's complete? She is now officially a house servant?"

"Yes, sir."

"Good. I've been thinking about her for days now. She in there?"

"She is."

"Well, wouldn't be prudent to have me walking in there now in broad daylight. But you tell her, I'll be paying her a visit this evening, soon as it gets dark."

"Well, I...uh. I've got some, uh..."

"Spit it out, Celia. What are you trying to tell me?"

"I'm afraid your long-awaited first visit may have to be postponed a day or two?"

"What? Are you being serious?"

"Yes sir, I'm afraid so. See, Miss Hannah having her some...woman problems, if you catch my meaning. The kind that come around once a month."

"Oh...that is...disappointing news. Extremely disappointing." He exhaled an audible sigh, then a groan. "Okay then, you let me know the moment the situation is...improved."

"I definitely will, Colonel."

The Colonel went back to the main house. Hannah watched him through the window. She couldn't believe what just happened.

Celia stepped inside, looked at Hannah. "I only bought you a little time, child. That's all. A little time."

"I know. And thank you."

42

The past two days had been mostly uneventful, spent traveling by train from Fredericksburg to Charleston. The original plan had been to get off the train in Columbia, South Carolina and take a carriage the rest of the way to Charleston. That was before John learned the distance between the two towns was over a hundred miles, which would've made it a two-day trip by carriage. Another train could get them to Charleston in half the time, so that became the new plan.

The train station in Charleston was on the northern end of town near Calhoun Street, renamed after the late Senator and former Vice-President, John C. Calhoun. A fierce advocate for slavery, he was also a native of the city, who died a few years ago. Laura had whispered these details to John as the train slowed to a stop.

It was just before noon. After they disembarked, they'd waited a few minutes for Micah and Eli to gather their luggage together and join them. John quietly reminded them they were officially in the deep south now and needed to be extra careful not to do anything to give away their true identities or purpose.

"While Daddy was asking one colored man," Eli said quietly, "about finding a stable nearby to lease a carriage, I was talking to another man about what it's like for folks like us in this town. Like, how many free versus how many are slaves. He said most who work outside of town on the plantations are slaves, but a good number in town are actually free. Thought there might be as many as three thousand, or more. He said, you see a colored man workin' as a carpenter or a mason, or some other trade, he's probably free. Course, the man said, that doesn't mean they get treated with any respect. But they are free."

"That's good to know," John said. "It means the people in this town are used to seeing Negroes who are free. We won't have to be as concerned about people being suspicious of you and your dad, if they see you on your own. Once we get in the carriage and out by the plantations, we'll have to be more careful. Micah, what did you find out about leasing a carriage?"

"There's a stable on a side street about three blocks down this main road, Calhoun Street. On the right. But the man say, the owner not likely to lease a nicer carriage to a colored man, even he has the money."

"That's okay," John said. "Eli and I will get it. You stay here, look after Laura and the luggage."

"Be my pleasure," Micah said. He looked around. "Hard to believe it, I'm seeing more new places these past few days than I've seen in thirty years. And up until this week, never rode on no train before. I've been on so many now, I've lost count."

"Yes," Laura said, "and so far things have gone remarkably well. Let's hope it stays that way, and that we'll find the slave-owner, and he'll be more than happy to sell Hannah back to us at a fair price."

John and Eli walked at a brisk pace west on Calhoun. After they crossed the second street, Eli said, "Just one more to go, then we turn right. Should be able to see the stable from there."

John decided to ask Eli something before their time alone ran out. "Say Eli, I've noticed when we're together lately, the four of us, you seem a little...detached. A little less talkative and more reserved. Are you okay? Anything happen when you went to your sister's old plantation?"

"Well, Mr. John, guess it's okay to tell you. But yeah, something did happen. Everything turned out fine in the end, like I said. So didn't see any reason to bring it up. Especially didn't want my Daddy frettin' over it. But I ran into a little trouble as I was making my way off the plantation."

Eli went on to explain what happened; about finding his brother-in-law, Lucas, whipped bad and hanging by his hands in a barn. Having to leave him there like that, which bothered him greatly. Then almost getting caught by the same slave handler who'd whipped Lucas, just as Eli was about to head back into the woods. Finally, how Eli had been able to turn the tables on the man, knock him out with his own rifle and tie him to the fence. John couldn't believe what he was hearing, and how close this entire trip had come to a sudden end. "Wow, Eli. That's terrible. So, I guess that's what's been bothering you? Having to hurt that man?"

John was surprised by his answer.

"No, sir," Eli said. "I wish that was the thing bothering me.

I'm struggling with how little it did. If I am being honest, truly honest...I wanted to kill that man there in that field. Not just knock him out. I wanted to keep hitting him so he wouldn't get up ever again. I thought about what he done to Lucas, and probably to almost every other slave in that place, week in and week out, for years and years. Laughing all the while, having not an ounce of concern for the pain and terror he caused those poor people every day of their lives."

Put that way, John could completely understand Eli's sentiments. "But you didn't kill him."

"No, I didn't. But not because of mercy. Only because I knew it would stir up ten times the trouble if I did. I didn't want to take a chance they'd come into town looking for a murderer. This way, I'm just a runaway slave that got the drop on a slave handler. He's probably leading a posse north right now, trying to find me."

"I don't know what to say," John said. "Seems to me you acted in self-defense and kept your composure in light of a potentially ruinous moment. I'm not hearing anything you need to apologize for. But I would agree, probably better if you keep this between us."

They came to the stable and John took the lead interacting with the proprietor. "Hello, my good man. The name's John Foster. This here's my driver, Eli. My wife and another of my slaves traveling with us are back at the train station. We've just come in from a long trip that started in Baltimore, where we live. We're down here a few days hoping to take in some of the lovely sites and scenery of your great town and the surrounding area. I was told at the station we might be able to lease one of your nicer carriages for a few days. Eli here is a remarkable and dependable driver. I vouch for him myself."

The stable owner was a middle-aged man dressed in reasonably nice clothes. Obviously, not a worker here. He looked John up and down, Eli as well. "I think something can be arranged. I always keep several of our finer carriages handy to lease to our plantation owners. From time to time, they'll have need of one for this reason or that. But these carriages don't come cheap, mind you. It'll cost you four dollars a day, upfront, plus a five dollar deposit. Which you'll get back when it's returned in decent order."

"That seems reasonable to me," John said. "Say, since you mentioned you service plantation owners in your business, perhaps you could help me locate one in particular. I'm a builder in Baltimore. We don't have plantations in town. Most, if not all, our slaves are domestic. Assuming like the kind that work in the big plantation houses around here. We were hoping to find a certain colored girl to serve as our nanny. She and my wife used to know each other as children. I understand she's recently been purchased by a slave owner named Clifton. That name ring a bell?"

The man smiled. "It does. Colonel Clifton has actually been a client of ours on occasion. Not recently, mind you. But he does lease carriages from us several times a year."

"Wonderful," John said. "Do you know where the Clifton plantation is? How would we get there from here? And about how long would it take?"

"I do know where the plantation is, pretty sure I can get you there. You'd go back on Calhoun Street heading west till you reach the last road, the one that runs along the river. That'll be the Ashley. Turn right, until you come to Spring

Street. Look left, and you'll see a drawbridge which'll bring you over to the mainland. Mind you, they'll be a slight toll. Bridge was just finished last year. Then follow the road to the right. It'll fork off a couple of times, but keep staying to the right. You'll come to Ashley River Road, and there you'll stay for the next ninety minutes to two hours."

"How will I know when I've reached it?" John said.

"When you come to St. Andrew's Church on the right, you're in the neighborhood. You'll pass Bee's Ferry, and you're getting much closer. Start looking for the sign up ahead on the right. Less than a mile. If you get to Drayton's Hall, you've gone too far."

"Will the sign be on the left or the right?"

"It'll be on the right. Most of the plantations are. Got 'em all up and down the river, on both sides."

"Thank you. Get that Eli?"

"Yes, sir."

"One last question, if you don't mind," John said. "We'll be in town for a night or two. What hotel would you recommend?"

"For you and your wife? You'll find plenty. Go south down Meeting Street. Plenty of good ones around there. For your slaves? They'll need to stay somewhere in The Neck. That's the area the coloreds stay in, unless they're in town to work."

"And where is this...Neck?"

"Not far at all. Actually, it starts pretty much anywhere's north of Calhoun. I'm sure your driver will have no problem finding a boarding house that takes in his kind." He looked at Eli. "Might have better luck closer to the east end of Calhoun, closer to the Cooper River. That's where all the ships come in from the harbor."

"Thank you kindly, sir," Eli said, then looked down.

"Well, you've been extremely helpful, my friend. A pleasure doing business with you."

John paid him the money. He went out and picked one of the carriages. Minutes later, the carriage and a team of fresh horses arrived out on the street where the man had asked them to wait. John was just about to hop inside when Eli reminded him. "Oh, quite right."

Eli opened the door, and John got in. "Did you really get all that? The directions?"

"Yes, sir. Being a driver, I'm good with directions. "

"Then let's go pick up Micah and Laura, and we'll be on our way."

"Well, sir. Let me sneak on back there to where some coloreds were working with the horses first. See if I can't find someone who maybe knows a little more about the Clifton plantation."

"Good idea," John said. "Don't take long."

43

After riding down Meeting Street in their carriage, John and Laura had decided to stay at the Mills House hotel, on the corner of Meeting and Queen, just six or seven blocks south of Calhoun. But before checking in, they continued a few blocks past Broad Street so Eli could find a more secluded private street where they could stop and formulate their plan.

Throughout the carriage ride, John could tell Laura was really taken with the town. They both were. The homes were simply lovely. John had pointed out to her this unique style of architecture he kept seeing, where a front door—which faced the street—didn't open inside a foyer or living area, as most front doors do. As they drove past, he saw they opened into an outside porch that ran the length of the home. There, in the middle of the porch, was the actual front door that led inside the house. And these porches were replicated on the second floor, even on a third floor with the biggest homes. "You could never get away with such a thing in the north," he'd said to Laura. She'd agreed, then added, "But I think they're so charming."

The home Eli had parked in front of was just such a home.

"So, Eli," John said, "as we got into the carriage, you said you had a plan we needed to discuss."

"Yes, sir. Because of what I learned talking to the fellow at the stable. And because I know my sister, Hannah. I figured, we heading out there tomorrow hoping to buy her back from that slaveowner, and we talking about the reason we picked her is because of this history she's got with Miss Laura, from when they were both children."

"Right. And you see a problem with this?"

"Well, first thing...she's gonna scream her fool head off with glee, the moment she sees me and Daddy. Gonna give away everything right then. Even if somehow she doesn't see us, when Miss Laura starts talking about her and Hannah being childhood friends, I can just see Hannah saying she never met this woman before in her life."

"I see your point," John said. "What do you suggest?"

"Well, only one solution I can see. I need to go out there first, see her in private. Get her ready for what's coming. That fellow at the stable I spoke with, he said he's made deliveries out to the Clifton plantation a number of times. I explained I was hoping to see my sister, who's still a slave out there. But that I needed to do it without nobody seeing me. He gave me the layout of the plantation, best as he remembered. He also said the stable got an old buckboard wagon they rent out to the colored folk for a dollar day."

"So," Laura said, "you're going to ride out there this afternoon, see if you can sneak onto the plantation to speak with her?"

Eli nodded. "Don't see any other way."

"You think you have time to go all the way out there and back?" John said. "In one afternoon?"

"Not quite. But the fellow at the stable say the curfew for Negroes is 9PM. Got more than enough time to do what I gotta do between now and then."

"You want some company, son?" Micah said.

"Well, Daddy. Maybe so. But I'd need you to wait out by the road with the horse and wagon, while I sneak onto the plantation. That way you could move it and come back if anyone comes by."

"I can do that."

"Okay then," John said. "That's our plan. I guess Laura and I will just wait at the hotel till you get back."

"Or maybe," Laura said, "we'll take a nice stroll down by the waterfront. A woman at the train station told me they have a beautiful park there, and some of the nicest homes in town."

"Okay," John said."

"Probably won't be back till after dark," Micah said. "But either Eli or me will get word to you when we safely back in town. So you don't fret none."

"Thank you, Micah. And Eli...well done. That's a great idea."

"Thank you, sir."

THINGS FOR MICAH and Eli had gone smoothly at the stables. They had changed into regular street clothes and were able to pay cash to the colored man Eli had spoken to before. Since the horse and wagon were nothing special, he was able to make the deal himself. No one in the Charleston area would think anything of two colored men riding in an old wooden wagon up Ashley River Road on a shady October afternoon.

Eli figured they had been riding about ninety minutes or so when they came to St. Andrew's Church on the right side of the road. A little further up, they came to an intersection with another dirt road. A sign posted on the corner read: Bee's Ferry. An arrow pointed toward the river. "Okay, Daddy. The man say less than a mile from here. Maybe I should ask about somethin' I been meaning to talk about next time I got you alone."

"We've been alone this whole ride, son. Must be something sitting heavy on your heart to wait this long."

"Guess you could say that." Eli sighed. "I've actually talked about this with Mr. John already. Well, partly. Has to do with, well, I guess the idea of loving or actually, *not* loving your enemies."

"Okay, we don't hardly ever talk about such things. So, go ahead."

"While we were in New York," Eli said, "it would bother me every now and then. But down here, being around all these slave-owning white folks, bothering me quite a lot. Sometimes, feels like it's getting the best of me. I see how they talk to us, how they treat us, like we're nothing but dirt. Makes me so angry inside. Find myself feeling the opposite of mercy, like all I want to do is hurt them. Pay them back for all the misery they're causing our people. But then I look at you, and it's almost like none of it affects you. Like you don't hate 'em at all. Like they don't even bother you. See, I don't get that. Where's that mercy come from? Seems to come so easy to you, and I can't find enough inside to fill a thimble."

Micah smiled. "Well, first off, son. You gotta know. It does come easy to me now, but it wasn't always so. Believe it or not, I used to be just like you. Felt everything just the way you described. Pretty much every day. But then I realized... I needed and wanted mercy from God for my own life. Turns out, he's happy to give it, but only if I'm willing to show that same mercy to folks who wrong me. If I hold it back from them, he got no choice but to hold his back from me. That's the deal. So, that one thing there, all by itself, helped me get a foothold on this thing we talking about. At first, seemed like the hardest thing to do. But I kept at it, and it came easier and easier to get hold of. Somewhere in there, I guess the Lord started helping me see things the way he see 'em, and see other things I was never thinking on."

"Like what?"

"Well, for starters, you do know Mr. John and Miss Laura, they white?"

Eli smiled. "Course I know they white."

"And their whole family is white. And so many of them abolitionist folks you working with on that Underground Railroad, they white too. They hate slavery 'bout as much as we do. And they doing everything they can to stop it. And giving all kinds of money, too. What does that tell you?"

Eli thought a moment. "That the real problem is not the color of a man's skin."

"That's right. You hit the nail on the head. Then let me tell you something else I seen since we been in New York. Seen it several times, in fact. I see an Irish man be treated by other white men just about as bad as any colored man get treated in the south. So, I'm looking at this Irish man, and he looks as white as white can be. But they talking down to him like he's nothin.' Just like they do to us. So now, that shows me…it's not even the color of a man's skin that brings all this meanness out."

"I seen that, too, Daddy. How the Irish get treated."

"Goes to prove…the real problem's on the inside," Micah said. "The condition of a man's heart. That's what Jesus says, too. I know you know this. If the problem were on the *outside*, how come that big colored man who took your sister for that slaveowner think that's something okay to do? He got the same skin color. You seen colored men just like this at them plantations we been on, beating on us, treating they own kind 'bout as bad as any white folks do. How can they do that? Why it don't bother them even a little? Because they got dead souls, son, that's why. Skin color don't change the color of a man's soul. Only God can do that. Fix a man on the inside."

They rode on in silence a few moments, then Micah said, "See, son, that's what you need Jesus to do for you. Fix you on the inside, like he's done me. Then every day you got someplace to go, someplace to take all them mean, hateful feelings get stirred up when you're treated badly. Whether by a white man, a black man, or any other man. I let it go, soon as I feel it growin' inside. And pretty soon after, the Lord fills up the space with his love and mercy. That's what's going on in here." Micah pointed to his heart.

"Makes all the difference in the world."

44

Micah and Eli finally saw the sign on Ashley River Road pointing to the turnoff for Clifton Plantation.

"Keep on going, Daddy," Eli said. "The man at the stable said the woods on the left side of the plantation are thicker than the right. Go 'bout another block or so, and I'll get out there."

Micah looked up at the sky. "How long you figure you need to get this done? Judging how long it took to get out here, I figure we got maybe two hours of daylight left."

"Don't know, Daddy. Thirty minutes? Maybe less. See that big tree laying on its side up ahead? Why don't you pull over there? When I'm done, I'll aim to get back to that point, stay hidden till I see you ride by."

Micah did what Eli suggested. Pulled off the main road, said a quick prayer and turned Eli loose to his task.

Eli headed through the woods in the direction of the river. After what felt like a block or two, he began moving right, till he could see through the woods to the cotton fields.

A little further, he got close enough to start seeing slaves working that part of the field. He slowed down, got lower and came nearer to the edge of the trees. Got his eye on a young lady in a row closer to the woods than the rest. He knew he was taking a chance but really didn't have a choice. He crawled out, got between the cotton rows not fifteen feet from where she was picking.

"Excuse me, Miss," he whispered loudly.

She jumped at the sound, turned and backed away.

"Sorry to startle you. Mean you no harm."

She calmed when she saw how he was dressed and the look on his face. "What you doing here?" she whispered.

"Looking for my sister. She got sold maybe a week ago. I'm told she was brought here. This the Clifton place, right?"

The girl continued picking and answered without looking at Eli. "This is the Clifton plantation. But the Massa didn't buy her to work these fields. Only slaves he bought lately work up at the big house."

"That's what we heard," Eli said. "That he didn't buy her for the fields."

"We all noticed Massa buy four girls, but sold off three already. Don't know if your sister gone, or she the one still left."

Eli hadn't figured on this. "We think maybe she's the one still here. Know where I can find her? Name's Hannah."

"Well, I never knowed any of they names, but the one still here stay up in one of those white painted shacks, closer to the big house. She in the one next to Miss Celia, who runs the house. Course, this time of day she prob'ly working in the big house, not in the shack where she sleep." She suddenly froze a second, then started picking faster. "You better git. Boss man just look this way. He catch you, you be in a world of pain."

"I'll get goin'. Thanks. So, she's in one of the white painted shacks?"

"Tha's right. They bigger than what most of us get. She be in the second one, if she there. But you better make sure Kitch don't see you. He the main Boss Man. Big as a horse, and the meanest man I ever knowed."

"I will. Thanks again."

Eli crept back into the woods then headed back the way he came. This time he kept closer to the edge so he could see the rest of the plantation through the trees. After a while, he got past the fields and saw the main house. Scanning the scene, he found two rows brick shacks, the kind slaves generally lived in. Found the barn surrounded by white fencing and filled with livestock. But it took a few more minutes before he found the white painted shacks the girl had described. They were off by themselves but still fairly close to the main house.

The problem was, while there were plenty of big live oak trees scattered about, they wouldn't provide any cover at this hour. No way to reach the white painted shacks without getting caught. Unless he waited till dark. Nothing else to be done about it. So, he made his way back out to the road, found that tree laying on its side, and waited.

Ten minutes later, his dad came by from the other direction. He smiled, pulled over when he got to Eli. "How'd it go?"

Eli filled him in on the situation.

"Well, that's some progress anyway. Guess we just gotta be a little patient. I found a nice place where we can wait till dark. Just up the way found a dirt road seems to lead nowhere but to a little creek. Water's nice and cold. Me and the horse had some. Didn't see a soul."

Eli hopped up in the wagon. "I could use a cold drink about now."

WHEN THE SUN had finally fully set below the horizon, Micah and Eli headed back to their rendezvous point by the fallen tree. There was still a little light left but plenty of shadows for Eli to work with.

"You got to be quick, son," Micah said. "Got to be back to the Fosters' hotel by 8:30, so we can make it back to where we supposed to be by nine. You maybe got thirty minutes."

"If she's there, Daddy, I'll only need half that much. If she's not, well...don't even want to think about that." He ran off, this time very clear about where he was going.

He came to the spot closest to the white painted shacks. He could see some people moving up by the main house, but no one moving down by the shacks. He ran quick as he could, stopping behind each of the big oaks to make sure the coast still clear. Finally, he came to the second of the painted shacks, saw it had a door in front and a lone window in back. He picked the window. Making sure there was no one nearby, he crept to it and peeked inside. Saw a gas lamp over in the corner, a colored girl sitting in a chair beside it.

Looked like she was sewing. Eli couldn't recognize her face. Glass was too blurry. Had to take a chance it was Hannah. He tapped on it. Too gently, at first, since no one came. So he tapped a little harder. The girl looked up toward the sound. He lifted his head a little further, and she was startled by the sight. He motioned with his finger for her to come closer. She got up from the chair, walked toward the window. Between the darkness and the blurriness of the glass, he wasn't totally sure it was Hannah until she slid the window open halfway.

"I don't know who you are," she said, "but you better not let Kitch —"

It *was* her. Tears welled up in his eyes. "Hannah, it's me. It's me. Eli."

She gasped, bent down to see his face. Her mouth hung wide open. "Eli, it is you. How...how?" She reached out for him through the window opening. He grabbed her hands and squeezed.

"My sister. My baby sister," he whispered. "I need you to come on out here, so we can talk in the shadows. Can only stay a few minutes. Daddy's here, too. Out by the road."

"You with Daddy? He's here? You comin' to take me home?"

"Yes, but not tonight. Tomorrow. Come on out here and I'll explain. Hurry."

She looked over to the right, saw a big shadowy area. "Meet you over there."

He stood where she pointed. Moments later, she came around the darker side of her shack, then hurried across to meet him. They hugged tightly.

"Can't believe it's really you," she said. "Just can't believe it. Lord, I wouldn't even have prayed for something like this to happen. Be too hard to believe."

"Well, I'm here. And we got a plan to bring you back with us, starting tomorrow." He quickly explained the scheme and how she needed to act and the things she needed to say when he, Micah and the Fosters returned together tomorrow.

As he spoke, the joy on her face steadily slipped away.

"What's the matter?"

"It's a good plan, Eli. But it can never work. I wish they was a chance. But knowin' what I know 'bout this man, Massa Clifton...he ain't never gonna sell me to your Mr. Foster. No matter how much he pay."

Eli sighed. "Well, maybe so. But we gotta try. Mr. Foster's a very generous man, he might meet his price."

"He not gonna sell me, Eli. Take it as gospel. He not gonna do it. Only way I get outta here is, you come for me in the night. Like you doin' right now."

"But I can't take you now, Hannah. I gotta talk this over with Mr. Foster. See what he say. Our whole plan's already set."

She looked down at the ground.

"But listen," Eli said. "I will tell him what you said. You be ready when we come tomorrow, in case you wrong and your Massa willing to sell. He don't, then you be ready 'bout this time tomorrow night. I'll come back to this same spot, only in the woods over there." He pointed. "You meet me there, and we run like the wind."

"Okay, Eli." Tears filled her eyes. "But you gotta know. Tomorrow's gotta be the day. Massa made it clear, he comin' back tomorrow night, make me one of his ladies. I won't let that happen."

He knew what she was saying. "I will come back for you, Hannah. One way or the other. I will *not* go back home less you with me. I promise you that."

45

When Eli got back to the rendezvous point, Micah was already there. They weren't likely to see much traffic on the road now that darkness had set in. Eli explained the things Hannah had said about her master refusing to sell her to the Fosters. Micah said he'd had a feeling things might go that way but reassured his son, "The Lord still in control, no matter what that man say."

They journeyed back to the edge of Charleston with about thirty minutes to spare before the curfew ran out, but they still had to get to the Fosters' hotel first. Fortunately, the drawbridge was down and, after paying the toll, they crossed right over. After strolling down Calhoun Street, well-lit by gas lights, Eli turned right at the Meeting Street intersection. A few blocks further, they passed by a bank, saw a wall clock.

"8:25," Micah said. "Cutting it close for that curfew."

"I know, Daddy. Going as fast as I can. We be in worse

trouble I hit somebody. Mr. John supposed to meet us at 8:30 in front of the hotel, right?"

"That's what he say."

A few more blocks and they saw the Mills Place Hotel looming up just ahead. Easy enough to spot at five stories high, the biggest building around. Only thing taller were the church steeples.

"I ain't never seen so many churches in the space of a few blocks before," Micah said.

"I know," Eli said. Then he leaned closer and whispered, "And every one of 'em filled with slaveowners, or folks that support it."

As they approached Queen Street, they noticed John standing on the corner talking to the doorman. He saw them when they crossed the intersection and waved. "Excuse me, sir," he said. "Enjoyed learning more about your fine town, but my two slaves are back, and I need to speak with them before the curfew starts."

Eli motioned with a head signal that they needed to talk further away from the hotel. John got the message and walked beside them two buildings farther. Eli pulled the wagon to the curb, in front of a tobacco shop long since closed for the night.

"Were you successful?" he asked.

Micah stayed in the seat. Eli got out and came behind the wagon, closer to where John stood.

"Partly," Micah said. "Eli got to see Hannah, got to explain what we doing tomorrow."

"That must've been exciting," John said. "Getting to see your sister after all this time. How is she doing? How's she holding up?"

"She looked good," Mr. John. "Considering all she'd been through. And like Daddy say, she knows the plan now and says she'll do her part, but..."

"But...what?" John said. "Is something wrong?"

Eli explained what Hannah had said about Clifton's plans to make her one of his ladies, and that she believed he'd never sell her.

"The scoundrel," John said then sighed. "The judgment these men will face someday."

"I agree," Micah said. "But I think Hannah might be right."

"But I'm prepared to pay handsomely for her," John said. "I know what the going price is for young slave girls now, and I'm willing to pay a good deal more."

"And we are so grateful," Eli said. "But I'm not sure, considering his plans for —"

"What my boy trying to say," Micah said, "is that sinful desires are a powerful thing. We should try things your way tomorrow. But maybe have us another plan, case he won't budge. Should get ready for that, too."

That seemed to sink in. John took a few steps away, then came back. "Well, we haven't come all this way to go back without her. The only other option—if that happens—is to steal her in the night and flee to the north."

"Me and Eli been thinking the same thing," Micah said. "That gonna increase the danger of getting home safely by a good measure."

"It's a sure thing," Eli said, "that man gonna come after us with a fury. He gonna hire a posse, maybe more than one, put out a huge reward, too."

"And if we caught," Micah said. "Well, Eli and me gonna

be slaves again. After we get the whippin' of our lives. But you and Miss Laura? Down here in the south, you doing what you doing? They surely put you both in jail. That is, if we get caught."

"Then we won't get caught," John said. We can't let it happen."

"But Mr. John, Daddy's right. It's one thing him and me gettin' caught. But we can't let you and Miss Laura take that risk."

"I understand, Eli, Micah. But hear me out. If we do have to flee, it won't be anything like the time you ran away, Eli. You and Sally. You had to run on foot, through the woods. We'll be in a carriage on good roads. And if we came back for her as soon as it got dark, we could run the horses all night. The weather will be cool. There won't be anyone else out on the road. And when we come to the first town, we'll trade the horses and carriage in for a new set. Get right back out on the road. We'd build up such a large lead, they'd never be able to catch us. Besides, if this Clifton fellow does turn us down, we'll act disappointed then leave the way we came. He'd never suspect that a wealthy gentleman traveling with his wife in a fine carriage would ever take part in stealing a slave at night. He'll think Hannah ran off on her own...on foot. That's what his posse will be looking for. Don't you see? I really think it could work."

Micah and Eli looked at each other then back at John. "I suppose it could work," Eli said. "But it's still so risky. I'd hate it if anything ever happened to you or Miss Laura on account of us."

"I appreciate that, Eli. But I am still hoping the man will come to his senses and take my offer. But just in case, tomorrow you, Micah, and I will head to that city market area we saw a few blocks north of here, and stock up on supplies...as if we were taking a lengthy trip."

"Okay, Mr. John," Eli said.

"If you say so, sir," said Micah.

"Now you two better get back to wherever you're staying tonight before the curfew starts. I'll go up to our room and explain all this to Laura."

46

The following morning, John and Laura enjoyed a fine southern breakfast at the hotel restaurant. Except for the grits, it wasn't all that different from what they were used to eating. That, and seeing so many Negroes serving at the establishment. And only Negroes. Laura kept wondering which of them might be slaves and which ones were free. Of course, she'd never consider asking. While trying to remain in character, she did her best to be courteous toward them all.

As he ate, John read several articles in the local newspaper. Waiting till there was no one near their table, he leaned over and said, "The outright hostility toward the northern states reeks in almost every paragraph I read. There's not even an attempt to mask it."

"It almost feels like a foreign land," she said.

Last night, she'd fallen asleep while John waited up to meet Micah and Eli, so John couldn't tell her any of the details about how things went. "While we were getting dressed, you said Eli was able to make contact with his sister and prepare her for our visit this afternoon. But you didn't tell me much more than that. Did he feel like we could expect any problems, or was he more optimistic when he returned?"

John set the newspaper down, took an unusually long pause, like he was trying to figure out the best way to say something.

"I'm guessing there were problems then," she said.

"Afraid so." John spent the next five minutes explaining the mostly discouraging details. The more he talked, the more anxious she felt inside. "Do you even think there's a chance this Mr. Clifton will accept our offer to buy Hannah?"

"I don't know, Laura. I've done enough research into the going price for a healthy slave girl, that I felt quite confident this matter would reach a quick and peaceful resolve. I was willing to pay that much and more. It never dawned on me that this man might reject my offer. After listening to Micah and Eli last night, I feel our chances are fifty-fifty at best."

"You must have come up with some other solution?"

"I have. Really, there's only one. If he won't sell her, we'll have to steal her. We can't go back without her. I feel even more firmly about that now that we know what his intentions are."

"I completely agree," Laura said.

He spent the next ten minutes explaining how—if it came to it—this rescue-and-escape plan would work. "I'm actually waiting on Eli and Micah to arrive. We're heading over to the City Market to stock up on supplies, in case we have to start our flight to freedom tonight."

Laura felt her stomach churning in knots. "When you go to the market, I'd like to come with you. I could pick out all the food items we'll need, while you men get everything else.

"Thank you," John said.

"I'm happy to help."

"No, I mean thank you for taking this news so well."

TWO HOURS LATER, John and Micah were walking through one end of the Charleston City Market — the side closest to the harbor — while Laura and Eli shopped at the other end. John had decided to have Eli accompany her, realizing the food she'd be buying would become too heavy for her to carry. The area where John and Micah shopped contained mostly dry goods and nonperishable supplies.

As they browsed, John couldn't help but admire the design of the market area. Ever since he'd adopted this role of being a southern builder, he found himself more attracted to the architecture and design of things. This City Market was significantly more impressive than the market areas he'd seen in Baltimore or New York. "Say, Micah. These things we're carrying are getting a little heavy. Why not ask that woman making baskets over there how much they cost? Here's three dollars. See what that'll buy. If there's change left over, let her have it."

"Yes, sir, Mr. John. Be right back."

Moments later, Micah returned with four big baskets. "Two for you and two for me," he said. "They were fifty cents each. She said I made her day when I insisted she keep the extra dollar." They stopped a moment to put their purchases in the baskets. "Say, Mr. John. You come to me for advice now and then. Last night on the ride home with Eli, found myself struggling with something. Didn't feel right asking Eli about it. Thought maybe you could help, since I know you read your Bible every day."

"What is it?"

"I guess, I guess it's about...all the lying we doing every day since we been on this trip. I know we both believe lying's wrong. I know it says so in the Bible. But I don't feel wrong about what we doing on the inside. I guess because I know we saving Hannah's life. But I'm wondering if the feeling I got inside that God don't mind is just me hoping it's so, or it's the Holy Ghost saying it really is okay, on account of the reason why."

John smiled. "You really are quite the thinker, Micah. You know that? And for once, I think I might actually be able to help you. One of the good things about being able to read the Bible every day is, you come across all kinds of stories, especially in the Old Testament, that you don't hear preachers talk about very much. So, before I tell you what I'm thinking, I'd like you to give serious thought when we get home to letting your son teach you how to read."

"I been thinking the same thing myself," Micah said.

"Laura and I were talking about this very thing when we first came up with this idea, because we knew it involved us pretending to be different people than we are, and telling all kinds of fibs to make the whole thing work. Then I remembered this Bible story about the time Pharaoh was killing all the firstborn Jewish males, as a way of keeping them from growing more in number than the Egyptians. It says the Jewish midwives disobeyed Pharaoh's order, and when he asked why, they said the Hebrew women bore children much quicker than the Egyptian women did — which wasn't true — so their babies kept being born before the midwives could get there."

"So," Micah said, "the midwives were fibbing to old Pharaoh to save those babies' lives?"

John nodded. "Then Laura remembered another story about the time when Rahab hid the two Jewish spies in Jericho on her roof. When the king's soldiers came looking for the spies, she told them they had come but had already left, and she didn't know where they were."

"But that wasn't true," Micah said. "They on her roof."

"Exactly. So, it wasn't the kind of lie that's a sin, because she was trying to save the lives of those two men."

"And we trying to save Hannah's life," Micah said. "That's all we doin'."

"Then there's another story," John said, "about the time David was fleeing from Saul, who was trying to kill him. David lied two different times then. I could explain how, but...you get the idea." Suddenly, John could tell something else had grabbed Micah's attention. He was looking over John's shoulder.

"Well, I'll be..." Micah said. "Excuse me, Mr. John. But, I...I can't believe my eyes. That look like...it's got to be him.

"Who is it, Micah?"

"It's Mr. Smitty. The cook from my old ship, The Cutlass. He's just over there, at that first table across the street. Okay if I go see him? I'll be quick."

"Certainly," John said, turning to see who Micah was looking at.

Micah was already headed in that direction. John

followed a few steps behind. He found Micah talking to a man who was either in his mid-fifties or aged to look so by a lifetime on the sea. He seemed genuinely happy to see Micah.

"Micah, heavens man, look at you. Wasn't it a month ago, you were swabbing our decks. Now you look like some British dandy ready for a fancy ball."

Smitty laughed out loud. "I know, Mr. Smitty. Hard to believe what the good Lord done for me in so short a time."

"But I thought we'd left you in New York City," Smitty said. "Why am I finding you here in Charleston?"

John walked up and extended his hand, "Mr. Smitty, don't know if I look familiar to you, but I'm the gentleman who took Micah off your Captain's hands back in New York. Micah is helping my wife and I as we journey through the South. At home, he still looks after the horses but here he's serving as my valet."

"My valet," Smitty repeated. "Certainly coming up in the world. Well, good for you, Micah. Good for you."

"You here buying supplies for the ship?" Micah said.

"Aye, I am. The plan is to set sail tomorrow. Trying to make do with the money the Captain gave me, but I'm not sure it'll be enough. He was supposed to give me twice as much, but yesterday we learned a major shipment got canceled. Now our hull's only half full for the voyage home."

"Where's the captain now?" Micah said.

"If he was successful, he'd be back on the ship. If not, he'd still be knocking on doors at one of these wharf warehouses, trying to drum up some business before we have to set sail."

"Well, it's been great to see you, Mr. Smitty," John said. "But Micah, we probably better go."

"Aye," Smitty said, "nice to see you, sir. And you, Micah, the way things are goin', the next time I see you, I might be asking you for a job."

Micah laughed. "You tell Captain Meade, Micah sends his regards."

"Listen to you now...sends his regards. I'll tell 'im, Micah. Off with you now."

John and Micah crossed the street and headed back to the part of the market where they'd been shopping moments ago.

But Micah stopped walking. Got this odd look on his face. He turned back to look at Smitty.

"What is it, Micah?'

"I don't know, Mr. John. But an idea—a mighty big one—just popped into my head.

47

"So," John said, "Tell me. What's this idea you just had?"

Micah was looking back toward Smitty. "Take me a moment to explain. But if Mr. Smitty starts to move, I'll need to chase after him, so's I don't lose him. He's a big part of the idea."

John looked over at Smitty, who seemed to be paying a merchant at the moment. "Okay, I got my eye on him. Tell me this idea."

"Well," Micah said, "maybe us bumping into Mr. Smitty no accident. Maybe it's something else, something the Lord did to help us in our time of need."

"Go on."

"Think about it. Last time I see Smitty we was way up in New York, a thousand miles away. Pretty much thought I'd never see him again. Yet here we are at this market, sharing the same space at the same time. Captain Meade sail all up and down the East Coast, even goes over to England at times. But here he is, right where we is...at the same moment in time. What are the chances something like that happen by itself?"

"I agree, it's an amazing coincidence. So, what are you thinking?"

"Maybe the Cutlass supposed to be our Plan B. That is, if that slaveowner won't sell Hannah to us. Maybe we don't steal her and start riding north in a carriage, with all kinda folks chasing us all the way back to New York. Maybe we ride back into town, all of us climb aboard the Cutlass, let Captain Meade take us north by sea. He losin' money with half his hull empty. That might be the Lord's doin.' We could offer him the money you be givin' to the slaveowner."

John saw Smitty begin to move away from them, into the crowd. "Quick, there he goes. We've got to catch him." They hurried toward Smitty to close the gap.

"So you like this idea, Mr. John?" Micah said as they picked up the pace.

"Actually, I hate it. But I think you're right. It's too outlandish to consider our crossing paths with Mr. Smitty's to be merely a coincidence. It's got the fingerprints of providence all over it."

"Not sure I understand what that means," Micah said, "but can I ask why you hate it? The plan, I mean."

"The idea is totally sound. It's just one part I hate. The part about escaping to the north *by sea*."

AFTER CATCHING up with Smitty and discussing Micah's idea, Smitty said the captain might agree to the scheme but only if he wasn't able to secure enough cargo to turn a profit on the trip home. He told them there were seven or eight ships docked in the harbor, and they could find the Cutlass in the middle of the pack. "Course, you know what she looks like, Micah," he'd said. "Looks the same now as the last time you were on her."

John glanced at his timepiece and made a quick decision. They were supposed to rendezvous with Laura and Eli an hour from now. Smitty said it was a ten minute walk to the ship, maybe a few more. Knowing how much Laura dreaded getting back on a boat —any boat, for any reason — he decided to chance that he and Micah could find the Cutlass, talk with the captain, and get back to the rendezvous point in time. That way, if the captain turned them down, John wouldn't have to worry her with the rest of the details.

After five blocks, John and Micah started to see ship masts rise above the buildings on East Bay Street. Right past Broad they turned left and were soon walking on the docks. A busy and active scene. Obviously, most of the men dressed the way you'd expect dockworkers to dress. John looked like any other white plantation owner or warehouse manager, but Micah's appearance drew a lot of stares. If Micah noticed this at all, he didn't let it show. Fairly quickly, he pointed out which ship was the Cutlass and headed right for it.

As they turned down the walkway leading to the gangplank, Micah smiled and said, "She hasn't changed a bit."

One of the men on board was rolling up a length of rope when he noticed the two men looking as if they wanted to board. "Help you folks with something?"

"You must be new," Micah said. "Don't recall ever seeing you before?"

"Well, that makes two of us. I'm on the crew about two weeks now. And who might you be?"

John decided to answer. "Hello, my good man. My name's John Foster. I am acquainted with your captain. The last time he and I spoke the Cutlass was docked in New York City. This is Micah. Up until just over a month ago, he had been part of this crew for three years. We just bumped into your cook, Mr. Smitty, at the market. He's the one who told us where to find the ship."

"Smitty? He sent you here? And you want to see Captain Meade?"

"Yes," John said. "But not just to exchange greetings. We have a significant matter to discuss with him. Is he on board?"

The young man came down the gangplank stood just a few feet away. "He just got back not ten minutes ago. Considering what you said, and that your man here sailed with him that long, I'll ask him if he'll speak with you. But don't get your hopes up. He's in a pretty foul mood."

John answered back in the same quiet tone. "Would this have anything to do with a canceled cargo shipment, and the captain not being able to secure a replacement?"

"Smitty tell you about that?"

John nodded and said, "I'm sure the Captain will want to speak with us. We may be able to solve his financial problem."

The man's eyes widened. "In that case, I'll go speak to him now. What's your name again?"

"Micah."

"Wait here." He hurried back up the gangplank and headed toward the back of the ship.

Moments later, the young crewman returned followed by Captain Meade. He wore a curious expression until his eyes finally focused on Micah. The look changed to shock. "That can't be you. That can't be my Micah." Now a great big smile.

"Permission to come aboard, Captain," John said.

"I remember you, Mr. Foster. Permission granted, to the both of you. Let's head back to my cabin where we can talk."

The cabin looked just as John remembered. It was hard to believe the last time he'd been in this room was less than six weeks ago, where he had paid Captain Meade a hefty sum to purchase Micah's freedom. So many things had changed since then.

"So what brings you to this fine southern city?" Meade said. "And I must say, Micah, if I'd have seen you on the street, I'd have never known it was you. I'd love to hear the story about how you came to be wearing such fine apparel."

"I'm happy to fill you in on both accounts," John said. "But did your crewman mention we have a business proposition to offer?"

"He did. And he said Smitty had informed you of our recent...financial disappointment."

"Yes," John said. "But before I go any further, do I have your word as a gentleman, Captain, that this conversation will go no further than this cabin?"

"One of those kinds of propositions, eh? Okay then, you have my word."

John spent the next ten minutes filling him in on their situation, their need of his services, and their willingness to pay him handsomely if he'd agree to help. "I know there is some risk involved in this endeavor, but I believe they are minimal. If the man will not sell her, our intention is to rescue Micah's daughter secretly tonight and for all of us to come directly here to board the Cutlass. If you can be prepared to set sail immediately, we will be far out at sea before anyone at the plantation even knows she is gone. And even then, the plantation owner would be sending his posses north to search for her by land."

Captain Meade took a long time before answering. "I am not unwilling to consider your offer, Mr. Foster. I'm also very sympathetic, Micah, to your daughter's plight. And it is true, at this point I haven't been able to secure enough cargo to make our return trip profitable. But there are still several good hours left in the day. So, as of now, I must turn you down. I would much prefer to fill my hull with cargo that won't see me put in prison, should this plot be uncovered by the law." He stood as if that word was final.

John and Micah stood, quite dejected.

Micah walked over to a shelf and pointed to a well-worn Bible. "See, you still reading the Good Book, Captain. And I know, you a praying man. You understand what Mr. John here say, what this plantation man intend to do with my girl, Hannah. That's why we here. That's why we need your help."

Captain Meade sighed. "I'm sorry, Micah. Truly, I am. And I will pray that your efforts to secure her release — legally — will go well. If they do not, and if I am *not* able to secure legal cargo to fill the rest of my hull, I may be tempted to reconsider. But for now my answer must be no."

48

John and Micah hurried back to the rendezvous point at the City Market and found Laura and Eli waiting for them there. As they'd walked, John had explained to Micah the depth of Laura's fear about getting on a ship, because of the ship-wreck experience. Which is why John didn't want to bring up their visit with Captain Meade aboard the Cutlass. Especially now that he had refused to help them. Micah, of course, totally understood but said he hoped John wouldn't mind, but "he prayin' the good Lord change the Captain's heart on this thing."

John had smiled and told Micah to go on praying however he chose. He also said that Micah could feel free to share everything regarding the Captain Meade idea with Eli, just as long as Laura couldn't overhear it.

As soon as the four of them were all together, Eli left to get the carriage, parked at a nearby stable. When he returned, they loaded up all their purchases and headed back to the hotel.

Inside the carriage, Laura talked freely about how much she enjoyed shopping at the market and how much better some of the prices were for some of the same things back in New York. John explained it was because many of those things were grown locally and didn't have to be shipped in like they did in New York. That, and the sad fact that here in the South most, if not all, the work was done by slave labor, which cost the plantation owners nothing. Whereas the farmers and growers up North had to pay for all their labor, which of course factored into the higher cost for the food.

"Now see," Laura said, "you just spoiled the whole thing."

"I'm sorry. I really am glad you enjoyed your time, but I just didn't want you to entertain any illusions about it being better here. It's only better for some of us."

She sighed. "I know. You're right. So, speaking of plantation owners, when are we heading out to the Clifton plantation to try and buy Hannah back?"

"I thought we might as well leave right after lunch. It'll take quite a while to get there and back."

"And hopefully," she said, "there will be five of us on the return ride home."

"Yes, hopefully," John said.

DURING THE RIDE out to the Clifton plantation, the sun was high overhead. The temperature was cool, even inside the carriage. The clerk at the hotel had said October was generally like this. September could be hit or miss in terms of the heat. But normally in October, this is what you could expect. As they got closer to the place, though, John felt like it had suddenly gotten warmer. He knew it was probably just his nerves, the stakes being so high. What happened in the next thirty minutes or so is what the entire journey had been about.

Of course, Eli and Micah knew exactly how to get there and had made better time than they did the night before.

The little wooden door slid open. "We turning into the Clifton place now," Micah said. "Can't quite see the house just yet. I'll let you know when we do."

"Thanks, Micah," Laura said.

The further they drove from the main road, the shadier things got.

"I have to say, I've really grown to love these big Live Oak trees," John said. "Wish they had them where we live."

"And the palms," Laura added. "Wish we had those, too."

But the enjoyment of the southern scenery was soon marred by the appearance of these little brick slave shacks on either side of the road, just beyond the trees. And the pitiful looking people sitting or standing around them. Not one of them smiled. Not even the children.

"Every time I get a thought," Laura said, "about how I might want to live here someday, a few seconds more, I'm reminded why it could never be."

"I know," John said.

The little door slid over. "We coming up on the big house up ahead," Micah said. "She's a beaut.' Nicer than any of the ones I've been on."

Out the window, John could see a barn and livestock off in the distance. Then he remembered, it was in a barn just like this where Eli had found Lucas hanging by his hands that night. They passed a garden area where three Negroes worked. They stopped briefly only to notice the carriage go by. The road curved and now John and Laura could see the big house, standing majestically in the center of it all. Two stories, lots of windows, lots of tall Gothic pillars from top to bottom. Painted white except for the black shutters, surrounded by more oaks and maple trees, as well.

"Can I help you folks?" John heard a booming voice coming off the porch. He looked out the window and saw a large Negro coming their way.

"Hopefully you can, sir," Micah said. "My name's Micah. Our driver here is Eli. Our master and his missus are in the carriage. We come a long way hoping we can speak with the owner of the plantation. This here's the Clifton place, is it not?"

The man came down the steps, stood at ground-level. "It is. My name is Kitch. I kinda run things around here for Massa Clifton, on the outside anyway. What business does your Massa have with mine?"

John decided to insert himself and got out of the carriage. "Hello, Mr. Kitch. Happy to make your acquaintance. My name is John Foster." He pointed toward Laura. "That lovely young lady in there is my wife, Laura." John extended his hand.

Kitch looked at it for a moment, then shook it. "Nice to meet you, Ma'am. So, you hoping to speak to Mr. Clifton? Can I ask what this is about? Because he sure gonna ask me when I go fetch him."

"Certainly," John said. "Our reason for being here is no secret. We have come a long way in hopes of securing a certain slave girl, and we're willing to pay a very fair price for her."

"Well, we got lots of slave girls here at the plantation.

Don't know which ones are for sale, but I best go get Massa Clifton, let you talk to him directly." He walked up the porch steps then turned. "Be right back."

While they waited for Clifton to come, John helped Laura down from the carriage. He thought things might go over better if Clifton could see her while John spoke.

A few minutes later, a tall man wearing a wide-brimmed hat and clothes equally as nice as John's but all in gray, came out of the front door and walked to the edge of the porch. "Afternoon folks. I'm Colonel Clifton, the owner of this plantation. My man, Kitch, informs me you are interested in buying a slave girl. As it turns out, we don't have a surplus at the moment. If anything, with all the work we got going on here, I could use a few more slaves myself. So, I'm sorry you have come all the way out from town in hopes of buying one, but I'm afraid I —"

"Well, Colonel," John interrupted. "We aren't just looking for any slave girl, but one specific slave girl. We've been searching for her a good while and have reason to believe she's here. You see, my wife Laura here is with child, our first. As you can tell from my accent, I'm not from the South. I'm a builder from Baltimore, still south of the Mason-Dixon line. But I did marry this fine southern girl, who was raised on a plantation in Virginia. All throughout her childhood, she was best friends with a little slave girl on her plantation, and she had always hoped that when she grew up and started to raise her own family, her best friend—this slave girl—would serve as her nanny."

"I see," Clifton said.

"So, we went back to that plantation in Virginia only to find my wife's childhood friend had recently been sold. We were informed that she had been purchased by you, sir. So, we've come all this way hoping to buy her, and I'm willing to pay you a good deal more than you recently spent to acquire her. Her name is Hannah, I believe you bought her in Fredericksburg not long —"

"Hannah!" Clifton said, his whole expression turning sour. "Hannah, you say? This is the slave girl you've come here expecting to buy?"

"Why, yes, Colonel Clifton. So, you do have her?"

"I'm afraid I do," he said. "And I use the word *afraid* only in the sense that I'm afraid I will have to disappoint you, sir. And your lovely wife. Regardless of her touching story, there is absolutely no chance you'll be leaving here today with Hannah in your carriage. She is not for sale."

As if on cue, Laura instantly became emotional at this news.

John looked at her, then said, "As you can see, Colonel, my wife is heartbroken over this. We simply must have the girl. I will double the price you paid for her in Fredericksburg."

"You can double it, or triple it, sir. The result will be the same. Hannah is not for sale. I have plans for the girl. Big plans. And I need her to fulfill those...plans. She will not be leaving my plantation. My word on that is final, sir. I'm sure you passed a number of plantations on your way out here from Charleston. Perhaps on your way back, you will have more success buying a slave girl from one of them to serve as your nanny. But Hannah is staying here. Good day, sir."

He touched the brim of his hat, turned, walked back into the house and slammed the door behind him.

49

After Eli turned the carriage around, they rode past the brick slave shanties then down the shady lane of live oaks that led to the main road. Eli was furious but did his best to keep it in. He looked at his dad in the seat beside him. His eyes were just sad. Then Eli saw movement in the woods just beyond the oak trees. A girl running. He pulled the carriage over slightly.

"What is it, son?" Micah said.

"I think it's Hannah, Daddy. Look, it is."

She ran out and hid behind a big oak. She was crying.

"You stay there, Hannah. Don't want anyone seeing you."

"I heard what the Massa said. He ain't never gonna let me go. Can't I go with you now?"

John answered her from the carriage. "Hannah, we haven't met. I'm John Foster. My wife Laura and I are the ones who bought your dad's freedom and organized this trip. We did it for one reason. To bring you home. But if you come now that awful man back there will win. He'll immediately know you've left and come after us. But we will come back for you tonight. As soon as it begins to get dark. Like last night, Eli will come back to that same spot where you met him. We'll be waiting in the carriage out by the road. You be ready to leave as soon as you see him. Then we'll take you away from here for good. I promise. But you need to go back right now, and act as if you don't know a thing. Can you do that?"

"Yes, sir, Mr. John. I guess I can."

"Go on now, my little girl," Micah said, his voice choking. "We'll be back for you. Don't you worry."

She waved and hurried back into the woods.

"You better keep going, Eli," John said, "before we draw any unwanted attention. When you get to the main road, turn right. I don't want to head back to town. We've only got a few hours before it starts getting dark. I want to be ready to move as soon as it's safe."

"I know a place we can go while we wait," Micah said. "Found it last night while I was waiting for Eli. Nobody see us there."

THE HOURS WAITING at the quiet spot Micah had found went by slowly. Laura was glad John had the foresight to pack the carriage as though they might not return, so there were plenty of provisions. But Laura was too nervous to eat. She couldn't believe that man wouldn't even take three times what he'd paid for Hannah. That could only mean one thing...he'd become obsessed with her, which is why they had to get her out of there right away.

Eli and Micah passed the time fishing with poles they'd

bought at the City Market. John spent the time going over a map he'd purchased, trying to figure out the fastest routes north by carriage. Laura had pretended to read the book she'd been reading, but the topic made her too anxious. They were living something of the nightmare the author of *Twelve Years a Slave* had experienced themselves. Potentially, things were going to get even more perilous from here.

The time came to turn Eli loose on his rescue mission. They rode the carriage back to within a hundred yards of the plantation entrance. Eli pulled it off to the side of the road and handed the reins to his father. At the hideout, they had already changed out of their fancy clothes.

As Eli got down, Micah set the reins on a hook and followed him. "Mr. John, do you think you'd be able to drive this carriage without me? Got a strong feeling inside I'm supposed to go with my boy this time."

"I'll be fine, Micah. You go ahead."

"You don't need to come, Daddy," Eli said. "I know exactly what I'm doing. Went the exact same way last night."

"I know, son. It's not that I don't trust you. But I've come to depend on these strong nudges I get from time to time. Usually turns out, it was the Lord trying to direct me or protect me from something."

"You two go on ahead," John said. "Laura and I will be fine. Used to drive my own carriage back in San Francisco all the time. How much time do you think you'll need?"

"Should be less than last night," Eli said. "Hannah's supposed to be waiting for us. No more than ten, fifteen minutes."

"All right then. We'll just ride up and down this road a bit, keep our eye out for you."

"And praying," Laura said.

Micah did his best to keep up with Eli as they ran through the woods. When they got to the spot where they expected to find Hannah, she wasn't there.

"Something's wrong, Daddy. You saw how much she wanted to leave this afternoon. She'd have been here early before she'd be a minute late."

"You know where she stay?" Micah said.

"Yes, it's not far."

"Lead the way. I'll keep up." Micah said a quick prayer as they ran.

When they came to two small white buildings, Eli stopped by the oak trees behind them. "She's been staying in the one on the left. But the light shouldn't be on inside. Something's wrong. I know it. She wouldn't be in there unless somethin' was keepin' her."

Just then they both heard someone talking inside. A man's voice coming through the half-open window. Couldn't see much because of the curtain.

"Now, I told you Hannah I'd be coming back yesterday morning, when Celia was here. Remember? She said you needed a couple more days for your woman issues. Well, a couple days has passed."

"I still ain't ready, Massa Clifton. Almost I am. Maybe one more day, is all."

"Now Darlin', I think you might be fibbing me. I wasn't too sure I believed Celia yesterday, but I gave her the benefit of the doubt. But I'm through waiting. I paid good money for you. Today I turned down more than twice as much to a man ready to take you off my hands. But you ain't going anywhere. Except in bed with me."

Micah had heard enough. "We going in. We going in now."

They hurried around the back wall, then down the side wall toward the front. Staying in the shadows. They were stopped in their tracks when they saw that big colored slave, Kitch, standing guard by the front door.

"Lord have mercy," Micah whispered. "Okay Eli, you go around the other side. Get ready to go in through the front. I'll distract this big man, get him to come my way. Soon as he does, you rush in there and save your sister from that evil man. Do whatever you gotta do."

"Yes, sir, Daddy." He hurried toward the back, then went right and disappeared.

Micah felt the dirt around him, found a few pebbles. He waited another moment to make sure Eli was in place, then threw a pebble hard against the white building in front of him. The noise even startled him.

"What the...?" Kitch said, then started walking toward the noise.

Micah stayed flat against the wall of Hannah's place and watched as Kitch walked past. When he'd put enough distance between them, Micah ran toward him fast as he could, then leaped on his back, causing Kitch to slam against the far wall. Micah swung his left arm under Kitch's neck, grabbed hold of his wrist with the other arm and pulled tight. Kitch instantly started to choke and gag. Micah then wrapped his legs around Kitch's waist and squeezed hard.

"Who ith thith?" Kitch yelled. "I'm gonna—"

Micah squeezed tighter on his neck, until he could speak no more. Kitch tried slapping behind his head to hit Micah, but it was no use. Seconds later, he passed out.

Micah heard his son Eli kick down Hannah's front door with his foot.

ELI COULD NOT BELIEVE the scene.

Hannah was backed into the corner, a look of terror on her face, wrestling with Clifton's hands, his body pressed up against her. When he heard the door fly open, he turned, saw Eli. "What are you doing here? Get back to where — wait... you're not one of mine."

"You got that right, *massa*." Eli rushed him.

Clifton spun around, took a swing at Eli's face. Eli ducked. It missed. He buried his fist into Clifton's left side with all his might. Clifton gasped and fell to his knees. A perfect liver punch. Clifton doubled over, holding his side. Eli yanked his head up by his hair. "Not the big Boss Man now, are ya'?" Eli punched his face hard and Clifton fell to the floor.

Eli turned him over, sat on his chest and punched him again. "That ones' for all the pain you caused Lucas when you stole his wife." He punched him again. "This one's for all the pain and fear you caused my sister."

Clifton, half-conscious, said, "Who's Lucas? Who is your sister? I don't know them, I didn't do any—"

"THAT'S my sister," Eli shouted, pointing at Hannah. He punched him again. "How's it feel, bein' on the other end of one-a-your beatin's? Doesn't feel so good, now, does it?" He punched him again, and again, and again.

"Stop, Eli," Hannah yelled. "You'll kill him."

"I don't have a problem with that." He punched him once more.

Hannah grabbed his wrist. "But I do. You kill him, and they won't stop looking for us till the world ends. He's out. Look at him. He's not getting up. Let's leave now, before someone else comes."

"Too late," a woman's voice said from the front door. "Someone's already here." She stepped inside.

"Celia," Hannah said.

A moment later, Micah came in behind her.

"Just met your, Daddy," Celia said. "He's old, but you shoulda seen what he just did to ole Kitch outside. Never seen anything like it." She had a smile on her face.

"You ain't gonna turn us in?"

"Turn you in?" She looked down at Clifton, unconscious and bloody on the floor. "Child, I been wantin' someone to do that to that man long as I can remember. Kitch, too. I asked your Daddy if he wouldn't hit him with a stick in the face a few times, but he refused."

Micah walked toward Hannah. "My girl," he said, tears streaming down his face. She ran toward him, and they embraced.

"Okay now," Celia said. "This all very sweet and touching, but you three better make your way off this property, quick as you know how. I got some rope next door. I'll tie 'em up real good and gag 'em. No tellin' when they come to, but that'll slow 'em down plenty. I'll stay next door till they ask me about it, hopefully not till mornin,' and I'll say I slept through it all. So, you go on and git now, Miss Hannah. You go and give all that love you got to that man you found, whatever his name is."

"Oh, Celia." Hannah ran over and hugged Celia.

Celia blinked back a rush of tears. "Go on now, git. 'Fore anybody else wanders over this way."

Micah and Eli thanked her again and, together with Hannah, fled into the night.

50

"John, something's wrong. They should have been back by now, shouldn't they?"

John had just turned the carriage around again and was heading back toward the rendezvous point. "I don't know, Laura." He glanced at his timepiece. "It definitely feels longer than it's supposed to." He hadn't included in their plans anything for the possibility of them being caught or captured. He tried to suppress feelings of panic rising to the surface. What good would it do to give in?

"Oh, Lord," Laura said. "Keep them safe, please."

They rode the next few minutes in silence and were both relieved to finally hear some noise coming from the woods as they approached the spot. A little closer, and it definitely sounded like people running.

John just hoped they weren't being chased.

"There's Eli," Laura said. "I can see him. And there she is. That's got to be Hannah behind him. But where's Micah?"

John pulled the wagon over. He was grateful for the

amount of light provided by the moon and the stars, because he dared not light the lantern.

"There's Micah," she said. "I see him a few yards behind. Thank you, Lord."

When they broke into the clearing between the woods and the road, Eli and Hannah slowed to let Micah catch up.

"I'm coming," he said. "Don't worry 'bout me."

John could already see his smile, even from here. He climbed down off the wagon, helped Laura to do the same. They hugged Micah and Eli and stood in front of Hannah.

"Here she is," Micah said. "My girl, Hannah. Took some doin', but we back, safe and sound."

She held out her hand and John shook it. Laura pulled her close into a hug."

"Thanks so much for comin' back for me," Hannah said. "Don't think I would-a made it through the night, if you didn't."

"Question now," Micah said, "is which way do we go?"

"I don't understand," Laura said. "Aren't we going north? What other direction could we go?"

John looked at Micah and then Eli. He could tell they had something on their minds that needed to be said. "Did something go wrong? Is that why you were longer getting back?"

"Yes, sir," Eli said. "Fact is, couldn't have gone much worse than the plan we made." He took a few minutes to describe the terrible scene that had just unfolded. John and Laura were shocked by the account. "If Daddy hadn't had that nudge from the Lord, as he calls 'em, we wouldn't be here right now. Don't think I could've taken on that big fellow Kitch by myself and Clifton, too." He looked at Micah. "How did you take down the big man, Daddy? I didn't hear anything sounded like a fight, and he was twice your size?"

Micah smiled. "He was. But no matter how big or small they are, everyone need to breathe. I learned me a wrestling move when I was on that ship. Have to teach it to you sometime. Just jumped on his back, locked my arm 'round his neck, and down he go. Just like a tree. But see, another way the Lord was surely with us was sending that woman from next door to help."

"That was Celia," said Hannah. She went on to explain what Celia had done for them.

"The problem now is," Micah said, "this situation may force us to change our plans. That's why I said we got to decide which way to go. Going north might not be the best thing anymore."

"But why?" Laura said. "I don't see how it changes anything."

"Because," Eli said, "with the plan we made, we'd have already gotten Hannah back and been on the road twenty minutes. No one would've known she was gone till morning. We be riding all night before anyone at the plantation figured out what happened."

Laura looked at Hannah. "Do you think your friend Celia would turn us in?"

"She never do that," Hannah said. "But—"

"But the way we left that slaveowner, Clifton," Micah said, "and his man Kitch...don't expect they'll keep for more than a few hours. Could be less than that for Kitch. The chokehold I put him on don't put your lights out long as the beating old Clifton got from Eli. Point is —"

"The point is," John interjected, "instead of a ten-to-fifteen-hour head start, we might have more like two or three. That makes the odds of them catching up to us dramatically greater." John felt his stomach tighten in knots.

"But what choice do we have?" Laura said. "Seems like we need to stop talking and get on the road as soon as possible."

John looked at Micah, who nodded. "What are you thinking, Micah?"

"I'm thinking 'bout where you and I went after the market today."

"But that door closed on us," John said.

"It did," Micah said. "Earlier today. But I'm getting one of them same nudges, telling me the door may have opened up again."

"How strong is that nudge?" John said.

"Pretty strong. Maybe stronger than what I had a little while ago, telling me I better go with Eli to fetch Hannah."

"You know if you're wrong," John said, "and we go back into Charleston, we'll be trapped. We'd lose even the tiny lead we have now, since we'd be heading the wrong direction."

"I know," Micah said. "I know."

"But you still think we should try it?"

"You the Boss, Mr. John. I'll do whatever you say. But if it was me..."

"What are you two talking about?" Laura said. "I don't understand a word of this. Where did the two of you go after the market today. I thought you just met back up with Eli and me."

John sighed. "I didn't tell you, because as I said, the door seemed to have closed shut. Since it did, I saw no reason to worry you."

"What door? How did it close? John, would you just tell me what's going on?"

"I will, but...it's going to be a serious leap of faith...for both of us."

"For all of us," Eli said. "If'n that ship captain says no again."

"Ship captain?" Laura said.

THE NINETY-MINUTE RIDE back to Charleston seemed to fly by for Laura, compared to the earlier trip out to the plantation. John had decided that on something this significant he didn't want to be "the Boss." He put the choice whether to head north as originally planned or south toward Charleston harbor up for a vote. Hannah had abstained, saying as long as she was free she didn't care which way they went. Laura realized right after she said this, that Hannah's best chance of staying free was in the choice to sail out of Charleston tonight aboard the Cutlass.

So, the vote had been unanimous.

At least for now, her dread of sailing on a ship seemed kept at bay. Likely in the face of the more ominous option of being captured by ruthless slave hunters sometime tomorrow. And at this point, there was probably no one whose ability to discern the will of God she trusted more than Micah.

After crossing the drawbridge, Eli steered the carriage all the way down Calhoun Street to East Bay. They passed hardly anyone on the streets or sidewalks of town. They continued past the intersection of Broad when Micah said, "Just another block further, then park the carriage."

After the carriage was secured in an open spot along the curb, Micah led them down a side road toward the waterfront. "Not much more from here," he said. They only carried their personal things, left all the provisions in the carriage.

When they reached the wharves, it took Micah a few moments to catch his bearings. Each of the ships had lanterns on their bows, but there was precious little light beyond that. "I see her," he said. "I'm sure that's her. This way."

They rushed down the docks past two other ships then stepped carefully down the wooden walkway that led to the Cutlass gangplank. At first, they didn't see anyone on board. Then Smitty walked by. He glanced down, startled to see the small crowd that had formed there. He didn't recognize John or Micah in the shadows.

"Mr. Smitty, it's me, Micah. And Mr. John. The man you met with me at the market."

"Micah? What you doing here at this hour? I remember John. Who these other folks with you?"

"My boy, Eli. My daughter, Hannah. This other lady is Miss Laura, John's wife. Can we speak with the captain?"

"Let me check. Just went by his door, still saw the light on."

"Thank you, Mr. Smitty," John said. "Our situation is very urgent."

"Okay, I'll hurry."

John put his arm around Laura to offset the night chill. He said a silent, quick prayer for mercy.

Moments later, the captain came out with Smitty right behind.

He looked down at the group, focused on Micah. "My, my," he said. "What have we got here?"

"May we come aboard, Captain?" John said. "The matter is delicate. We don't want to yell."

"Fine."

"Should we leave our things here?" Micah said.

"No," Meade said. "Might as well bring them with you. I had a feeling you'd be back as the day wore on. Every other deal I'd been working on to fill the hull fell flat. Had all the earmarks of the Almighty forcing me into a corner...on your behalf, I suppose."

51

3 Days Later, on the Atlantic
75 Miles East of Cape Hatteras

IT WAS JUST AFTER SUNRISE, so John went up on deck to find Laura. When he awoke, she wasn't beside him. Neither of them had been sleeping well, mainly due to the motion of the ship. Thankfully, it wasn't because of bad dreams. Except for that first night when they'd left Charleston in such a hurry. John had to wake Laura up twice because of her loud moaning and thrashing about. Only one of the dreams involved being on a ship, though. The other wasn't much better; she was being chased in a carriage by men on horses...who were shooting at her.

He found her at the stern leaning against the rail, sipping hot tea. A thick shawl was wrapped around her shoulders. He didn't see Micah, Eli or Hannah yet but they were sleeping in a different part of the ship. Happily, not because of their race. Captain Meade had made it clear to his crew the very first night, that Micah and his family were on board as his guests, and that they would be treated with respect. Any infractions on this point would be met with the lash.

When John reached her, he decided not to embrace her from behind, which he genuinely desired to do, for fear of startling her. "Good morning, my love."

She turned and smiled, still looking quite tired. "So good to see you," she said.

Now he embraced her. "How did you sleep?"

"Not badly. Not great, either. But I did sleep. And if I dreamt anything, I forgot it almost immediately after waking up."

"That's a good sign," John said. That's how most of his dreams behaved.

"And for the first time since coming on board," she said, "I don't feel any anxiety or fear. On one level, I know we've been quite safe since we sailed past Fort Sumter out into the open sea, but now I suppose all of me believes it."

"I'm glad to hear it. Because we really are okay now. I'm sure of it. If you think about it, Hannah's owner — or should I say former owner — would have no reason to imagine we would flee to the north by sea. My guess is he and his posse have probably already given up trying to find us some time yesterday, after scouring the countryside throughout the Carolinas without finding a single trace. He may have hired some slave catchers to continue on, but he thinks I'm a builder from Baltimore. He'd have no reason to venture further north than that."

She took another sip of tea. "You should get a cup of

coffee. Warm up your insides. Smitty's isn't that bad. I tried some yesterday afternoon."

"I think I will. I guess Micah and his children are sleeping in this morning. Haven't seen any sign of them yet."

"Micah and Eli might be, but Hannah is already up. She was getting tea at the same time as I. I'm not sure where she went after that, but I'm growing concerned about her."

"What's the matter? Guess I haven't noticed."

"She's very depressed. Each time I see her, it seems her melancholy grows worse."

"But why? She knows she is safe now, right?"

"John, tell me you can come up with another reason for her sadness."

He thought a moment, and it came. "Her husband, of course. I'd completely forgotten. He's still stuck at their old plantation in Fredericksburg. I'd forgotten that our new plan of escape meant we wouldn't be coming back for him on our return trip home."

"I'm sure she believes she's lost him for good," Laura said. "She looks just like I felt the last time I sailed aboard this ship. I'm sure the only reason I'm doing so well is I have you beside me now. She is free, but she's still all alone."

"Something has to be done," John said. "We have to find a way to save him."

"I've been thinking about it since I awoke," she said. "I can't think of a thing."

THE SOLUTION to their dilemma presented itself shortly after John left Laura to get a cup coffee. After pouring it, he decided to check on Hannah and walked to the bow of the ship. There he found Hannah sobbing, her arms wrapped around her brother Eli's neck. He was patting her back. As John got close, he heard Eli say, "You don't need to thank me. I made a promise to him. A promise I intend to keep."

"Is everything okay?" John said.

"I'm sorry, Mr. John," Hannah said. "I'm just so happy now. Scared, but happy."

"Why? What's going on?"

Eli released Hannah from the hug. "Mr. John, good to see you. Saves me from having to come find you. I come up with a new plan, to fix something that our sea voyage sort of messed up."

"Are you referring to Lucas being stuck in Fredericksburg?"

"Yes!" Eli and Hannah said in unison.

"See, I told Lucas we'd be back for him. Five days after we last spoke. That's what I said. You wait five days and come meet me at this certain spot. Soon as it gets dark enough. You don't see me, come back the next night. Cause I wasn't exactly sure how long it would take. But now?"

"I know," John said. "So what are you thinking?"

"That I get off this ship, by myself, make my way to where he is, and rescue him."

"But if you succeed, how will you get from there back to New York?" John said. "You won't have any transportation. And without a doubt, his owner will come after him soon as he realizes he's gone."

"Same way I got there the last time...with these two feet. But now, I know the route, so we'll make even better time. Only thing I need is for you to talk to Captain Meade for me.

Maybe you and Daddy. See if you can talk him into getting me onshore, close as we can to Fredericksburg."

OF COURSE, John immediately agreed to Eli's request. And Eli had already spoken with Micah before approaching Hannah with the idea. He asked Eli to have his father meet him outside the Captain's cabin in ten minutes to allow him time to speak with Laura, see what she thought of the idea.

Laura completely agreed that it was the right thing to do, even though she feared for Eli's safety. But when she'd heard Eli was completely resolved to do it, she felt they had no options but to approve.

Presently, John and Micah were standing outside the captain's cabin. "Now, don't you hold back if you have something to say," John said to Micah.

"I won't, Mr. John."

"Micah, we're no longer in the South. We don't have to pretend you're my slave anymore. Can't you at least try to start calling me John?"

Micah smiled. "I'll try, Mr. John."

John shook his head and knocked on the door. He heard the captain yell for them to enter. He opened it and found Captain Meade sitting at his desk reading his Bible. This could only help, John thought.

"Gentlemen, how are you both doing this fine morning? Glad I was able to provide another night of calm seas. Just kidding. We all know who to thank for that." He laid his Bible on the desk. "Have a seat."

"Thanks, but this should only take a moment of your time. First off, I want to thank you again for reconsidering our appeal a few nights ago in Charleston. It's probably fair to say, you may have saved our lives. At the very least, our freedom."

"Well, I'll just say you're welcome and leave it at that. In some ways, we've helped each other. The money you paid for your voyage is allowing me to at least break even on this trip. Always helps with the crew's morale when they get paid in a timely manner."

That gave John a thought. It seemed the captain's generosity could be encouraged by a healthy dose of self-interest. "We've been discussing a certain situation that has been left unattended by our rapid departure from Charleston. A serious situation. You've met Hannah."

"She seems like a lovely girl, Micah. Although I've been puzzled why she's not in better spirits considering her newfound freedom."

"Thanks, Cap," Micah said. "Her sadness is all about the serious situation Mr. John wants to talk about." He nodded for John to continue.

John explained the whole situation with Lucas, doing his best not to leave out any detail that might stir the captain's compassion. "So, our proposal is this. We'd like to ask you to consider heading back into shore, as close to Fredericksburg as possible. Perhaps Norfolk or whichever is the best port for you. That way, we could release Micah's son, Eli, to go and rescue Hannah's husband, Lucas. Thereby fulfilling our promise to come back for him on our return."

"You said this was some kind of proposal," said Meade. "You spelled out what I would do. What would your part of the proposal be?"

"Well," John said. "I gave you all the cash I had to pay for our trip. But I was thinking, you mentioned you still had significant space in your hull left to fill. We would be willing to wait a day or so at port, whichever city you pick, to see if you perhaps could find another merchant with cargo they'd like to ship north. That way you wouldn't just break even but turn a tidy profit."

"And I know the men's morale," Micah said, "be improved even more getting a few days shore leave they didn't expect."

Meade sat back in his chair, a smile crossed his face. "Gentlemen, I accept your proposal. I have made some profitable deals in Norfolk before. I could check some of my old contacts, see what turns up. You go get your boy ready for his mission, Micah. It'll take us most of the morning, if not half the day to get there. But I'll get up and give the order now to set sail for Hampton Roads."

52

2:40 PM, James River
North of Hampton Roads, Virginia

THE TIME HAD COME for Eli to head ashore and begin his perilous mission to rescue Lucas.

Captain Meade had agreed to sail past Hampton Roads, the harbor area near Norfolk, and go north up the James River as far as he could. He did this as a favor to Micah. He should've turned the ship south over an hour ago and headed straight into the Norfolk port. But he knew doing so would add at least an extra day to Eli's journey toward Fredericksburg, all the while traveling through enemy territory, so-to-speak. All of Virginia was still committed to slavery.

More than that, Meade had explained, since the James River was so deep, ocean-going ships could sail right through Hampton Roads and travel up and down the river with relative ease. This resulted in dozens of plantations being established all over the area with docks built right to the river's edge.

Plantations filled with slaves...and slave hunters.

Presently, Eli was climbing over the rail down a rope ladder to board a shallow rowboat. One of the ship's crew was already on board. Standing at the rail were Meade, Micah, John and Laura, and Hannah.

"I'm sorry, lad, I couldn't have brought you further north. But after Burwell Bay the river starts to narrow, and I really need to get settled in at Norfolk before dark."

"That's fine, Captain," Micah said. "We appreciate you doing this much."

"I definitely appreciate it," Eli said. "Now I figure I might be able to get to our old plantation sometime tomorrow. Only be a day late, instead of two."

"Best I can remember," Meade said, "you go ashore here, it's just woods. Next plantation is maybe a mile north. Should be enough provisions in that sack to hold you over for a few days."

"That's very kind of you, Captain," Laura said.

"I could give him more, but it would just slow him down. Besides, we were talking about the time three years ago when he fled here for New York. He knows how to forage and live off the land."

"That he do," Micah said.

Eli made it into the rowboat, took a seat in the front.

"Thank you so much, Eli," Hannah said. "What you doing for me, something I'll never forget."

"You're welcome, little sister. I know I couldn't be happy back in New York, knowing we left Lucas stuck on that plantation without any hope. Now there's one favor maybe you could do for me when you get settled in up there."

"Anything, just say it."

"I got this girl in New York, named Bella. She fixes clothes at this shop owned by a big colored woman name Ella Mae. On 7th Avenue, I think. Mr. John could probably show you where that's at."

"What you want me to tell her?" Hannah said.

Eli looked up at everyone staring down. Seemed to get a little embarrassed. "Just tell her what's going on. Why I'm not there with you. But you tell her, I am coming back. Tell her I don't want her seeing anyone else but me. And if that makes her smile, you can also tell her I got something special I wanna talk about when I see her again."

"What if it don't make her smile?" Hannah said, smiling now herself.

"Well then...I don't know. I'm hoping it will. If not, well then...I guess —"

"I'm sure she'll be smiling," Laura said. "Don't think you have to worry about that."

"Okay then. Well, we best be off," he said. "Y'all pray for me. Feel like Daniel heading into the lions' den."

"We'll be praying, son," Micah said. "Every day. As I recall, that story ended pretty well for Daniel. We'll pray yours will, too."

They all waved goodbye as Eli headed off toward the shore.

53

The rest of the day as well as the day following were spent in Norfolk. When they set sail on the third day, the captain was in good spirits because his hull was brimming with new cargo. Everyone wondered how Eli was making out. By now, he had probably reconnected with Lucas near Fredericksburg. If so, Micah said he'd be traveling mostly by night the rest of the way home.

They would, of course, get to New York long before Eli did. The captain had said if the winds kept blowing as strong as they were, they could make up to a hundred and fifty miles a day. They might actually be sailing into New York harbor three days from now.

On that first sunset back at sea, John and Laura went out to view it on deck. "It really is an amazing sight," she said, "seeing the sunset over the water."

"So, this last part of our journey hasn't been the horror that you feared," John said.

"No, it hasn't. But that's the thing about the sea, isn't it? It could be as majestic and wonderful as it is now for several days in a row. Then all of a sudden, everything changes and it's trying to kill you."

"I know this has been a crazy trip," John said, "but we've had some quieter times aboard this ship since Charleston. Have you given any more thought to the idea of staying in New York. Or do you think you'd rather brave the trip home to San Francisco?"

She shifted her gaze from the sunset to his eyes. "I've actually been thinking about something a lot lately. Really, two things. Even before we left Charleston. But since then, I've thought about them even more."

"What are they?"

"Well, both would definitely involve us staying in New York. But not because I'm afraid that the San Francisco option requires getting back on a ship."

"Then...what?"

"I know you'd have to go to work with your brother and father, if we stayed. So, I wouldn't want you to take this as me making any demands on you. If you'd rather go back to San Francisco, I'm more than willing to do that now."

John smiled. "I guess after what we've been through, the fears of sea travel don't seem near as ominous as they did before."

"That's partly it," she said. "But what we've been through has definitely affected me. More deeply than I expected. I don't believe I can simply go back to doing the things I did before. It was pleasant and satisfying, I suppose, on some level. But now..."

"I think I know where this is headed," John said. "You want your life to count for more."

"Well, that's definitely true for one of the two things I want to say. But the first one is...well, it's just...I don't want to be so far away from your family. If we don't have to be. I was thinking about this before we left, but seeing the level of love and sacrifice Micah and Eli went through to get Hannah back, and how happy Sally is going to be when she gets home...it makes me realize how important family is. And we're getting along with your family again. I've actually missed them on this trip."

"Oddly enough," John said, "So have I."

"And when we start having children of our own, I want them to be able to see their grandparents, and uncles and aunts and cousins. Often. Not once every four or five years."

"Okay, so...what's the second thing you wanted to say?"

"Well, I can't ignore how terribly Negroes are being treated in this country. Not anymore. It's not okay for me to just leave everything in my life in nice little compartments. I want to make a difference somehow."

"What are you thinking?"

"I'm thinking when we get home, I want to go down and talk to those folks who work with the Underground Railroad. See if there's anything I can do to help. If not there, then maybe talk to some abolitionist groups in the city. I'm sure they could use some volunteers."

John leaned over and kissed her.

"What's that for?"

"Because you look so beautiful against the backdrop of this setting sun. And because I love who you are on the inside. That this is where your thinking would lead, the conclusions you'd come to, after the harrowing times we've just spent together."

"So, you'd be okay with this? With what I'm thinking?"

"More than okay. If possible, as much as my work will allow, I'd like to join you in this endeavor. We'll both become abolitionists when we return. We'll stay in New York, and do whatever we can to fight this terrible injustice."

Just then, Micah walked up behind them. "Beggin' your pardon, I was just comin' to see the sunset myself before it got too late. Couldn't help overhearin' what you been saying about helping to fight against the way my people been treated. Just want you to know...whatever else you do from here, I'm sure it's gonna be a blesssin'. But what you folks already done?" Tears filled his eyes. "I just left my girl, Hannah, taking a nap down below. Sleepin' like a baby. All safe and sound. She free now. Never gonna be a slave again. And I'm free, because of you two. That's the God's-honest truth. And I got faith my boy, Eli, gonna get Lucas free. And somehow they gonna make it back to New York one day soon. And my other girl Sally will be waitin' there for us. Get to see her sister once more when just a little while ago, we's all afraid we never gonna see her ever again. And we'll be a family...all together in the same place."

He wiped his tears on his sleeve, but they kept coming. "That's all account of you two, John and Laura. What you already done for me and my family. I won't ever forget it. I'm tellin' you. None of us will."

John and Laura were crying now. They hurried over and gave Micah a big hug. When they finally let go of each other, John said, "Wait a minute...I just realized something. Micah, you called us John and Laura, not Mr. John and Miss Laura."

Micah smiled. "Yeah, I know you been wantin' me too for some time. Figured now's a good a time as any. Because we most definitely friends, and with you folks stayin' in New York now, looks like the Lord makin' it so we get to be friends for life."

54

2 Weeks Later
New York City

ELI AND LUCAS were weary to the bone.

But they were both as happy as could be. The happiness began on that first night in Fredericksburg when Eli had gotten to the rendezvous point and found Lucas waiting for him there. Of course, Lucas had been disappointed not to see the rest of the family there, especially Hannah. But he was relieved to learn she was at least safe on a ship sailing for New York. He was also disappointed that he wouldn't be making the trip in a carriage but on foot, mostly running through the woods at night. Still, he must've thanked Eli a dozen times in the past two weeks for coming back to get him. And it had given him strong confidence knowing Eli had made the same trip three years prior.

The second wave of happiness washed over the two men the night they had officially crossed the border into Pennsylvania. They were not entirely out of danger, but they were no longer in a slave state, and it was nice to know most of the people they'd see from then on would be sympathetic to the cause.

But the greatest dose of happiness greeted them both this morning when they'd read the sign, "Entering New York City." They'd found a merchant heading into Manhattan with a half-empty wagon, who agreed to give them a lift. Eli had to tell him where Gramercy Park was. He'd said he could get them within a five-minute walk, which was fine with them.

Now that they were getting close, all Eli could think about was seeing Bella again. She was the thing he thought about the most on the last leg of this trip. Lucas couldn't wait to see Hannah, of course. It was great hearing him talk about their future, knowing they could finally have one together. While he'd talked, Eli enjoyed just looking at Lucas' face. He had never seen anything like New York City before. The tall buildings, the crowded streets, the noise, the smells and all the rest that go with being in that remarkable place. Made Eli remember how he'd felt pretty much the same way three years ago, the first time he'd run away to freedom.

The merchant stopped the wagon by a curb near 14th Street and 5th Avenue. "Guess you better get off here. From the directions you gave me, that place you wanna get to shouldn't be too far from here."

Eli and Lucas hopped out of the wagon. "It's not," Eli said. "I know where we are now. Thank you so much for the ride. Wish we had something to give you."

"Happy to do it, young fella. You two have a nice day." He drove the wagon off, heading north.

"I can't believe these houses, Eli. They so big. Some are like the Big House of a plantation, except they all pressed together."

"Wait till you see the Foster place. I think it's the biggest one in all of Gramercy Park. It's just a couple blocks from here. I think that's where Hannah is. I'm their driver. My sister Sally works in the house. We both have nice rooms we stay in above the carriage house. Daddy takes care of the horses for another family a couple blocks away. And John and Laura, the couple I've been telling you about, they live in the big house. So, that's where we're headed."

They crossed an intersection. "Say, Eli. Before we go any further, something I need to ask you about. Been trying to get it out of my mind ever since we started out from Fredericksburg, but it won't let me go. You never gave me any details about this evil man, Clifton. And that man Kitch. I need to know...what they did to my girl, Hannah. I need to know...what kind of shape she's in. Did they —"

"You got nothing to worry about, Lucas. I ain't saying that what you thinking wasn't on their minds. Matter of fact, the night I came there to get her, he was already there, about to have his way." Eli could see the anger rising in Lucas' face. "But nothing happened. I got there in time. Well, something did happen."

"What?"

"I gave that white man a whupping like he'd never had or maybe ever seen."

"You did?" Now a big smile.

"I did. Hit him with a liver shot so hard, doubled him

over. Then I kept punching him in the face, over and over. Hannah had to make me stop. Didn't even look like the same man when I got off him. The whole while I was thinking about what he did to you and Hannah."

"What about that fella, Kitch?"

"I didn't see what happened to him. Daddy took care of it. Now you know he ain't one to boast but that Celia, remember I told you about her?" Lucas nodded. "Whatever Daddy did to him, she said he was out cold. I could tell one thing, for sure."

"What's that, Eli?"

"The smile on Celia's face that night...you could tell she was glad both men got what they deserved. And you just know she'd have spread word about the beating they took to every slave on that plantation before lunchtime the next day."

Lucas laughed. 'I know that's right."

55

It was shortly before lunch.

Sally was out in the kitchen getting things ready. Hannah was probably still in Sally's room, where she had been staying since she'd arrived. John was escorting Laura down the stairway. Mother and Allison were out on the veranda, enjoying the cool weather. Micah was actually in the carriage house. Since they'd arrived home last week, he had agreed to come look in on the horses for them, until Eli returned.

Everyone still held out hope that he would. Return, that is. He and Lucas. Yesterday, John had gone down to speak with the people who worked at the Underground Railroad, to ask if they had heard any word. Any word at all. No one had. John then asked how long did such a trip typically take. They asked how long Eli had been gone. Then said, "That is a little long if they're only coming from Fredericksburg. But not terribly so. There's any number of reasons they could be delayed."

That provided at least a ray of hope.

Just as John and Laura reached the base of the stairs, the doorbell rang. Beryl went to answer it. John and Laura continued toward the veranda, where they intended to eat lunch. Just before leaving the living room, John heard Beryl say, "Why, Master Eli. It is you. I barely recognize you. I do believe everyone in this household has been awaiting your return."

John and Laura stopped, turned and hurried to the door. Beryl stepped out of the way to allow two very tired and rough looking young men through to the foyer. "May I present, Master Eli and his friend, a Mr. Lucas."

"Eli," John and Laura yelled in unison. "You're home!"

Laura gave no thought to their appearance and gave Eli a hug. She turned to Lucas and extended her hand. "I'd hug you too, but we've never met. I have heard so much about you. Welcome to the Foster home, finally."

"Thank you, Ma'am."

"Eli, Lucas, welcome," John said. "We're so glad you finally made it home. Had us a little worried."

"Ran into a few close calls," Eli said. "One at the border of Virginia and the other just before we got into Pennsylvania. Had to spend a few days hiding in the woods till the coast cleared. But we made it."

Just then, Sally came out from the kitchen having heard all the commotion. Tears filled her eyes as soon as she saw the two young men. "I knew you'd get home. I just knew you would." She ran to them, hugged them both and cried some more. After hugging Lucas, she pulled away. "I gotta go get Hannah. She's up in my room. Be right back."

"Please," Lucas said.

She literally ran back toward the kitchen. A back door there led to the carriage house.

A few moments later, they heard almost a squealing sound coming from the kitchen. It was the high-pitched sheer delight and joy of Hannah, giving no thought to manners or protocol as she raced through the kitchen and hallway toward the front door.

Lucas stepped toward the sound into the living room. Hannah broke through the doorway entrance, saw Lucas and shrieked again. John thought he'd never seen a happier face. Lucas ran toward her, she toward him, and then they embraced. He swung her around and set her feet down again. Both were crying and goin' on and on about how much they loved and missed each other.

Finally, Hannah broke free and ran to Eli, hugged him just about as hard. "No girl ever had a brother like you," she said. "No one. You risked your very life to bring my man back to me."

Eli was tearing up. "Had to do it. You my baby sister."

"Well, we gonna name all our kids after you," she said, "soon as we start having 'em."

"Please don't do that," Eli said.

John decided to duck out and get Micah. Told Laura he'd be right back. He went out through the veranda, met his mother and sister, Allison, coming in to see what was going on. John quickly filled them in and headed for the carriage house.

When he opened the side door, he could hear Micah in the back singing some hymn, while he brushed one of the horses. "Hey, Micah!"

"Yes, sir, Mr. John. Uh...I mean, John."

"You're wanted in the living room. Everyone's waiting for you."

"Say what?" He came walking toward John. "Why they waiting for—" He looked at John's face. "They back?"

John nodded.

"Eli and Lucas, they back? And they okay?"

John nodded again. "Come see."

The two men rushed up the steps, across the short lawn, through the veranda and the two hallways, and into the unfolding scene in the living room. When everyone saw Micah, they stopped to take in the moment.

"We made it, Daddy," Eli said. "Lord got us home, just like you said He would."

"Yes, He did, son. So good to see you. Both of you." Micah held out his arms and Eli walked right into them. They hugged for several moments, not a dry eye left in the room.

Even Beryl wiped tears from his eyes.

When Eli pulled back, he looked at Hannah. "Say Hannah. Since you been back, did you get a chance to go see Bella, the girl I told you about?"

"I did. Maybe two, three days after we got here."

"You give her the message I told you to give her?"

"You mean about you not wanting her to see anyone else but you?"

"Yeah, that," Eli said.

"You wanna know was she smiling after?"

"Yes."

"Umm-hmm. She was. And that ain't all."

Now Eli was smiling. "What else?"

"She say, '*Why would I ever go and see anyone else?*'"

"She said that? So, you told her the second part?"

"About you havin' something special you wanna talk to her about when you git home?"

"Yeah."

"I did. And that smile on her face grew wider still."

Everyone laughed at this exchange.

Eli looked at them all. "Excuse me folks. I am so happy to be back and to see y'all, but there's someplace else I gotta be. I won't be gone too long."

"You better go get yourself cleaned up first," Hannah said. "You gonna do what we think you gonna do."

Eli headed toward the kitchen. "Oh, I intend to. I will see you all real soon." After a few steps, he came back pulled Micah aside and whispered. "Daddy, you okay if we grow this family a bit? I intend to ask Bella to marry me. It's all I been thinking about since we got on that ship."

Micah smiled. "You go on ahead, son. Bella's a fine girl. You got my blessin.'" Eli took a step back. "And son?"

"Yes, Daddy."

"That's a fine thing you done, going after Lucas like that. I couldn't be more proud. Look at us now. Just look. All together again. In one room. Never thought I'd see the day."

Eli did look. "Thank you, sir. And I'm proud you're my Daddy. God has been good to us. I can see that now. Even this morning, when Lucas and I were sitting in a wagon, I kept thinking of that Bible verse you always quote. From an Old Testament story, I think. Something like, '*What man meant for us as evil, God used it for our good.*' Seemed to fit what we all just been through."

Eli smiled. "Think you right, son. And listen, when you get settled in, maybe in a few days, think you could start teachin' me how to read?"

"Really? Yes! I would love to do that. But, right now?"

"I know," Micah said. "Someplace else you gotta be."

WANT TO READ MORE?

We hope you enjoyed *The Longest Road*. If you didn't know, it's actually a sequel to Dan's Bestselling Award-winning novel, *The Deepest Waters*. If you read them out of order, not a big problem. Readers say they still very much enjoyed reading *The Deepest Waters* as a "prequel" to *The Longest Road*. You'd be reading the exciting story of what happened to these same characters in the weeks and months before *The Longest Road* began.

Here's a link to *The Deepest Waters* on Amazon. As of this moment, it's received over 1,200 Amazon reviews (with a 4.8 Star Avg).

https://www.amazon.com/dp/B07CK6KKHL

LINKS TO DAN'S OTHER BOOKS

Dan has written over 20 other novels, all available on Kindle (most on Kindle Unlimited).

Combined, his novels have received over 11,000 Amazon reviews (4.7 Star Avg). All are written in Dan's unique style and voice, though he writes in more than one genre (Example, 5 of his books are Christmas novels and 8 are suspense). Some have more romance than others. Some have are more inspirational or have more of an emotional punch than others. All of them can be considered "clean reads."

The 2 things reviewers mention most with all of Dan's books are: 1) How much they love the characters and 2) They couldn't stop reading once they started.

Some quick links to *some of Dan's other novels*:

- The Reunion - https://www.amazon.com/dp/B07X4BJTTN
- The Discovery – https://www.amazon.com/dp/B07XSP51G1

The Forever Home Series (*over 2,200 Amazon Reviews, 4.8 Star avg*)

- Rescuing Finley – http://amzn.to/1Hn0vrg
- Finding Riley - http://amzn.to/2c7xdWY
- Saving Parker - http://amzn.to/2g9vKkA

The Jack Turner Suspense Series (*over 2,200 Amazon Reviews, 4.7 Star Avg*)

- When Night Comes - http://amzn.to/1xNat4G
- Remembering Dresden - http://amzn.to/1RO7WvN

- Unintended Consequences - http://amzn.to/2pvSvmG
- Perilous Treasure - https://amzn.to/2HOgpl7

You can check out the rest of Dan's novels by going to his Author Page on Amazon. Here's the link:

https://www.amazon.com/Dan-Walsh/e/B0024JAOZ6

If you'd like to contact Dan, feel free to email him at dan@danwalshbooks.com. He loves to get reader emails and reads all of them himself.

WANT TO HELP DAN?

If you enjoyed reading *The Longest Road*, the best thing you can do to help Dan is very simple—*tell others about it*. Word-of-mouth "advertising" is the most powerful marketing tool there is.

Leaving good reviews is the best way to insure Dan can keep writing novels full time. He'd greatly appreciate it if you'd consider leaving a rating for this book on Amazon and writing a brief review (even a sentence or two will help).

Here's the Amazon link for *The Longest Road*. Scroll down on the left side to the area that says **"Customer Reviews,"** right below the graphic that shows the number of stars you'll see the words: "Review This Product, and below that is a box and says: **"Write a Customer Review."**

The Longest Road Link

AUTHOR'S NOTE

Unlike the first book in this series, *The Deepest Water* (inspired by a true story), *The Longest Road* is entirely a work of fiction. It's fair to say the inspiration for this second novel was the first. After I'd written *The Deepest Waters* back in 2009 (came out in 2010), I wanted to write a sequel, and the main ideas for it were already in my head.

By the time *The Deepest Waters* hit the shelves, my first 2 novels had released to rave reviews from critics and readers alike. My publisher decided they didn't want me to write any more historical novels set that far back in time (the 1800s). So, reluctantly I wrote down my ideas for the sequel and set them aside, hoping someday I'd be able to write it. I was nowhere near ready to be done with the lives and the story of John and Laura, Micah (and the rest).

Literally, 20 books later I got my chance. In 2019, I got the rights back to *The Deepest Waters* from my old publisher and was now free to do whatever I wanted. I immediately made plans to finally write the sequel, *The Longest Road*.

Will there be a 3ʳᵈ book to the Epic Journey Series? Possibly. We'll see.

One final note, people have asked me which of the characters in this series do I mostly connect with on a personal level. Hands down, Micah is my favorite. But if I'm being honest, I have more in common with John. As I wrote both books, like John, I found myself greatly encouraged by Micah's insights and sometimes even, greatly helped.

I also found it somewhat ironic, diving into the research for this book, how similar the times were back then to what's going on today, even though the story takes place well over 150 years ago. Sadly, our country (as of this writing) is almost as polarized and divided as we were in John and Micah's time. And because of this, I found myself greatly drawn to Micah's words, as well as his deep, abiding faith in God to lead and sustain him, regardless of his circumstances.

I hope you will be blessed as much as I was as you read his story.

Dan Walsh

SIGN UP TO RECEIVE DAN'S NEWSLETTER

If you'd like to get an email alert whenever Dan has a new book coming out or when a special deal is being offered on any of Dan's existing books, click on his website link below and sign up for his newsletter (it's right below the Welcome paragraph).

From his homepage, you can also contact Dan or follow him on Facebook, Twitter or Goodreads.

www.danwalshbooks.com

ACKNOWLEDGMENTS

There are a few people I absolutely must thank for helping to get *The Longest Road* into print. First is my wife, Cindi. Not just for her encouragement and support. But over the years, Cindi has become a first-class editor. Her editorial help and insight was indispensable with the storyline and characters in this book.

Then, of course, there is my proofreading team: Terri Smith, Debbie Mahle, Jann Martin, Betty Vallery, and Rachel Savage. These ladies scour the manuscript trying to pick out any errors, typos, wrong words, missing words, etc. before it goes to print. They do a great job and we're so grateful for their work. If somehow, after all this, we still miss a typo or two, please feel free to email the author at dan@danwalshbooks.com.

In this digital age, it's fairly easy to correct mistakes, and our goal is to make all of my novels error-free.

Thanks so much,
Dan Walsh

ABOUT THE AUTHOR

Dan was born in Philadelphia in 1957. His family moved down to Daytona Beach, Florida in 1965, when his father began to work with GE on the Apollo space program. That's where Dan grew up.

He married Cindi, the love of his life in 1976. They have two grown children and four grandchildren. Dan served as a pastor for 25 years, then began writing fiction full-time in 2010. His bestselling novels have won numerous awards, including 3 ACFW Carol Awards (he was a finalist 6 times) and 4 Selah Awards. Four of Dan's novels were finalists for RT Reviews' Inspirational Book of the Year. One of his novels (The Reunion) is being made into a feature film by Oscar-winning screenwriter and producer, Nick Vallelonga (Green Book).

CPSIA information can be obtained
at www.ICGtesting.com
Printed in the USA
LVHW051512131220
674072LV00016B/1810